# TO THE CITY, WITH LOVE

## Volume I

by

# Steve Slavin

*Martin Sisters Publishing*

TO THE CITY, WITH LOVE

Published by
Martin Sisters Publishing Company
Kentucky, USA

Martin Sisters Publishing Company
ISBN: 978-1-62553-097-4

Literature & Fiction/Contemporary/Short Story Collection
Printed in the United States of America

Visit our website at www.martinsisterspublishing.com

# ACKNOWLEDGMENTS

I had a lot of help. My high school friend, Linda Sperling, not only edited most of these stories, but she supplied scores of extremely helpful suggestions.

Over last three years, hundreds of literary agents and editors turned down this book. But Mike Stringer, an acquisitions editor at Martin Sisters Publishing, just said "yes." In addition, he did a great job of editing my manuscript.

The heart and soul of short story publishing are the literary magazines. Nearly all will consider submissions from unknown writers. Most of the stories in this book first appeared in one of the magazines listed here. I want to thank each of their editors for publishing my work.

*Across the Margin, Against the Wall, Birmingham Arts Journal, Bitchin' Kitch, Cactus Elbow, Chicago Record Magazine, Corvus Review, Danse Macabre, Down and Out, Down in the Dirt, Downstate Story, Eskimo Pie, FICTION on the WEB, Fifth Estate, Free Focus, Friday Fiction, Green's Magazine, hackwriters, Half Tones to Jubilee, Jewish Currents, Near 2 the Knuckle, Nerve Cowboy, New Pop Lit, Nuthouse, Open Magazine, Potluck, Punchnel's, riverSedge, Section8, Shalla Magazine, Short Stories BiMonthly, Skylark, The Ecphorizer, The Literary Yard, The Path, The Pointed Circle, The Tower Journal, Through the Gaps, Tucumcari, Up Front Muse International Review, Winamop, Work Literary Magazine, and Ygdrasil.*

Chuck Stickney, another of my high school friends, after patiently listening to me read these stories, suggested that I put them into a collection. He made many very helpful suggestions, and makes appearances in some of these stories.

Vanessa Cano did a fine job transcribing my older (pre-computer day) stories from more than a dozen literary magazines into modern day text. Fred Cerniglia managed to convert typed pages into Word documents.

I'd also like to thank all my friends who provided story ideas. Among them were Barbara Hanna, Christian Hanna, Gail Olson, Janet Kwasman, Henry Lewy, Arnie Schwartz, Irina Mahitov, Margo Feiden, Marilyn Sochalski, Andy Kent, Bernie Sanders, Nadine Goode, Jack Nowinsky, Len Friedman, Kathy Rehm, and Eve Hinderer.

My parents, Ethel and Jack Slavin, told me stories about our extended family, little suspecting that they would one day be put to this use. So to them both – a belated thank you! And to other family members whose recollections I shamelessly expropriated – Barbara Slavin, Betty Slavin, Laura Slavin, and Vera Zorn.

And finally I want to thank my sister, Leontine Temsky, for taking the cover photo, and my nieces, Eleni Zimiles, Liz Zimiles, Justine Zimiles, and Sophie Zimiles, for their comments about my stories.

# TABLE OF CONTENTS

# INTRODUCTION

Can you remember Saul Steinberg's iconic map of the U.S? On the left is New York with its towering skyscrapers, and then, looking to the right the viewer sees a few other cities shown in Lilliputian dimension. The entire expanse between New York and San Francisco is depicted as fly-over country.

But there's a fatal flow in Steinberg's map – a flaw that would be detected only by the eye of the true New Yorker. New York is shown as the *biggest* city – and that's completely wrong! New York is the *only* city.

Just as a stage set facilitates the production of a play, our City is the setting for innumerable stories. In fact, our City itself is very much the sum of all the stories that New Yorkers tell about themselves, their friends, and their families. The stories in this book are my own, and soon they shall be yours too.

# Part I

## DOWN ON THE LOWER EAST SIDE

If you're old enough, you can probably sing the first line of *The Sidewalks of New York.* "East side, West side, all around the town." For centuries, New York has been a city of neighborhoods. Prominent among them is the Lower Eastside of Manhattan.

In the 1880s, real estate developers began to construct what would become the City's largest concentration of five-story, walk-up tenements. Built mainly for the waves of immigrants from Southern and Eastern Europe – largely Italians and Jews – these buildings were divided into three-room railroad apartments, with very primitive plumbing.

A century later the neighborhood housed dirt poor families, many of them on public assistance. There was also a sprinkling of artists, writers, actors, and students. This first group of stories takes place in the neighborhood where I lived for five years when I was a struggling graduate student.

# THE PRINCE OF SIXTH STREET

If you're a New Yorker who loves Indian food, then the chances are you've been to what may be termed "Indian restaurant row." Situated on Sixth Street, between First and Second Avenues, there are said to be more Indian restaurants than in all of Mumbai. They were started by a handful of graduate students at nearby NYU, who hoped to parlay their culinary skills into making a few bucks to help them get through school.

It was possible in those days to rent a squalid basement for less than $100 a month, and by the late 1960s, the block was lined with restaurants bearing such names as *Taj Mahal, Bombay Palace, The Royal Bengali,* and *The Prince of India.* Considering the locale, these names, which hinted at royal lineage, had obviously been chosen tongue-in-cheek.

The arrival of the restaurants coincided with a budding real estate boom in that part of the Lower Eastside, which the local brokers had renamed, *the East Village.* The rents shot up, artists, hippies, and then, yuppies started moving in, and the restaurant owners themselves began to believe in their *own* royal lineage.

Before the block had become transformed, there lived, at number 314, a young prince. How long ago *was* this? It was so long ago that the young prince, a graduate student at NYU, was paying just $40 a credit. I was that prince.

From the 1890s until the Great Depression, most of the people living in the neighborhood were Eastern European Jewish immigrants. Second Avenue, which was lined with

11

kosher restaurants, was also home to the world's largest concentration of Yiddish theaters. Perhaps the most popular actor was the amazingly versatile and talented Boris Thomashefsky, who was equally adept at playing women's roles as men's roles. He starred in *The Jewish King Lear, Faust, Uncle Tom's Cabin*, and even a somewhat altered Yiddish version of *Hamlet*, in which the Danish price attended rabbinical college. By the 1930s, most of the Jews were moving out, their places taken by Ukrainian immigrants, Puerto Ricans, blacks, and other folks who could not afford to pay much rent.

By the time I arrived, Sixth Street was just a collection of run-down tenement walk-ups, a few pathetic storefronts, absolutely no street life, and not a single tree on the entire block. The Ukrainian National Home, a rather strangely named restaurant just around the corner on Second Ave, was still serving its perogies and borscht to its mainly non-Ukrainian clientele. Rappaports and Ratners, two kosher dairy restaurants, still did a thriving business.

On a steamy June afternoon in 1962, I moved into a "two-room" apartment, which included a bathroom that had been added years before as an apparent afterthought. It was so narrow that I was able to fit my chinning bar directly over the bathtub. And when I ran the hot water, I could actually take a steam bath. Mr. Stahlman, who also owned a couple of neighboring buildings, rented the place to me for exactly $62.33 a month.

He had taken some considerable license calling this a two-room apartment, but this was some time before a creative real estate broker had coined the term, "studio apartment." A previous tenant had divided it with a bookcase made of orange crates that had been nailed together – an excellent place for my "library," which consisted of my economics textbooks and a dozen paperback novels such as *Catch 22, The Naked and the Dead*, and *Raintree County*.

During my first visit to the local hardware store, I was advised to buy long thick screws for my windows, which were very effective in keeping out burglars, who regularly made their way up and down the fire escapes. My windows faced the backs of perhaps another two dozen tenements. The adjacent backyards were all strewn with garbage. On the Lower Eastside, following a custom dating back to the Middle Ages, people threw their garbage out the window. We called it *night mail*.

For a short while that summer, I had a girlfriend named Sunny, who truly lived up to her name. She would tell me stories of her adventures, including overcoming her fear of flying by getting so drunk before boarding, that she would pretend to be an invalid, and manage to get wheeled onto the plane.

Sunny's favorite drink was tomato juice, even without vodka. I can still picture her sitting on the windowsill, sipping from an aluminum cup I had just bought. When I heard the cup hitting the concrete in the backyard I asked her why she threw it out the window. "I didn't," she said, and held it up for me to see. Then we heard another sound of metal smacking the ground, seconds later followed by another, and then, still another. We soon figured out it was just another warm night on the Lower Eastside, and my neighbors were tossing their empty beer cans.

Not surprisingly, Sunny was an artist, and lived with her parents in a New Jersey suburb. They decided to move to Australia, and Sunny would move there once they were settled. On their way, they had a stopover in Hawaii, and loved it so much that they decided to move there instead. The last time I heard from Sunny, the family was living on Waiholo Street in Honolulu. I still miss her.

In fact, my love life suffered for months after she left. I became friendly with a woman in the building, Emma Brown, who claimed she had once been the Madam of a brothel in Cuba. She lived a couple of floors below me with her two young daughters, and subsisted on welfare. I, however, was a prince, the recipient of a $45 weekly unemployment check. Emma decided that the young prince needed a new girlfriend, and she thought that her good friend, Flo, would fill the bill quite nicely.

So it was all arranged. I would drop by Emma's apartment when Flo was there, we would hit it off, and Emma would suggest that I show Flo my apartment. When I knocked on the door, Emma asked me to come in, and there was Flo, a fairly attractive woman about twice my age, with very short frizzy orange hair and a thick West Indian accent. I was a horny young man, so when Flo agreed to come upstairs with me, I had all my moves already planned.

Keep in mind that this was all taking place a few years before the onset of the sexual revolution, free love, and everything that entailed. Most guys still considered the steps of the seduction process analogous to rounding the bases in a Dodgers vs. Giants game.

I opened a bottle of wine, which we drank out of my aluminum cups, and not long after a few gulps we were locking lips. I had reached first base and was heading for second when Flo asked me an unexpected question. "How is your heart? Is it OK?"

"Of course!"

"You never had a heart attack?"

I was 23 years old. "No! In fact I was a long distance runner in college.

"So you were in the Olympics?"

"No, Flo. I wasn't nearly good enough."

Flo seemed satisfied with my answer, but then she asked me why I had so many books. So I told her I was a graduate student, and she said something like, "I see."

Well, by now the mood was lost and Flo mentioned that she needed to go downstairs to say good-bye to Emma, because she had to get up very early for work the next morning. I, of course, being a prince, usually stayed up till around six am.

When she left, I wondered to myself whether the game would be resumed at a later date, or if it was simply rained out. The next afternoon I went downstairs for the post-game analysis. Emma, who had a certain flair for the dramatic, summed up the previous evening quite nicely: "Steeeeeeeve, did youuuuuuuuuu mess up!"

14

"Yeah, but I can't figure out what went wrong. We were making out on my bed, and then she started asking me some strange questions. Like, did I ever have a heart attack?"

"Oh Steve, I should have warned you! Flo was dating this guy called "old man Jack." She really liked him, and he had a lot of money. But one night, when they were doing it, he clutched his heart and told her to call an ambulance. He was having a heart attack and he died on the way to the hospital."

"That's awful! Well, did he at least leave her any money?"

"That's the sad thing. It turned out he was married. Actually he was married to three different women. In the end, Flo didn't get a penny.

"But she wasn't scared off because she thought you would have a heart attack. In fact she was really impressed that you were in the Olympics."

"No, I told her I was a long distance runner in college. So I wasn't likely to have a heart attack."

"Well anyway, that's not what had Flo worried, and that's not why Flo changed her mind about doing anything with you. She told me that you really scared her!"

"How did I do *that*?"

"Well, she was looking at all your books."

"My *books* scared her? They're economics textbooks for my classes."

"Steve, Flo thought you were a policemahn."

"What do economics books have to do with policemen?"

"I don't know either, but when Flo saw all those books, she was sure you were a policemahn, and if she did anything with you, you would arrest her."

"Is she a prostitute?"

"Are you crazy, mahn?"

"Well, why was she scared?"

"Look, Flo knows a couple of cops, OK? And both of them have books. So she figure, *you* must be a cop."

Well, I thought to myself, even princes can strike out on occasion. The big question was how long I'd have to wait

15

before returning to the batter's box. In the meanwhile, I made a couple of new friends.

Diane and Marlene were two struggling artists – a blatant redundancy – I had met at a party just down the block. In fact, they might have been the only women there, which was typical of the Lower Eastside "scene" in those days. Almost no single women – except welfare mothers – lived east of Third Ave. They shared a three-room railroad apartment, with a bathtub in the kitchen, which, when covered with a door, served as their kitchen table. By far, the most interesting thing about their apartment was the sometimes overwhelming presence of their next-door neighbor, a six foot four African named Nonkabruce.

In traditional societies, the richest man often had the most desirable women. Nonkabruce, an illegal immigrant, worked a couple of days a week for Budget Movers, an outfit that paid the almost unheard of hourly wage of $5 an hour. Best of all, it was off the books. With tips, Nonkabruce earned well over a hundred dollars a week, probably making him the highest earner on all of Sixth Street. But I suspect that it may not have been just his money that attracted the women. There's just something about a man who can climb five flights of stairs with a refrigerator strapped to his back.

If I was indeed the Prince of Sixth Street, then surely Nonkabruce was the King. The man probably had the most active sex life on the entire Lower Eastside. Evidently the shortage of women was absolutely no problem, because virtually every night, for hours, Diane and Marlene would be forced to bear witness to the sounds of Nonkabruce pounding some poor girl, his steel bedframe rhythmically slamming into their own bedroom wall, accompanied by the appreciative screams of a very grateful young woman.

Marlene well remembers the night she found herself locked out of her apartment. After trying every possible means of getting back in, in exasperation she began throwing herself against her door – again, and again, and again. After a while Nonkabruce's door opened and he stepped into the hall, wearing just a pair of white skivvies. He was sweating so profusely that his body actually gleamed.

Marlene glanced at him and then went back to throwing herself against the door. Nonkabruce stood there, hands on his hips. Then she saw he had a big smile on his face. This infuriated her and she actually backed up a few feet from the door, got a running start, and slammed herself against the door. As she bounced off the door, Nonkabruce burst into laughter. Soon he was doubled over.

Marlene glared at him. Finally, he just shook his head, went back into his apartment, closed the door, and within minutes the familiar sounds resumed. About an hour later, when Diane got home, she found Marlene sitting on the hallway floor, her back against their door. When they got inside their apartment, Nonkabruce's bed frame was slamming against the wall. Marlene told Diane what had transpired out in the hall. Diane started laughing.

"Diane, it isn't funny!"

"I know, I know! But I just thought of how Nonkabruce might have helped you."

"That man would not help his own *mother*! That man has only one interest in life – and we both know what *that* is."

"Don't you see? *That's* how he could have gotten you into the apartment."

"Be serious, Diane."

"I *am* being serious. You could have asked him to bring his bed out into the hall and put it right next our door."

"Oh no!"

"That's right, Marlene. He could have gotten the door open in five seconds."

I never actually met Nonkabruce, but I did know one of his neighborhood rivals, a guy named Perry Gewirtz, aka Sonny Williams, who lived just around the corner from me on Fifth Street. In 1969, Perry had a bit part – playing Sonny Williams, a flasher clad in just a raincoat – in what became a cult movie, *Putney* Swope. A very short, extremely skinny pale man with thick glasses, a long beard, bald except for shoulder length hair growing from the sides and back of his head, Perry looked a lot more like a Talmudic scholar than an exhibitionist.

Perry came by his unusual looks quite honestly. Growing up in Brooklyn, he was sent to yeshivas all the way through high school. But he found a future in orthodoxy unappealing, perhaps because of his extremely amorous nature. After short stints in the Post Office and in an Off Track Betting Parlor, he found his true calling acting in pornographic movies. He was reputed to have the largest schlong in the industry, at least according to the testimonials of his legions of female admirers. And to be objective, there was certainly a clear record of photographic evidence. Still, Perry may have been the real Sonny Williams, but he was no Nonkabruce.

Perhaps Nonkabruce's other great competitor was a man with no known first or last name; he was sometimes known as *the father of the Lower Eastside.* or just simply, *the stud.* Both titles were quite apt. His exploits were well documented in the case files of the New York City Department of Welfare. Scores of unwed mothers listed him as the father of their children. None of them knew his actual name. But, listed on the birth certificates of their children next to the word, "father," were the words, "the squirrel. "No, I am not making this stuff up.

By the spring of 1963, it was time for a change. I was finishing up my Master's thesis and had secured a job at the U.S. Communicable Disease Center in Atlanta. When I left, I gave my apartment key to a guy named Bill, who desperately needed a place to stay. Although I barely knew him, I said that if he kept paying the rent, the landlord would probably let him stay.

Well, as luck would have it, things did not work out for me in Atlanta, and six months later I was back in New York. I moved into an actual two-room apartment in an elevator building down on Norfolk Street, just off Delancey. This area would continue to be called the Lower Eastside, and would not become gentrified for decades. I felt at home here, and resumed my studies at NYU, even though the tuition was creeping up towards $60 a credit.

18

One day I decided to visit my old apartment on Sixth Street to see if Bill was still there. He wasn't, but Emma invited me in. "Steeeeeve! I never expected to see you again! Are you OK?"

I filled her in on my adventures in the South, and then she asked me if I had heard the news?

"*What* news?"

"The news about Bill."

"No, I was wondering if he kept the apartment."

"Steeeeeve! The police came. I think he was arrested. One night about 10 policemahn, they bang on his door."

"Why?"

"You didn't hear? He was running some kind of flop house. Your apartment was filled with bums. Mr. Stahlman must have called the police."

"What happened to Bill?"

"I don't know if they arrested him, but he was gone. Mr. Stahlman had the apartment painted and now there's two guys living there. I think they are students like you. They're from India and they go to NYU."

"Are you friendly with them?"

"They're OK. But they're a little crazy. One of them said they wanted to rent a basement on the block and open a restaurant."

"On *this* block? Emma, no one's going to come to Sixth Street to eat Indian food!"

# SCHWARTZ

## 1

When one of Schwartz's drawings was published in a literary magazine, an editor wrote this biographic note: Arnold Schwartz is a man of letters. He works in the post office.

In a way, that pretty much summed up Schwartz's life. Here was a guy who had a fair degree of talent, but like the rest of us, he needed to make a living. Sorting mail may have paid the bills, but it's not what any person would choose to do for eight hours a day. You can ask any actor who waits tables or tends bar the same question.

Schwartz, which is German for black, always saw the dark side of life. And his observations were often conveyed through black humor. One of his cartoons shows several people dressed in rags, all of them lying in the gutter. His caption reads, "Bangladesh has developed a bad reputation because so many of our citizens lie around starving to death. But that is not a completely accurate picture. Some of us have the strength to stand up and beg."

Another cartoon shows two vertical lines and a jagged horizontal line connecting them. The caption reads: You put up your first building. But it falls down. The second panel is a repeat of the first with the caption: You put up your second building. But it, too, falls down. The third panel shows just two vertical lines – and no jagged horizontal line. The caption: You put up your third building and it does not fall down. You have just won your Brazilian architect's license.

21

During the last couple of years of his life, he was in and out of hospitals. Once, when I was visiting, a woman with a thick Indian accent entered his room and announced, "I am your psychiatrist. I see in your records that you are depressed. So tell me, Mr. Schwartz, how long have you been depressed?"

"All my life," he answered with a smile. The three of us burst out laughing.

## 2

After high school, when the rest of us went on to college or got some crappy job, Schwartz and his friend, Mel, took different paths. In our yearbook, instead of "college" or "business", Mel wrote, "French Foreign Legion." He ended up working in the family oil delivery business, which went by the reassuring motto, "We'll be right over." Schwartz added, "but don't hold your breath."

The yearbook editors provided just three options – college, business, or military. At least Mel *did* choose the military option, even if he never exactly followed through. Schwartz created his own fourth option: he wrote "nothing."

What he actually did was attend the Brooklyn Museum Art School on a full scholarship, and then set out to become a painter. He found a really cheap apartment on Manhattan's Lower Eastside – just $40 a month for three rooms – which, of course, he painted black. Once, when he was out, someone broke into his apartment and stole – absolutely nothing. As Schwartz observed, "If artists are starving, then how are burglars supposed to make a living?"

One day, after his unemployment checks ran out, he managed to get an appointment for a job interview. For this he needed a clean shirt and an unstained tie. And so, with his last dollar, he walked down the block to the unclaimed laundry. In those days, there were stores that sold laundry that no one had retrieved, for just the cost of the cleaning. The shirts were twenty cents and the ties were a nickel. Schwartz picked out a shirt and tie and brought them up to the cashier.

"That'll be thirty cents."

"Thirty *cents!*" yelled Schwartz. "Your shirts are twenty cents and your ties are a nickel."

"You're right! But that shirt is a nickel extra."

"Why?"

"Just look at the label. B *Altman's!*"

## 3

Schwartz's fascination with black was apparent not just in his paintings, but in his moods as well. There was an old joke in the art world and beyond about the no-talent aspiring artist who schmeared black paint on a canvas and entitled his masterpiece, "Blackout in a coal mine." Schwartz, perhaps because it reflected his own bleak outlook, used a lot of black in his paintings. He also hated most of the paintings he saw in the galleries he visited. He would typically walk into a gallery, look around, and then announce: "All of this is *shit!*"

One day I accompanied him to see his friend, Ibrihim Ibrihim, who, Schwartz whispered confidentially, was a Christian Arab. He also turned out to be devilishly handsome, like a movie star whose name I could not quite recall. He lived in a very long railroad apartment, just a few blocks from Schwartz. We walked through the entire apartment to the back bedroom.

And then, as we stood just inside the room, Ibrihim Ibrihim said to Schwartz, "I'd like you to take a good look at the painting on the opposite wall." As we approached, it appeared to be one of the most depressing paintings I had ever seen. It was, in fact, reminiscent of the fabled "Blackout in a coal mine." But it was much, much more subtle, with perhaps a dozen different shades of dark, ominous gray.

The three of us stood there staring at the painting, as Ibrihim Ibrihim began to smile. "So Schwartz," he asked. "What do you think of it?"

Schwartz didn't answer. He just stood there staring at the painting. Finally, after a couple of minutes, he was ready to render his judgment.

"It's *shit!*"

"Well," said Ibrihim Ibrihim, "It *should* be! *You* painted it!"

Schwartz didn't say anything. But then, when we were ready to leave the room he turned to Ibrihim Ibrihim and said, "It's *still* shit!"

## REMEMBER IRINA MAHITOV

Back in the mid-1960s the Lower Eastside was a fairly friendly place. Where I lived, just off Delancey Street, there was a sprinkling of hippies, blacks, and old Jews in a sea of Puerto Ricans. The Winston Theater played three movies – at least one of which was a western. The Puerto Ricans loved westerns and always laughed when the tenderfoot would try to mount a horse and fall off.

Except for the movies, there was almost no air conditioning, so on spring and summer nights people used to drag out their kitchen chairs and sit in front of their tenements drinking beer, bullshitting, and listening to the ball game. Sometimes on a weekend afternoon a caravan of cars would make their way through the neighborhood, horns blaring, to announce that another couple had just become hitched. Or were forced to get married. Whatever.

It was a friendly place. Bodegas and abogados on every block, and always a guy selling ices. My friend, Schwartz, insisted that the filthy towel the guy used to cover the ice block gave the ices their flavor. Day or night, there were always people out on the street. There were plenty of burglaries, but almost no one ever got mugged.

One day I was coming up the subway stairs and saw this woman struggling with a huge suitcase. She was going to this guy's place on Norfolk Street, so I offered to carry her suitcase. Who knows, maybe I'd get lucky.

She was a political organizer and knew this dude from California. I can't remember if they were anarchists, Spartacists, hippies, or diggers. The diggers, by the way, ran a free store, and would just give things away. When we got up to the apartment, which happened to be a fifth floor walkup, there were several mattresses on the floor, kind of your standard crash pad. A few people were hanging out, smoking, and maybe just waiting for something to happen. Albert Solomonow was their leader; it was his apartment.

One of the women there was Irina, but I didn't find that out until years later. I do remember that Albert was mad at her because she owed him rent money. I mean, how much could it have been, an eighth share in a sixty-dollar-a-month apartment? It was getting to be a pretty bad scene, so I split.

What's kind of funny is that even though I lived down on the other end of Norfolk Street, I never ran into any of those people again. Except Irina. It turned that she knew Schwartz, my artist friend. Schwartz kept debating with himself whether or not he actually wanted to go out with her. He asked his shrink, Sergio Rothstein, what he should do. "I don't see anyone falling out of your closet, Schwartz."

So he asked her out. But she said, why spoil a perfectly good friendship? Irina had been in a soft porn flick, "Lust Weekend," which ended as a naked couple waded into the ocean and drowned themselves. And that may have been the best part.

Schwartz was friendly with some guys who called themselves, "The League for Lousy Lovers," all of whom were so depressed they couldn't even get themselves laid in the late-1960s. Their meeting place was an apartment whose only furnishing was some couches with broken legs. If you sat down, you'd fall asleep in seconds.

The high point of the League's meetings was when they were addressed by Valarie Salonis, the woman who shot Andy Warhol. She was the president of SCUM, the Society for Cutting Up Men. She told them they were a bunch of losers. Marshall, their leader, said that they could not agree more.

26

Irina, who had long since left the Albert Solomonow apartment, ended up staying with Marshall for a week or so. When Schwartz went to visit, the place was dark, and Marshall and Irina were lying on couches across the room from each other. Schwartz sunk down into another legless couch and the three of them spent the rest of the afternoon asleep.

One day Marshall told Irina that he was thinking about getting a phone. "Who would call you?" she asked. So he never got one installed.

Irina was 25 when she died. They found her in her room at the Evangeline Residence for Women, on West 13th Street in the village. She washed down a bottle of sleeping pills with a fifth of scotch.

Irina never made it as an actress, and she and Schwartz never made it with each other. But who knows – maybe in another life.

He had a death notice printed on the theater page of the Village Voice, "Irina Mahitov, 1945- 1970, actress."

Irina would have enjoyed reading that. But she would have enjoyed the rest of the story even more. She told me that Albert Solomonow kept all her stuff until she paid him the rent she owed him. Even though he had told her that she could stay there for free. "He was just this horny little guy," she told me.

Well, it turns out that years later and hundreds of miles away, it all caught up with Albert Solomonow. He had crashed a party somewhere in Ohio and met a woman who seemed pretty hot to trot. They drove up to an isolated hilltop a million miles from nowhere. This woman could really pick her spots. So they exited the car and walked to the edge of a cliff. Way off in the distance, they could barely make out the lights of the city. The woman said to him, "I'll be right back. I just need to get something from the car."

When he heard the engine start up, Albert knew right away he was definitely not going to get laid that night. He went running up to the car just as it started to pull away. "'What's the matter?" he screamed. "Did I do something wrong?"

As she pulled away, she rolled down the window, and called out: "Remember..... Irina..... Mahitov."

# THE TENANTS' PATROL

## 1

I grew up in the '50s in a nice, boring subdivision way out on Long Island. In the words of Malvina Reynolds' song (made famous by Pete Seeger), the houses "were all made out of ticky-tacky and they all looked just the same."

Of course, I had never heard of Pete Seeger, nor did I begin to suspect just how boring the 'burbs were until I went away to college. Before that, about the only time I was actually off the Island was when I accompanied my parents on their bimonthly pilgrimage to see *Zaydeh* Beryl. (In case you're not from New York, *zaydeh* is Yiddish for grandfather.)

We always went on Saturday, because Sunday the Lower East Side was full of *meshuggeners* (loonies) looking for bargains on Orchard Street. And they were perfectly happy waiting on line for two hours to get a table at Ratner's.

*Zaydeh* sat in the lobby of his co-op with all his cronies. They were the building's "Tenants' Patrol." They sat in camp chairs, beach chairs, and even in wheelchairs. Not one of them was a day under seventy.

Eight-year-olds are not the most tactful people in the world. I asked them if they were serious. How could a bunch of old people stop a criminal? Of course, I *was* tactful enough not to call them "old geezers" or "old farts," for that matter.

"David, are you kidding?" a woman they called Tsippie asked me. "We have a very serious crime problem right here in this building." And the others all nodded. "The other day some kid tried to snatch a woman's purse. But we raised such a holler, he left her alone."

"Really?" I asked. They all smiled and nodded.

"David," my grandfather said, "you see these jackets?" A couple of the men slowly got up out of their chairs. And they turned around. On the back of their blue satin jackets, in big yellow letters, it said "Tenants' Patrol." I read the words out loud. The men smiled, turned around, and slowly sank back down into their chairs. A few minutes later I noticed they were both asleep.

My parents confirmed for me that the Lower East Side was indeed quite unsafe. "Why do you think we got out of there?" my mother asked. "Do you think we wanted you and your sister to grow up in a place like this?" added my father.

"We fought to get out of this neighborhood," my mother continued. "As soon as your father and I could afford it, we put a down payment on a house and moved out to the Island."

"And never looked back," said my father. "Amen!" my mother always liked to get in the last word.

Even an eight-year-old could see that the Lower East Side was not a very attractive neighborhood. Too many houses looked like they might fall down. The streets were filthy. People were talking strange foreign languages. And not just Yiddish.

And now my grandfather and his cronies were worried about crime. I wondered why they still lived there. "I'll tell you why," said my father. "Because they can't let go – that's why!"

"You see, David," my mother added, "most of them grew up in the neighborhood. Their roots are there. So there's nothing for them on Long Island."

"Just their children and their grandchildren," said my father.

"What's wrong with that?"

"Nothing, David," answered my mother. "We had *Zaydeh* out to the house a couple of times before you were born. But he couldn't wait to get back on the train. He kept checking the timetable."

"Why didn't he like it?"

"Who knows?" answered my father. "I think he's a little meshugge, if you ask me."

My mother just shook her head. "Your *Zaydeh* never approved of our buying the house. He said that we would live to regret it."

"Did you?"

"Are you kidding? What's to regret? Believe me, every day I thank God we had the sense to get out while we could. A bad element was moving in. People on relief. Bohemians. Hippies. Drug addicts. Criminals. Believe me, we got out just in the nick of time."

My mother was probably right. And even *Zaydeh* said the neighborhood was unsafe. But I still couldn't understand why he stayed. Whenever I asked him, he would say, "Because I like it here. Someday, maybe you'll see for yourself."

## 2

As fate would have it, I did get that chance. Right after college, I got a job in the city. I tried living at home, but the commute was over an hour. One day, I got a great idea. Why not live near *Zaydeh*? Apartments were really cheap in his neighborhood, and I wouldn't have to live with a roommate.

"David, have you taken leave of your senses!" my mother asked me again and again. "We fought to get out of that neighborhood, we scrimped and saved to send our son to one of the best colleges, and this is how he repays us?"

"Ma, you didn't have to scrimp and save. I had a scholarship and student loans."

"That's not the point! Your whole education is wasted! But why listen to me? You'll see for yourself. Don't worry, in a month you'll be begging to move back into your old room."

My father kept quiet. I guess he had finally gotten used to my mother having the last word.

So I moved into a tenement on East Sixth Street, very close to *Zaydeh*. Believe it or not, he was still on the Tenants' Patrol, which still met every evening in the lobby. Some of the faces had changed, but they still wore their blue satin jackets. I hadn't been around much for the last six or eight years, but they were very glad to see me.

"David you're all grown up now, "one of them observed. As if I hadn't noticed myself.

"Thank you," I said lamely. *Zaydeh* was now one of the oldest. He had arthritis and his memory was starting to fade. I wanted to get to know him better. I wanted something to remember.

He told me stories about my mother, how she was the prettiest, smartest girl on the block. How he and *Bubba* always regretted not sending her to college. But what could they do? They had two sons to send to college, so there just wasn't any money to send my mother. Their other big regret was telling my mother that my father wasn't good enough for her. *Zaydeh* would stop and make sure I was listening. Then he would say, "Your father is a *mentsh*, David."

"I know that, *Zavdeh*. Tell me about *Bubba*." ·

"You know she died before you were born. She saw your sister when she was a baby. Anyway, your *Bubba* made the best *tayglach* in the whole Lower East Side. Did you know that Ratners, Rapaports, Moscowitz and Lupowitz, and even Glucksterns – they were all begging her to bake for them? But your *Bubba* said no. She would cook and bake only for her family. And that was it! She was a very stubborn woman. And your mother took after her."

## 3

*Zaydeh* would tell me the same stories again and again, and I was getting bored visiting him. I was working full time, going for a master's at night, and I was enjoying a pretty active social life. I mean, what was I supposed to do – bring my dates to meetings of the Tenants' Patrol? So I visited less and less often.

One night, just as I was leaving his lobby, we all heard a crashing sound against the outer door. I ran outside and saw two kids running down the block. I started running after them, but then I thought, "What for?" I came back into the lobby,

32

carrying the brick they had thrown against the door. It hadn't done any damage.

They all greeted me like a hero. "Those lousy bums! They'll think twice before they come back here again," said one man. *Zaydeh* patted me on the back, then hugged me for a long time.

Just a few weeks later, *Zaydeh* died in his sleep. It made absolutely no sense to sit *shiva* out on Long Island, so my parents and my sister agreed to come to *Zaydeh's* lobby each night. Everyone brought food and *schnapps* and it turned into a regular party. Hundreds of people I had never seen before came by to pay their respects. People who hadn't seen *Zaydeh* in thirty, forty, or fifty years would tell me stories about him and my *Bubba*.

On the last night I walked my parents to their car. I could see they were glad it was finally over, relieved they didn't have to come back to the neighborhood. Even though they were resigned to my living there, they came to my apartment only once. I knew that if I were to see them, it would have to be out on the Island.

As I walked back to *Zaydeh's* lobby one last time to help everyone clean up, I realized that I would never see any of these people again. I had known them all my life, but I had no reason to ever go back. I opened the door of the building. There were just a few people still there. They had already cleaned up.

When they saw me, they crowded all around. "David, David," one of them said, "we have something for you. It was your *Zaydeh's* and we know he wanted you to have it." And they presented me with a blue satin jacket. On the back, in bright yellow letters, it said, "Tenants' Patrol."

# CHRISTIAN AND THE SANTA CLAUS BUMS

Christian is a five-year-old boy who lives on the Lower East Side of Manhattan. He has only one problem. Christian is sometimes a little too smart for his own good.

One winter morning Christian was on his way to kindergarten with his mother. They passed a building with a big window. Inside Christian saw twenty or thirty men dressed as Santa Clauses. They were all eating breakfast.

"Mommy! Mommy! Why do they have all those Santa Clauses?"

Christian's mother was just as surprised as he was. Why indeed *did* they have all those Santa Clauses?

"I guess they're all having their breakfast," was all she could reply.

"*That's* no answer!" said Christian. "I asked you why they have all those Santa Clauses. I thought there was only *one* Santa Claus."

"You're right, Christian. There *is* only one Santa Claus."

"Well who *are* those guys in there eating breakfast?"

"I don't know who they are, Christian, but I can tell you *one* thing. None of them is Santa Claus."

That answer seemed to satisfy Christian for a few minutes, but when he got to school, he told his friends what he had seen.

"*I* know who those men are," said Adam.

"Who are they?" everyone wanted to know.

"They're bums!" shouted Adam. "That's who they are!"

"Bums?" everyone asked. "Bums? Then why are they dressed up like Santa Claus?"

"No one had an answer for *that* one. When Christian's father picked him up from school that evening, Christian told him about the Santa Claus bums.

"Christian, don't call them the Santa Claus bums."

"Why *not*?"

"Well, it isn't nice to call someone a bum."

"If it isn't nice, daddy, then how come *you* do it?"

"Well, the guys I call bums are *real* bums. Remember that guy who tried to clean our windshield yesterday? *He* was a bum."

"*That's* no answer!" said Christian. "If it's not nice to call *one* person a bum, then why is it OK to call *another* person a bum?"

"Christian, when you are older, then you will understand things better. But right now I don't want to hear you call anyone a Santa Clause bum. All right?"

Christian knew he'd better pretend to agree with his father, so he didn't say anything. He just nodded "yes."

His parents had mostly forgotten about the Santa Claus bums, when, just one week later, Christian and his mother were on their way to kindergarten. Well, you can probably guess what they saw.

There were about twenty Santa Clauses walking across the street, and then getting on a bus.

Christian began to shout. He forgot his mother was standing right next to him. He forgot what his father had told him.

"Those guys aren't Santa Clauses! They're *bums*! They're just dressed like Santa Clauses. Those are fake beards. They have pillows under their coats. Those guys are Santa Claus bums!"

Christian's mother was shocked, but most people passing by stopped and laughed. One man knelt down to talk to Christian. He was wearing a business suit under his coat. He told Christian, "You're right, son. Those men *are* bums. I want to thank you. You've made my day." Then he shook Christian's hand, stood up and walked away.

"Christian! How could you *say* such an awful thing?" asked his mother.

Christian was confused. Nearly everyone had laughed. The man had told him he was right and even thanked him. But now his mommy was mad at him. And he had a feeling that when his daddy heard about this, he would be madder than his mommy.

Now remember that Christian is a very smart little boy. Christian thought to himself – "Hmmmmm. Mommy's mad. She'll talk to daddy. So I better do what they told the president to do when he did something bad and everybody yelled at him. I think they called it 'damage control,' whatever *that* means."

"Mommy," Christian said, "I'm sorry I called those men bums."

His mommy just looked at him.

"Hmmmmm," Christian thought. "She's not going for that excuse." "Mommy, why do those men dress up like Santa Clauses?"

"That's a good question, Christian. Those men in Santa Claus suits go all over the city to raise money for poor people."

"Really? But aren't *they* poor?"

"Well, yes, Christian. I think some of the money they raise goes to help them as well."

When he got to school, Christian told all his friends what happened. Everybody laughed and laughed when he yelled again and again: "Those guys aren't Santa Clauses! They're *bums!*"

His teacher overheard Christian and felt very bad. Mrs. Grady had lived in the neighborhood for many years and she had seen the men dressed like Santa Clauses every year during the weeks just before Christmas. They always made her sad because she knew they were really poor men who dressed up like the real Santa Claus, and stood outside on the streets all day ringing bells, and saying "Ho, ho, ho, merry Christmas," over and over again, asking passersby to give money to the less fortunate.

Mrs. Grady knew it couldn't be very pleasant work and she often wondered what these men did the rest of the year, where they lived, and if they had families. She also knew that Christian and his friends didn't mean to be cruel. Children are basically honest, and they were just telling each other what their parents and other adults said to themselves – that these were not *real* Santa Clauses, but only poor men, or as Christian called them, "bums," dressed up as Santa Clauses.

So Mrs. Grady decided she would have a talk with all the children about the Santa Clauses. "Children! Children! Is everybody ready for a story?"

Of course they were. Everyone stopped what they were doing and sat around Mrs. Grady. When everyone was settled, she began.

"A long time ago there was a musician with a very funny name. His name was Offenbach. He had moved to a city that he loved very much, and he wrote a song about it. The first two lines went like this:

'Winter has come to the city.

The pavements are icy and cold.'

"Offenbach wrote those words a long time ago. But they could describe what New York is like right now. The streets are so cold that no one is outside who doesn't *have* to be. But on the Bowery there are still a lot of people who stay outside. Do you know who lives on the Bowery?"

"Drunks!" "Drunken old men!" "Bums!" called out most of the children.

"That's right! They are very sick men. And very poor. And they are all out there in the cold. While everyone else is in their nice warm homes."

"Don't they *want* to be out there? Someone said on television that they *like* to be out there," said Beth.

"Would *you* like to be out there, Beth?" asked Mrs. Grady

"Nooooooooo!" answered Beth, hugging herself.

"Would *any* of you like to be out there all day and all night in the rain and snow?"

"Nooooooooo," they all replied in a chorus.

"Well then," said Mrs. Grady, "I guess they don't want to be out there either."

"Aren't there places for them to go?" asked Ricky.

"They call them 'shelters,'" said Christian. "We used to live near one. There were drunks on our block all the time."

"That's right," said Mrs. Grady. "Ricky and Christian are both right. They *can* go to shelters. Have any of you ever been inside a shelter?"

Nobody said anything. Most of them just shook their heads. They were waiting for Mrs. Grady to tell them what it looked like inside a shelter.

"Well, to be truthful, I've never been inside a shelter myself. But from the pictures I've seen of them in the newspapers, I don't think I'd ever want to sleep in one. They are usually in very large buildings, with row after row of small beds all in one big room."

"Do any of the men snore?" asked Amy.

The children started to giggle. "My daddy snores," volunteered Ricky, "but then my mommy pinches his nose, so he stops."

Now everyone was giggling, even Mrs. Grady.

"Well, I'll bet," she said, "that most of them snore. In fact I'll bet they all snore so loud that you'd think the whole building would fall down!"

"Now everyone was laughing. Several of the little boys started to make snoring noises. This went on for a couple of minutes. As it began to die down, Mrs. Grady asked the children, "Now how many of *you* would like to sleep in a shelter?" Only Ricky raised his hand.

"I don't mind snoring, Mrs. Grady. I don't think anyone could snore louder than *my* father." A few of the children giggled at this.

"Well, how do you think all those poor homeless men feel? They can't go to the shelters because they can't get any sleep. So they have to take their chances sleeping out on the street."

"But it's so cold out there," said Anthony. "Especially when it snows," added Beth.

"Why would anyone want to sleep in the snow?" asked Christian.

"That's a good question," replied Mrs. Grady. "Why *would* anyone want to sleep in the snow?" she asked. "Unless he *had* to. Unless he didn't have any place to *go*."

"I'm glad *I* don't have to sleep in the snow," said Jennifer.

"Me too! Me too!" echoed the other children.

"That's right," said Mrs. Grady. "None of us has to sleep outside in the snow. Do you know *why* we don't have to?"

"Because we have mommies and daddies," said Adam.

"And our own homes," said Ricky.

"I have my own room," said Jennifer.

"So do *I*!" echoed most of the other children.

"I have to share my room with Kathy. She's my sister," whined Danielle.

"Well," said their teacher, "that is still a lot better than sleeping out in the snow, isn't it Danielle?"

"I guess so, Mrs. Grady."

"Well then, children, do you understand why these men have to sleep outside in the street, even when it snows?"

They all nodded their heads.

"Actually there are other things that are very bad in the shelters. Some of them are very dirty."

"Dirtier than the street?" asked Amy.

"Yes Amy, even dirtier than the street. Now that's pretty dirty, isn't it?"

Everyone agreed.

"And some of the shelters are very unsafe. So a lot of the men are afraid to go there."

"Aren't there ladies out on the street?" asked Christian.

"Yeah," said Adam. "They're shopping bag ladies."

"There's this lady who stays down the block from us," added Jennifer. "Boy, does she *stink*!"

This made everybody laugh. A few of the children held their noses. "Peee-you!" yelled Ricky.

When they finally calmed down Mrs. Grady continued. "There are a lot of poor women who live on the street. And the reason they are called shopping bag ladies – "

"*I* know! *I* know!" yelled Adam. "Because they keep all their stuff in shopping bags!"

"That's right, Adam," replied their teacher. "These women keep all their things with them because they are afraid someone will steal them. Everything they have in the world is in those plastic bags."

"Why don't they go to the shelter?" asked Amy. "Because of the snoring?"

"Maybe the snoring bothers them, Amy, but I think it's mainly because they're afraid they'll be robbed in the shelters."

"Why don't they move someplace else?" asked Christian.

"There isn't any place they could afford. Remember that they are very poor. Do you know how expensive it is to live in New York?"

"My daddy says it cost a thousand dollars to live in New York," said Beth.

"That's *cheap*! A thousand dollars! You know what my mommy says? You can't get a hole in the wall for a thousand dollars!" exclaimed Danielle.

"Children – a thousand dollars is a lot of money. And none of these poor people has a thousand dollars. If they did, they wouldn't be poor. Anyway, they don't have enough money to live anywhere, except out on the street. So now you know why these people have to sleep out on the street even when it snows."

They all nodded their heads.

"This makes me very sad," said Jennifer in a very soft voice.

"Me too!" said Ricky.

"Me too! Me too!" said all the other children.

Mrs. Grady waited until they all quieted down. When they finally did, she said, "Well, then, we all agree that it is very sad that these people have to sleep out on the street, even when it snows… Now I want to tell you about some people who are trying to help all these homeless people. Would you like to hear about that?"

"Yes, Mrs. Grady!" all the children exclaimed.

"I'm going to ask Christian to help me. Christian, do you know the street where all the Santa Clauses live?"

"Santa Clauses!" yelled Ricky. There is only one *real* Santa Claus. Everybody knows that!"

"Children! Ricky has made an excellent point! There is indeed just one real Santa Claus. So let's see if we can find out why all those other men are dressing up to *look* like the real Santa Claus.

"Christian, do you know the name of that street where you saw all those men?"

"It's the wide street with the big church. Maybe three blocks from here. Not far. They have a whole big pile of those Santa Clauses – well they're dressed up like Santa Clauses. I saw them eating breakfast."

"They're *bums*! They're Santa Claus *bums*!" some of the other children shouted.

When they finally quieted down, she said to them: "I'm going to tell you something very sad. Are you ready?"

It was so quiet you actually *could* hear a pin drop.

"Those men who dress up like Santa Clauses are very poor. But they are not bums. Those men put on their Santa Claus costumes and they stand out on the street all day. Do you know what they do?"

"They ring bells. Like this – ding-a-ling! Ding-a-ling!" said Anthony. "And they say, 'Ho, ho, ho!'"

"That's right, Anthony. But why do they stand outside all day ringing their bells and saying 'Ho, ho, ho?'"

"*I* know! *I* know!" yelled Danielle. "They ask everyone for money."

"You're absolutely right, Danielle! Now here is the hardest question of all. Is everybody ready?"

Everybody was ready.

"Very well, then. After they collect all that money, what do you think they *do* with it?"

That *was* a very hard question. Even Adam, who had an answer for almost everything, could not think of one. He just shrugged his shoulders.

"Do they take it home with them?" prompted Mrs. Grady.

"I don't think so," answered Beth.

"Good!" replied Mrs. Grady. "Now if they don't take it home with them, where do they take all that money?"

"*I* know! *I* know!" shouted Christian. They bring it to that building where they eat breakfast."

"That's right! That's where they bring it!"

"But what *do* they do with it?" asked Amy.

"Now that is a very good question. Doesn't everyone think that's a very good question?" All the children nodded "yes". Well, what do you think they do with all the money?"

Again, everyone just sat there trying to figure out the answer. Finally Jennifer blurted out: "They *give* it away to poor people!"

"That's *right!* Jennifer's *right!* They give away the money they collect to poor people."

"But *those* guys are poor!" objected Ricky.

"They are," said Mrs. Grady. "So they get to keep some of the money they collect."

"Why can't they keep *all* of it?" asked Beth.

"Because they are collecting to help a lot of poor people – especially the homeless people you see sleeping out in the street. It wouldn't be fair for them to keep all the money for themselves."

"But if they are collecting so much money, how come there are still so many people out on the street?" asked Ricky.

"Because, children, the men dressed as Santa Clauses can't collect enough money to help all of the people out on the street. Do you know why?"

"*I* know! *I* know!" yelled Amy. "It's because people don't give them enough money. Sometimes my father throws a quarter into the chimney."

"My mother throws in her change from her purse," said Danielle.

"I put a dime in once," said Beth.

"Well," said Mrs. Grady, "It is good that you and your parents give money to those Santas to help the poor, but it isn't enough to help everyone. There are hundreds and hundreds of people who have no place to live, and not enough to eat, and no warm clothes to wear."

The children grew very quiet and very sad. Finally Christian spoke up. "I think we should help them."

"Yes!" everyone agreed, "Let's help them!"

"Let's be the Santa Claus's helpers," said Adam. "We can help them collect money!"

"And we could dress up like Santa's helpers," added Amy.

"My mommy can make me an outfit on her sewing machine," said Danielle. "She made Dracula costumes on Halloween for me and my sister."

"It'll be as much fun as Halloween!" exclaimed Christian. "Besides, I was sick on Halloween and I couldn't go out trick-or-treating."

"This time," said Mrs. Grady, "you'll be collecting money for poor people."

"That's better than getting money and candy and stuff for ourselves, isn't it, Mrs. Grady?" asked Christian.

"Yes, Christian, it certainly is!" she replied. "Now that you have decided to be Santa's helpers, the next thing is to see that everyone gets their outfits to wear. That's very important, you know. Those Santa Clauses you've seen have very good costumes, and if we're going to be Santa's helpers, we will need very good costumes indeed."

"*My* mommy will make *my* costume," said Danielle.

"And *my* mommy will make *mine*," said Adam.

"Here's what we'll do," said Mrs. Grady. "I will give you each a letter to take home with you this afternoon. And in the letter I will ask your parents if they can make you a Santa's helper costume. Or buy one for you. I even know the name of a couple of stores in the neighborhood that sell them."

"Mrs. Grady," said Jennifer, "when everybody has a costume, will we go out and help Santa collect money?"

"That's right, Jennifer. With all of us helping Santa, we'll be able to collect a lot of money to help all the poor people who have to sleep out on the street. OK now, I'm going to write that letter and you can all go back to playing."

A few days later, when everybody had a costume, Mrs. Grady explained to the children how they would work as Santa's helpers. "Tomorrow afternoon we'll all be going to help one of the Santas. The school has made all the arrangements. Right after lunch a bus will pick us up and take us to Park Ave. Does anyone know where Park Ave. is?"

"Is that where Central Park is?" asked Beth.

"It's a parking lot!" exclaimed Christian.

"How can you have a park and an avenue at the same place?" asked Ricky.

"That's were all the rich people live," said Amy. She was very sure of this because her father had said this many times.

"That's *right*, Amy! A lot of very rich people live on Park Ave," replied the teacher.

"And they're going to give us a lot of money," said Anthony.

"I hope so, Anthony. Now does everybody understand what we're going to do tomorrow?"

Everyone nodded. The children knew that tomorrow they would all be going to Park Ave. They would all be dressed as Santa's helpers. And they would collect a lot of money from the rich people and give it to the poor homeless people.

The next day right after lunch, a yellow bus pulled up in front of the school. The children all got on the bus. So did Mrs. Grady and two parents. They were the only ones who weren't dressed as Santa's helpers.

It was a beautiful afternoon. The pale winter sun shined as the bus made its way uptown. Pretty soon they arrived at Park

Ave. Everyone saw the man dressed as Santa Claus ringing his bell. But even though they knew he wasn't a *real* Santa Claus, no one said anything. One by one, they went up to him and introduced themselves. He patted each one on the head, and said, "Ho, ho, ho! How are *you* today?" He even told them that he wasn't really Santa Claus and that his name was Bill. He learned everyone's name and could make funny faces.

Mrs. Grady handed each child a little chimney and reminded everyone to say, "Please give to the homeless. Please help the homeless."

"And what do you say when they put money in your chimney?" she prompted.

"Thank you!"

"Very good," replied the teacher. Now I want everybody to stay very close to Santa. All right, children?"

"Yes, Mrs. Grady!" they shouted.

Soon a whole crowd of passersby had gathered around Santa and his helpers. A very well dressed man knelt down and said to Ricky, "I haven't seen any of Santa's helpers around these parts. I've seen plenty of Santa Clauses, but never a Santa's helper. How are you helping Santa?" he asked.

"We're collecting money to help the homeless."

"Are *you* homeless, young man?"

"No!" Ricky laughed. "Not *me*! But I'm collecting money to help all the poor homeless people who live out on the street."

"In that case," said the man straightening up and reaching into his pocket, "I'd like to contribute." He pulled a $20 bill from his wallet and put it into Ricky's chimney.

Just then a red faced lady in a mink coat got out of a chauffeured limousine. "Wait right here, James." Then she saw the Santa Claus and all the children. "What's all this?" she asked.

"We're Santa's helpers," Jennifer replied. "We're giving the money we collect to the homeless."

46

"What a good idea! "Here's a nice shiny new penny. And with that she went over to each of the children and put a penny in each of their chimneys.

Jennifer made a face behind the woman's back and so did some of the other children. They knew that a penny wasn't very much to give. But their teacher saw what was going on, and she asked all of the children to gather around her. She wanted to talk to them.

"Now children, we have to remember why we are here."

"To collect money for the homeless!" said Adam.

"That's right, Adam. Now we're here to collect money. Even if it's a penny. Every little bit helps."

"But she could have given us more than a penny, Mrs. Grady," protested Jennifer.

"Yeah," added Danielle, "did you see her car? And that soldier she had with her?"

"That man isn't a soldier, Danielle. He's her driver. And I agree with Jennifer that she *could* have given more than a penny. But if we make faces at the people who give us only a penny, then other people will see this, and they may not give anything at all. OK?"

Everybody said "OK."

"Good!" said Mrs. Grady, "Now children, let's collect some more money for the poor homeless people."

For the next hour the children collected money from the passersby. When they were finished, they emptied out their chimneys into Santa's big chimney.

"All of you have been a very big help," Bill said. Then he said "Ho, ho, ho – have a merry Christmas! Oh, I almost forgot!" And he gave each of the children a piece of candy.

All the way back downtown to the school, the children chattered excitedly about what they had done. Everyone remembered the woman who gave them the pennies. But most of all, they talked about the poor homeless people who would have to spend Christmas out on the street.

When they got back to the school they took off their Santa's helpers outfits. They would be using them the next day and the day after that. Mrs. Grady had made arrangements for them to help a different Santa every day for the rest of the week.

Soon it was the day before Christmas, a very cold afternoon. The weather report said it might snow. But the children were very sad. Even though they would all be getting toys and other presents, they knew that there would be poor people out on the street tonight with no place to go.

When their teacher said that the bus was waiting for them, they all picked up their little chimneys and went outside. Today they would stand in front of Macy's – the largest store in the world.

Mrs. Grady understood why the children were so sad. On the day before Christmas, children are usually very happy. But she knew that they were thinking about all the poor homeless people, and that this afternoon would be the last time they would be helping Santa.

The whole city seemed like one big traffic jam. Many people were doing last minute shopping. Others were trying to get home early. Everyone was in a hurry to get someplace else.

The children introduced themselves to the Santa Claus. His name was Charlie. "Pull my beard," he told Christian, "but not too hard." Christian pulled it.

"It's *real!* It's *real!*" he squealed. Now all the others rushed up to Charlie and pulled his beard. It was real all right. They were so busy pulling Santa's beard, no one noticed that a television camera crew had set up and was taping all the Santa's helpers pulling Santa's beard. Of course Mrs. Grady noticed and she told the reporter who was with the camera crew that the children were helping Santa collect money for poor homeless people.

"This would make a wonderful human interest story! Would it be all right if I interviewed the children?"

"Are you *kidding?*" asked the teacher. "I'm sure the children would be delighted! Let's tell them!"

"Children!" she shouted. "This is Mary Beth, a television reporter. And guess what! She would like to interview you."

"Will we be on the six o'clock news?" asked Christian.

"Well," said the reporter. "I certainly hope so. I can't give you any guarantees, young man, but I will try to get all of you on the six o'clock news. Now I want each of you to tell me your name and what you're doing here today right in front of Macy's."

"My name is Christian, and I'm helping Santa Claus collect money to help poor people."

"And my name is Beth. I hope that all the poor people have some place warm to stay tonight."

Mary Beth told them that they were doing a great job, and then she asked Amy if she had anything to add.

"My name is Amy, and I think that everyone who has money should give some of it to help poor homeless people."

The interviews continued until each child had been introduced and had told the reporter something about helping the poor. The camera crew continued taping as the children returned to collecting money. After about half an hour Mary Beth asked the crew to pack up. Then she told the children that they had to rush back to the studio. "I can't make any promises," she said, "but all of you might be on TV tonight. At least you will be if *I* have anything to say about it."

The mood on the bus ride downtown was a lot better than it had been just a couple of hours earlier. It had even started snowing, so there it would be a white Christmas after all.

When their parents came to pick them up, the children excitedly told them they were going to be on the six o'clock news. All the way home Christian told his mommy about that afternoon, the reporter, the TV cameras, and he tried to remember what he had said to the reporter. "Anyway," he concluded, "we'll be able to see it in a few minutes."

Christian's daddy came home just before six o'clock, and they put on the TV. They watched and watched, but there was nothing about the children, nothing about Macy's, and nothing about Santa Claus except for an advertisement with a guy dressed like a Santa Claus screaming about a store named "Crazy Eddie's." Just before the news ended, one of the reporters announced that there would be a special program about Christmas at eight o'clock that everyone should watch.

"Maybe we'll be on *that* program." said Christian. He didn't really believe this. He just didn't want to give up hope.

Christian's parents said he could stay up since it *was* the night before Christmas. So they sat down to have supper, but this time Christian didn't want to talk about what had happened outside Macy's.

At eight o'clock they turned on the TV. The announcer said that instead of the regular program, they were going to show a special Christmas program. It would be about poor people and how they would spend *their* Christmas.

The first scene in the program was their own neighborhood, then the Bowery, a shot of some shopping bag ladies, a men's shelter, and then twenty or thirty Santa Clauses walking across a street. Christian almost blurted out, "*Look!*" Luckily, he caught himself just before he added, "the Santa Claus bums!"

Then the announcer came on again. "There are estimates that over 50,000 New Yorkers are homeless, and many of them will have to spend their Christmas out on the street. And while the snow continues to pile up, most of us are together this evening with our families inside our nice warm homes.

"But there are thousands of people in this city with no homes to go to, and no families with whom to spend the holidays. This program is about these people, and it is also about those who are trying to help them. One group that is helping is composed of five-year-old children."

"That's *us!*" shouted Christian. "We're going to be on television!"

And sure enough, there they were! "Our camera crew found this scene in front of Macy's this afternoon," he continued. "Mary Beth Jorgensen had a chance to interview these remarkable five-year-olds, who have been working every afternoon as Santa's helpers.

First Christian went. Then Beth. Then Amy. And the next and the next and the next and the next. Until everyone had been interviewed.

"Mommy! They did the whole class! Everybody! Even Ricky!"

Christian had never seen himself on TV. After all, how many five-year-olds were even on a kiddie show? There were pictures of the whole group with their chimneys, of Charlie the Santa Claus, of Mrs. Grady watching over them, and then there were pictures of people putting money into their chimneys. There was even snow falling. He hadn't noticed it was snowing until they were all back on the bus.

"In place of commercial messages, there will be listings posted of the agencies that help poor and homeless New Yorkers and their contact information. Please help them help those in need."

After the first listing, the announcer was back again, and there were clips of homeless shelters and of people sleeping in cardboard cartons on the icy sidewalks. There were scenes of soup kitchens and food pantries, and of the lines of people waiting to get inside.

Toward the end of the program, there was another clip of Santa and his helpers in front of

Macy's collecting donations from passersby. And then the announcer closed with these words: "What these children are doing is what all of us should be doing this holiday season. We should be helping those less fortunate than ourselves. After all, isn't that what Christmas is all about?

"So let me extend my thanks and those of Mary Beth Joregensen, her camera crew, and all the folks here at our station to Santa's little helpers who worked so hard to make Christmas a lot better for the City's poor people. And may you all have a merry Christmas and a happy new year!"

Well we're just about at the end of our story. We'd like to say that as a result of that TV special and the efforts of Santa's helpers, millions of dollars poured in to help the poor people of New York City. And who knows? Maybe next Christmas everybody in the City – even the poorest New Yorkers – will have a nice warm place to stay.

# Part II

## FRIENDS AND FAMILY

Just after the last guests had left an afternoon party I had hosted, my eight-year-old niece, Eleni, observed, "What a *crew*! Steve, you have some pretty strange friends." In fairness, she *did* concede that we also had a highly unusual family. But look at the bright side: my friends and family give me a lot to write about.

# FAT AND FORTY

When I was six years old, I got to meet my Aunt Edith. She wasn't exactly my aunt. Edith was my father's cousin, a jolly woman who described herself as "fat and forty." But when she said this, with her thick Boston accent, it sounded like "fat and farty."

Edith despaired ever getting married because of this unfortunate condition. She knew she had almost no chance of "catching a husband." I imagined her jogging down a street, pursuing frightened middle-aged husbands, who were fleeing for their lives in all directions. It puzzled me that she would want to marry someone who was already married to someone else. Besides, she certainly wasn't *fat!* And as for being farty? Well, I knew she didn't smell. So go figure.

During the Depression years, Edith and her younger sister, Grace, both public school teachers, supported the family, putting three younger brothers through college, and one of them all the way through medical school. On the downside, in those days the local school boards frowned on employing married women. The common wisdom was that married men needed those jobs to support their families.

The bottom line was that Edith was out of the matrimonial pool during her prime years. Near the end of the Depression, Grace, who was a great beauty, *did* get married – to a very handsome lawyer, no less – while poor Edith, admittedly no "knock-out," was well down the road to spinsterhood.

Aunt Edith was always there for us. Right or wrong, it didn't matter; if you got in trouble, if you needed help, Aunt Edith was always in your corner. She used to say that there is nothing in the world that is sadder than a child's tears.

It didn't matter that we weren't children anymore. While Susan's boyfriend broke up with her the day before prom and ended up taking her best friend, Susan stayed at Edith's house for the next few days. "Do you know, the exact same thing happened to me over twenty years ago?" But she still hadn't given up hope of finding a man. The only problem was that she was "fat and farty," which really limited the pool of available candidates.

When her nephew Fred dropped out of Yale three weeks into his freshman year, he turned up on Aunt Edith's doorstep. A week later he drove back to school. Edith had bought him an eight-year-old Plymouth.

She wasn't exactly rich or anything. Edith taught English at Classical High in Lynn, a decaying industrial town about ten miles north of Boston. She would sit on her porch every afternoon for years after she retired, and often some former student, or niece or nephew, would drop by.

She must have helped hundreds of kids through college. She figured out where they could get scholarships or loans, or she gave them her own money, saying it was depleting her dowry.

Everybody had to go to college. In a Jewish family, the minimum you settled for was a B.A., preferably from an Ivy League college. She talked for years about one of her nieces who was admitted to Brown "by the skin of her teeth." All of her students, most of whom, incidentally, were not Jewish, were expected to go to college, even if it was only to Salam State at night.

And so, her students would return and visit. They were still her students, even when they were in their thirties and forties. I guess she was the perfect maiden aunt school teacher. And maybe the fairy godmother as well.

Edith's parents came here from Russia in 1906. Her father I remember as a quiet, gentle old man. Her mother, Leah, was about five feet tall and had long, white hair which hung all the way down her back. She told us she was a bomb thrower during the 1905 revolution. I think that's why she left Russia.

The whole family had lived in a big old house on Ocean Street, just a block from the beach. There was a barn behind the house and a set of swings in the backyard. After her parents died and her brothers and sisters moved out, Edith kept up the house by herself. I suppose she was still hoping to "catch a husband" and live there with him.

One day I was driving through Massachusetts on my way up to Maine and decided on impulse to drop in on her. She hadn't seen me since I was a child. When I climbed the porch stairs and greeted her, she thought at first I was one of her former students. I was shocked to see how old she had grown. Edith asked how my parents were. I told her that I hadn't spoken to them in years.

"Your parents are old now," she said. "You know, I can remember your father when he was your age. Younger, even. And you look so much like him."

I hated to hear this. My father, the ladies' man. My father, the genius. My father, the eccentric. All the old stories. But I knew what he was really like. I had to live with him when I was a kid. They just saw one side, but they didn't know what it was like to be put down every day of your life.

"You know what you are, boy?" He never called me by my name. "You're mediocre. You're maybe just a drop above average." And then he'd stop and think for a minute. He was sorry. He was ashamed. "I'm ashamed that you're my son."

I was seven or eight years old then. When I was about twelve, I had a ready answer. "Excuse me for being born."

"Don't get impertinent with me, boy."

I poured this all out on Edith. "You know what your father called me?" she said.

"Yeah, he had a derogatory name for everyone. You were 'yenta.' In fact you were Aunt Yenta." (In Yiddish, a yenta is a gossipy woman.)

"Your father always did think I talked too much. And he used to make fun of me for always looking for a husband. Then, one day, I was forty. Fat and farty. That's how I described myself. And he got such a kick out of that!

"'Fat and farty! Fat and farty!' he would say, over and over again. And he would throw back his head and laugh. You never knew if he was laughing with you or at you.

"But I'll tell you something else about your father. And your mother. Your parents are very unhappy people. Their lives have passed them by. Their son won't talk to them. And they don't have much time left."

I had heard this all before. I knew exactly why I didn't talk to them. There is an old cliché – you can pick your friends, but you can't pick your family. Except, maybe, Aunt Edith. I'd have picked her any day of the week. It's not that I hadn't tried; but nothing I did was ever good enough. I mean, I couldn't even make honorable mention. What my father put into words, my mother would express in her own warped way. "Oh, Steve isn't doing that badly in school." Thanks a lot, Mom.

"I'll tell you something else," said Edith. "I'm going to be seventy-eight in a couple of months. How much longer could I possibly have? Most of my friends, my brothers and sisters, almost everyone I grew up with is gone. I've been to a lot of funerals.

"And I'll tell you something funny. There are only two kinds of mourners. Among the children, I mean. There are children who cry for their parents and the children who cannot accept the death of their parents. But it isn't what you'd expect. It's the children who have made peace with their parents who can accept their parents' deaths.

"Steven! How long has it been since you've talked with them?"

I thought for a while. "About eight years."

"Then I want you to do something. I want you to do something, not for me, and not even for them. I want you to do something for yourself."

"You want me to call them?"

"I want you to call them and I want you to go down to Florida and see them. I want you to see them while you still can."

"You want to know something, Edith? It's so ironic that you, of all people, should be giving me this advice. Do you know to this day they still call you 'Yenta' and that their worst fear is that you'll descend upon them in Florida, and want to stay with them?"

"I have to admit it. That *is* ironic. Well, you can tell them I have no intention of ever leaving this porch. My traveling days are behind me. But you can give them my regards. I've always been very fond of them both."

"I'll think about it. I'm not promising anything."

"Just remember what I said. And Steven, regardless of what your father said to you, I think you turned out just fine."

I hugged her. After I left, I realized that that I would probably be the last time I would ever see her. But I was still shocked to get a call just a few months later. She had died the day after her birthday.

I called my parents that day. They were surprised to hear from me. I decided to visit them. A week later I was in Florida.

I told them Edith had sent them her regards. "Yenta! The next thing you'll know she'll be down here with her suitcases. And she'll want to stay here. Rent-free! And then, she'll want us to introduce her to all the eligible bachelors."

No one had called them. I didn't know how to tell them.

"You know what she told me? She said that she was too old to travel and she anticipated you would say that. And, Dad, do you know what else she said? She said that you loved how she used to describe herself."

He threw back his head and laughed, and asked my mother, "Remember?" My mother smiled, nodding her head.

My father laughed again. "She was always looking to get married. But she used to say, who would want to marry a girl who was 'fat and farty?'" And he threw back his head and laughed. "Fat and farty! Fat and farty!"

# THE BROTHERS LEIBOWITZ

## 1

Almost everyone knows of a family with a crazy uncle they keep locked up in the attic – or in a mental institution. But my family is different. We have *three* crazy uncles – and none has spent a day in a mental institution – *or* locked up in an attic.

Meet the brothers Leibowitz – Jack, Dave, and Phil. They all held down jobs, supported their families, and as far as the rest of the world was concerned, they were not crazy. OK, certainly very eccentric – but not certifiably insane.

In fact, when you think about it, my mother should be included in this group. My brother Howard agrees, but our cousins insist that *their* fathers are in a class by themselves.

"Judy, your mom's not crazy – just highly neurotic" says my cousin, Elaine. "I think of her as Aunt Neurotica. And I don't mean that in a *bad* way."

"Elaine, from the time I even began to *think* about dating, my mom would warn me never to say anything about my uncles."

"Why, did she think their insanity was catching?"

"Almost! She told me that if I said anything, no nice Jewish boy would marry me."

"Judy, she probably wasn't that far off the mark. Imagine if there were a post office Most Wanted poster with a picture of the three Leibowitz brothers and a caption, "Are you a nice Jewish boy? Do *you* want to have insane children? Then don't marry their daughters.""

"Trust me, Elaine, my mom belongs on that Most Wanted poster with her brothers. It's just that she displays her insanity in subtle, understated ways. Like constantly nagging my dad to stop tipping back kitchen chair, because he'll fall backwards and split his head open."

"Judy, that's classical neurotic."

"Yeah, then how about when she made a combined affair – my sweet sixteen party and Howard's bar mitzvah?"

"You know, Judy, when I asked her why she was doing this, she told me, 'What are you complaining about? You're getting two for the price of one."

"You mean *she* was getting two for the price of one. Can you *believe* she did that to us? I was so embarrassed."

"Well, look at it this way: you and Howard both got presents, and *she* paid for just *one* affair. Look at all the money she saved. Maybe *not* so crazy."

## 2

The big debate among the cousins was: who was the craziest of the Leibowitz brothers? Opinion was pretty evenly divided. We agreed they were *all* nuts, but which nut took the cake?

Let's make the case for each of them. Uncle Jack gets points for doing crazy stuff all his life. But perhaps the most outrageous episode occurred during his early twenties while he was still living at home.

Being the oldest child, Jack long considered himself more a third parent than merely the most senior sibling. He would occasionally issue orders, which were always ignored. When he demanded that Phil stop caddying at a local golf course, Phil just laughed in his face. He was saving up for his own set of golf clubs, and if big brother didn't approve, that was just too bad.

I need to explain something extremely unusual about Uncle Jack. To say that the man hated golf would be the understatement of the century. He surely hated golf more than anyone else in the world. Just the mere mention of the word drove him stark raving mad.

So despite his brother's repeated warnings, when Phil had enough money, he went out and bought a fine set of used golf clubs. Every night, he would lovingly polish them, while his older brother huffed and puffed in the next room. One afternoon, when Phil was out caddying, Jack suddenly flew into a rage. He grabbed Phil's golf clubs, and one-by-one, he bent them over his knee. Then he gathered all the clubs and threw them out the window.

Years later, I asked Jack if his parents were home when he broke Phil's golf clubs. Yes, they were in the next room.

"What did they say about what you had done?"

"Boy were *they* sore!"

"Well of course, Uncle Jack. You had destroyed Phil's property."

He broke into a wide grin, "*That's* not what got them sore! It was because I threw the golf clubs out the window!"

"*That* got them mad? Not that you broke the clubs, but that you threw them out the window?"

"I was so mad that I didn't bother to open the window!"

Jack's son, Michael, once asked him why he hated golf so much. Jack went into a tremendous rage, which registered much higher on the Richter scale than his more customary tantrums. The whole basis of his anger was that golf was an effeminate sport. "Look how they dress! And they think they're athletes! But what are they actually doing? They're not playing against an opponent. A pitcher isn't throwing a ball at their heads! No one is trying to tackle them!"

When Jack finally calmed down, he explained that no activity could be called a sport unless there is a strong element of danger. The only danger in golf is getting run over by a golf cart. So what really got him mad was the presumptuousness of calling yourself an athlete and your activity a sport.

Michael's sister Arlene compared her father's outbursts with an aspect of *You Bet Your Life*, a TV quiz show starring Groucho Marx, which had been very popular in the 1950s.

During the show, if a contestant happened to say the magic word, a paper mache duck with one hundred dollars descended from above.

Arlene loved to draw this analogy: He could be anywhere, with anyone, and if someone said the word "golf," he would start yelling at the top of his lungs, often prompting those nearby to edge away from 'the crazy man.'

Once, when the family was having lunch in a Manhattan automat, a woman at the next table mentioned something about golf to her companion. Within seconds Jack was on his feet screaming that golfers thought they were athletes;, that he'd like to lock each of them in a room and go a few rounds with them, and that they should all be decapitated. Everyone stopped eating, and some people stood up to see what was going on. Jack's face had turned beet red and he was pounding the table with his fists.

A couple of automat workers approached him, but then backed off as he yelled something about performing a colonoscopy on them with a white hot iron poker. He then concluded his tirade, and sat down to finish his meal. New Yorkers being New Yorkers, realized the show was over, so they went back to their own meals as well.

Not long ago, Jack's grandson Jonah decided to videotape his grandfather. But Jonah realized that the video could really be enlivened if he could get Jack to talk about golf. Even though Jack must have realized that Jonah was baiting him, he couldn't help himself. So now his views on golf are preserved for future generations.

When Uncle Jack and Aunt Ethel retired and moved to Florida, they somehow ended up living next to a golf course. When he saw people playing, he would scream at them, "*Schmucks! Schmucks!*" Once someone yelled back, "Hey mister, I'm not even Jewish!"

One day, a grossly overweight man asked Jack for directions to the golf course. Jack replied, "Just stand right there. I want to do road work around your belly.

When the first President Bush took us to war against Saddam Hussein, Jack called it the "Golf War." If he thought you were stupid, he called you a "golf brain." And his favorite saying was, "Old golfers never die…. They just lose their balls."

## 3

Next up is Uncle Dave. Unlike his brothers, Dave never went to college. In fact he dropped out of school in the eighth grade. And yet his siblings always insisted that Dave was, by far, the smartest person in the family.

But Dave had two personality difficulties that held him back. He was deeply paranoid, and he could quickly become terribly belligerent. These two traits often led to his getting into fights – usually with complete strangers. His children remember his coming home from work hours late, with blood on his shirt, or with a black eye.

What happened? "Some guy was staring at me on the subway. So I sez tuh him, 'Who you looking at buster?' And then, outta nowhere, the guy sucker punches me."

"So you didn't start it, dad?"

"Ain't yuh listnin tuh me?"

And yet, this man was a self-taught Civil War scholar, probably the only person in the country with just an eighth-grade education who was published in refereed academic journals. In fact, he even taught a course at Kingsborough Community College until he was fired for throwing a chair at the Academic Dean, perhaps because of some scholarly disagreement.

Indeed, some of Uncle Dave's views on the Civil War were considered beyond the pale, except among certain diehard historians in the Deep South. He believed that General Robert E. Lee was our greatest military leader, and that he had never received his due among the war's historians. He also argued that the cause of the South was largely a noble one, and that General Sherman was a war criminal. Had the South won the war, Uncle Dave's views might have found more favor.

Dave insisted that his son be named after Robert E. Lee, but since the age of four, the boy insisted upon being called Robbie. After all, would *you* want to be addressed as Robert E. Leibowitz?

In an act of rebellion, when Robbie was about fourteen, he decided to buy a blue Civil War Union army cap, with a black leatherette visor. So he went to 29th Street and Fifth Avenue in Manhattan, an area with dozens of Korean novelty shops. Going from store to store, he finally found one that had a Civil War army cap in the window. The only problem was that it was a gray Confederate cap, which was still worn in many parts of the South.

So he went inside and told the owner that he liked the hat she had in the window, but wondered if she had any in blue.

"Why you want blue?"

"Well, blue was the color of the Union army and gray was the color of the Confederate army."

"What you talking about?"

"Our Civil War."

"Civil War?" It sounded to him like she had said "Cyral Law."

"You know, like the civil war in Korea?"

"Oh, I can remember war. I was little girl. It was terrible war. It almost destroyed our country."

"Look, can I just have a *blue* hat?"

The woman found a blue hat for him, and he tried it on. It fit perfectly. As he was paying for it, the woman asked him, "Why blue so important?"

"Well, in our Civil War, the North side wore blue and the South wore gray."

"What wrong with *South*? I from South *Korea*!"

Robbie wore the hat home, and it was still on his head when Dave returned from work. He took one look, grabbed the hat off Robbie's head, and marched into the kitchen. Robbie, his sister, and his mother looked at one another and just shrugged. It had been completely predictable that Dave would not be pleased, but what was he doing in the kitchen? Then they smelled smoke.

A minute later Dave came out of the kitchen with a big smile on his face. He looked at his wife, and then at his daughter and son. "If *Sherman* can burn Atlanta, then *I* can burn your hat!"

When Robbie was three, his mother, Maxine, got pregnant again. If the new baby were a boy, Dave had his heart set on naming him after another great Confederate general, Nathan Bedford Forest, a man who regretfully went on a second career as a founder and first Grand Wizard of the Ku Klux Klan. But when the baby turned out to be a girl, Dave quickly acceded to Maxine's wishes, and their daughter was named Elaine, after Maxine's grandmother.

But Dave's dreams were not entirely unfulfilled. To this day, Elaine's brother and cousins sometimes call her by her family nickname – Nate. General Forest rides again!

Dave's family lived in apartment overlooking Ocean Avenue, one of Brooklyn's most prominent thoroughfares. Every Memorial Day and Veterans Day, he hung a huge Confederate flag out the window. Not only did this attract a great deal of attention, but it incensed many of the neighbors. When his landlord demanded that he stop displaying that flag, Dave could have easily persuaded the American Civil Liberties Union and the Sons of the Confederacy to join in a lawsuit against the landlord. Clearly Dave's First Amendment rights had been blatantly violated. Displaying a flag – *any* flag – is a form of speech, so the landlord was trying to suppress Dave's freedom of speech.

But Dave preferred a different course of action. He went after the landlord with a sword that he claimed had once belonged to General Stonewall Jackson.

After his brothers and sister bailed him out of jail, Dave decided that enough was enough. He declared that his family would move out immediately. They could never live in a building owned by someone who was clearly on the wrong side of history.

## 4

Now meet Uncle Phil. Despite Jack's assault on his clubs, Phil remained an avid golfer. Having learned his lesson, he would lock up his clubs before he allowed Jack to enter his home. And at every opportunity, he would encourage his older brother to take up a sport – perhaps even golf.

Phil prided himself on his logical mind. And yet, despite this great gift, even his best laid plans did not always go well. Take, for example, his first marriage.

It was to be the perfect marriage. Phil loved Mildred: that was a given. There was nothing that wasn't too good for her. And then, Phil's logical mind figured out a way he could *really* demonstrate his great love for this woman. He would build her a dream house.

And so, he bought a lot near the top of a hill. It had a beautiful view, which he and Mildred could enjoy. Then he engaged the best architect in the entire New York area. Every evening on his way home from work, he would check on the progress. In fact, Phil managed to visit the site seven days a week, and made some very perceptive and useful suggestions to the contractor and the work crew. No detail was too small to consider.

One day, when he got home about an hour after super-time, he found a note on the kitchen table. Mildred came right to the point: "Phil, your supper is in the refrigerator. I moved back in with my parents. I need some kind of human contact."

He was heartbroken. He loved Mildred so much. And wasn't he building the dream house to prove his love? Go figure.

But love would find Phil once again. Shirley was twenty years younger, and the two of them were quite happy for a while. She would put up with his temper tantrums, and his growingly irrational behavior. After all, look at his brothers. They had a son, Mitchell, who, like his father, was a very good student. Then, one day, Mitchell's teacher accused Phil of doing his son's math homework. Phil was infuriated. He had certainly *not* done his son's homework. The whole idea was completely illogical. The teacher *knew* that Mitchell was an excellent math student.

That night he spent hours writing and rewriting a letter he would send to the local school board demanding that the teacher be fired. Only *that* would give him satisfaction – not a mere apology, or even a stern warning from the principal.

OK, maybe Phil's reaction was a little extreme, but he believed his logic was impeccable. Actions must have consequences. The teacher acted, Phil acted, and the school board must act. What could be any clearer than that?

Phil mailed the letter, and anxiously awaited a response. After waiting for almost a month, and not receiving one word, he went ballistic. He hired a lawyer, who wrote a threatening letter to the head of the school board. Only then was there a response – and a rather terse one at that.

But there had been a problem with the timing of Phil's letter. He did not mail it on the night he had written it. He did not mail it the next day, or even the day after that. When *did* he mail the letter? He mailed it exactly three years later.

Now Phil had told everyone in the family about writing the letter, yet somehow managed to leave out the part about not mailing it for three years. But Phil being Phil, he was threatening to sue the school board for their inaction.

"And what about *your* inaction, Uncle Phil?" asked Elaine.

"You mean: Why did I wait three years to mail the letter? Is *that* what you're trying to ask me?"

"Well, yeah."

"I had an excellent reason: I had no time."

"How could you not have enough time to just walk to the corner and drop the letter into the mail box?"

"Don't get smart with *me*, Judy! I used to change your diapers."

"And now you're changing the *subject*, Phil," said Jack. I think you owe us all an explanation."

"You want an explanation? OK, I'll *give* you an explanation! You remember the trip that Shirley and I took to Europe?"

69

"Vaguely."

"Well, what do you think I was doing during all those months before our trip?"

"Not mailing the letter?" I guessed.

"I'll *tell* you what I was doing. I was planning our trip. Do you have any idea how much money we saved because of all that planning? Well, I'll *tell* you how much! *Hundreds!* In fact, possibly it was over a thousand dollars. And you wanted me to drop everything I was doing to go out and mail that letter?"

## 5

Under Jewish law, someone who dies usually must be buried the next day. This places a great burden on the grieving family to make all the arrangements and notify all the mourners in less than twenty-four hours. And if the deceased was not religious, then she or he had probably never met the rabbi who would be officiating at the funeral.

Such was the case when Uncle Phil died quite unexpectedly. As Shirley explained, "One minute he was yelling at the TV, and the next he just keeled over. Except for his high blood pressure, clogged arteries, diabetes, emphysema, and a heart condition, he was in perfect health," she said, sadly shaking her head.

A few minutes before the funeral service began, the rabbi asked to meet privately with Phil's son, widow, sister, and two brothers. The rabbi said that he would like to learn as much as he could about Phil, so he could make his talk very personal. The others all looked at each other and smiled.

"I can see," said the rabbi, "that Phil was very beloved."

"*Beloved?*" Dave exclaimed. Would any of you guys say that Phil was *beloved?*" The others smiled and shook their heads.

"OK," said the rabbi. "I need all of you to work with me. Please, tell me *any*thing I can say about Phil. Anything that captures his soul, his essence."

When the group emerged from the office, everyone was smiling. Jack said that while he considered all clergymen "foreflushers," he was forced to admit that he actually liked this rabbi. And the others agreed.

Just then the funeral director asked all the mourners to please step into the chapel. When everyone was seated, the rabbi strode up to the front and began the service. And even though Phil had probably not been inside a shul since his bar mitzvah, the rabbi made him sound as devout as the Lubavicher Rebbe. Then he got to the part of his talk that will sound familiar to anyone who has been to a few Jewish funerals. It began with the boilerplate, "And while I was not privileged to have known Phillip Leibowitz, his wife, his son, his sister, and his brothers were kind enough to share with me some of their fondest memories. It was very touching to hear what a beloved father, husband, brother, and uncle he was. And when I asked if there were a few words that Phil would have wanted to say to all of you, I was told that there were."

He paused, and gazed out at the mourners. They were glancing at each other. Some shrugged, and others just shook their heads. The rabbi quickly realized that somehow, they truly believed that Phil would communicate with them this one last time. And that it was left to him to convey this last message to all Phil's loved ones.

"There was a phrase that Phil often used when addressing his friends, his family, and even people he barely knew. It was this phrase that defined him, his outlook on life, and how he felt about his fellow human beings – and perhaps most about those with whom he may have occasionally not seen eye-to-eye…. And so, from Phil's lips to your ears … 'You're full of *shit!*'"

# FAMILY CONNECTIONS

## 1

After graduating from high school, I worked for seven months as an office boy to save money for college. On the subway ride to and from work, my nose was buried in an economics book. I would be an economics major and save the world.

One day, my mother said that it was time for me to have a talk with her Uncle Paul, who taught economics at New York University. The word in our family was that had Governor Thomas Dewey been elected president in 1948, he would have asked Uncle Paul to be his Secretary of the Treasury.

Paul Studenski and Esther Rabinowitz had fallen in love at first sight during World War I – at least according to family lore. A pilot in the Polish Air Force, Paul woke up in a military hospital, and there was my mother's beautiful Aunt Esther holding his hand, while speaking to him in Russian. Whether or not it was love at first sight, they did get married, and would live quite happily for the next forty six years.

Although he had a Polish name, it turned out that Paul was actually Jewish. The name, Studenski, had been made up by his great-grandparents. During those times, Polish medical schools refused to admit Jews, so the family made this ironic name change. The Rabinowitzes all got the joke and welcomed Uncle Paul into the family.

One evening after work, I met my mother in Washington Square Park, and we walked over to Paul and Esther's apartment on Sixth Avenue. We had a pleasant dinner, throughout which Uncle Paul kept trying to ply me with wine. My mother would remind him that "Steve doesn't drink. He's only seventeen."

After dinner, Uncle Paul picked up a fresh bottle of wine and we adjourned to his study and talked economics for the next couple of hours. He was the first economist I had ever met, and was clearly even more knowledgeable than I was.

We had a wide-ranging discussion and often disagreed. He was "an Eisenhower Republican," and I was what would soon be called a "liberal Democrat." When we left, Uncle Paul smiled and said, "Steve, don't become an economist. It's a very controversial field, and you may be too emotional to handle it."

But I thought to myself, "What does *he* know?" Years later I learned that he was arguably the nation's leading expert in public finance.

## 2

After graduation from college and doing a short stint in the army, I enrolled in a couple of evening classes at NYU graduate school, where I would study for a PhD in economics. Uncle Paul had died just a few weeks before. No one knew who I was – not that it mattered. Still, I wondered how he might have felt about my ignoring his advice and then enrolling in his own department.

My more immediate concern was finding a full time job. So, once again we turned to my mother's family for help. Her cousin Bobby seemed like a good choice. A year or two out of law school, Bobby had secured a job at a large cosmetics company that was in the process of going bankrupt. He made a deal: He would work for one year with no pay in exchange for part ownership. In the course of that year the company became highly profitable and Bobby was made CEO.

One Sunday, my mother and I took a bus out to Bobby and Barbara's home in suburban New Jersey. The last time I had seen them, they were living in a basement apartment in the Sheepshead Bay section of Brooklyn. They didn't need to say that they had been both poor and rich, and that being rich was much better.

We had a nice lunch, and then sat out by the pool and reminisced. Finally, realizing that we had not said anything about why we were there, my mother mentioned that I was looking for a job.

"Yeah," said Bobby. "I remember when I was in your position. I had just gotten out of the army when I married Barbara." Barbara added, "We didn't have a pot to piss in." We all laughed.

My mother tried a different tack. "You know, Bobby, Steve is going to NYU to study economics."

"Really?" said Bobby." I'll bet Uncle Paul would have been proud."

"Well, actually he thought economics might be too controversial for me."

"Right! He probably said that to *anyone* he disagreed with. Now don't get me wrong – I truly loved Uncle Paul, but he *was* pretty opinionated."

"*And* a Republican," added Barbara.

"Anyway," said my mother, "Steve is looking for a job. He'll work days and go to school at night."

It was getting really embarrassing. "Bobby," she was practically saying, "please give Steve a job." I felt like the poor relation asking for a hand-out.

Bobby cleared his throat, smiled, and then he said, "Steve, I'm going to help you. I'm going to do for you what I wish to hell someone had done for me when I was your age."

My mother looked very hopeful. We waited. I can still remember his exact words: "Steve ... never work for an insurance company."

### 3

It took many years – going to school at night and working at an assortment of day jobs – but one spring afternoon I found myself just where I had often dreamed of being. I was

75

sitting in a room at NYU with five of my professors, and had just finished defending my doctoral dissertation.

The way the process works is that after your dissertation, you are asked to leave the room. The professors discuss the dissertation and its defense, and finally your advisor comes out into the hall and addresses you as "Doctor." Or not.

When we went back into the examination room everyone offered their congratulations. This is perhaps the happiest moment in academia. And then I said that I wanted to tell them something. "I know that most of you remember Professor Studenski."

Of course they did! They looked at me expectantly. "I really didn't know him well, but he was my mother's uncle. He passed away just before I enrolled at NYU."

They sat there in stunned silence. Then, one of the professors said, "You are so lucky to have had Paul as an uncle. He was so helpful, so encouraging, when I joined the department." The others remembered how nice he had been.

"Just out of curiosity – and by the way, it's too late for us to change our votes – but how come you never said anything about being related to Professor Studenski before this?"

"That's an excellent question. I wish I had an answer."

And then, one after another, they shook hands with me, and I was left in the room with my advisor.

"I want to buy you a drink," she said, which was another tradition. A few minutes later, as we sat at the bar, I told her how Uncle Paul had tried to discourage me from going into economics, and how we had never spoken about it again.

"Steve, if Paul could be here, I want to tell you what he would be doing. He would be doing exactly what I'm doing." Then she raised her glass and shouted, "Congratulations, Doctor Slavin!"

# MOTHER KNOWS BEST

## 1

My father almost never had a good word to say about anyone he knew, while my mother was nearly the opposite. But he reserved a special hatred for certain people whom he had never even met. Heading the list was Elvis.

One day, to see if I could provoke him, I asked my father whether he favored using a portrait of the young Elvis or the more mature Elvis on a postage stamp. And I got the desired result.

His face turned beet-red as he described what he would do to Elvis:

"First I'd decapitate him! Then I'd lock the door and go a few rounds with him."

"But Elvis is *dead*!" I pointed out.

"It doesn't matter!" he screamed.

My father had a more nuanced reaction to the college students on spring break, who often stayed near his Florida retirement community.

"*Students?*" he yelled. "Those aren't students, they're animals!"

"If you had a machine gun set up on the beach, would you mow them down?" I asked.

He scowled at me and then replied conspiratorially, "That would just be a waste of good bullets."

## 2

In comparison to my dad, my mother was sweetness and light. But on rare occasions, she stepped completely out of character. When I was fifteen, she brought me to her cousin's wedding. Helen, who was pushing thirty, was quite tall. By convention, the groom should be taller and somewhat older. Sol was about six inches shorter than Helen. But what he lacked in height, he more than made up for in years – and *then* some.

This was the first time my mother had met him. She kept referring to him as "the little refugee." The man was flitting around taking photos of all the guests. It turned out that he was a professional photographer; he either didn't trust anyone else to take pictures or he was trying to save money. Perhaps he took the first wedding "selfie."

Sol had a very thick Jewish accent, although he had been in this country for decades. Still, it seemed unnecessarily cruel for my mother to keep calling him "the little refugee;" even after I observed that, "Your parents and their entire families were refugees." But she would call him "the little refugee" till the day she died.

Years later, when my sister got married for a second time, my parents, who were living in Florida, were unable to attend the wedding. A month earlier, the bride and groom-to-be visited our parents. The trip seemed to go fairly well, although my sister suspected that Mother was somewhat less than pleased.

My future brother-in-law was between jobs. He had just been denied tenure at a branch of the State University of New York, and was trying to find another job. When they had a moment alone, my sister asked our mother what was wrong.

"He's a fortune hunter!"

"Yes, but where's the fortune?"

"Mark my words: he's after your money."

"*What* money?"

# 3

The wedding went off without a hitch. My sister's friend Dorothy advised the happy couple – who were in their early fifties – to "wait a few years before you start having children!"

After all the guests had left, my sister called our parents, and then put Alan on the phone with Mother.

Your daughter made a beautiful bride."

"Why don't you get a job?"

When my sister told me what Mother had said, I called her and asked how she could say such a terrible thing. But she kept asking, "Why doesn't he get a job?"

I love to use analogies, even if they sometimes don't exactly apply. "Remember how hard it was to get a job during the depression?" Of course she did. "Well, in college teaching, it's just like it was during the depression. Alan is trying very hard to get a job, but there are so few openings."

But she wasn't biting. "If he wants to work, he could find a job. It doesn't have to be at a college."

She really *did* have a point. But still, she had been so rude to Alan. He was a very likable guy, and I was pretty sure he'd find a job – even if it wasn't teaching in college.

My mother died just a couple of years later, still believing that Alan was a fortune hunter. My father, who hated people for even lesser offenses, had seemed much more tolerant. In fact, my sister and I had never heard a word from him about Alan – good *or* bad.

As things transpired, my mother *had* been right about Alan. While there *was* no fortune to hunt, the man turned out to be monumentally lazy. After settling down in my sister's home, over the next eighteen years he managed to get just a couple of part-time jobs, and was quickly fired from each of them. I would tell everyone that Alan had won an award – 'slacker of the year.'

But that was the *good* news. He had no interests – except for eating large quantities of food – and he turned out to be a complete bore. It got so bad that when he entered a room, everyone would flee.

# 4

One day, many years later, I got the phone call I had long been dreading. My father, who was now ninety-five, said that he could no longer care for himself. My sister and I flew to Florida, packed up his clothes, and brought him back to New York. As we were driving out of his housing complex, I asked my father if he wanted to take one last look. "*No!* Just throw me in that dumpster with the rest of the garbage."

Back in New York, we settled him into an assisted living facility, but a few months later, he needed to move into a nursing home. He was angry virtually all of the time. In fact, when we visited, his greeting was always the same: "Just give me a gun and a bullet!" This continued for a couple of months.

He was increasingly frustrated with his physical and mental deterioration, and often complained that he had become "useless." When people reached that state, he said, they should just kill themselves.

My father never told jokes, and in his later years, he stopped telling funny stories. He never laughed, and seemed to have an almost perpetual scowl. And then, when I least expected it, he said something so funny that I almost fell down on the floor laughing.

He was sitting in the hall and saw me coming. When I was a few feet from him he muttered, "Just give me *two* guns and *two* bullets!"

"Why *two* guns and *two* bullets? Are you afraid you'll miss?"
"I won't miss!"
"Then why do you want two guns and two bullets?"

He just glared at me as if I were missing the obvious. And then he said, "One for me … and one for Alan."

I couldn't stop laughing. When I told my sister, she was less than pleased. He had said the same words to her.

# 5

Several years ago I took on the job of family historian. I managed to get almost everyone's contact information; I was missing two cousins. They were the daughters of Helen and

Sol. Helen had died a few years before, and I had been given Sol's number.

I called Sol, told him I had been to his wedding, and had put together a family tree. I needed to add his daughters' contact information and the family tree would be complete.

Sol kept going on and on about his condominium and the swimming pool, his accent even thicker than I had remembered. "Look, I'll tell you what, Sol. I'm going to mail you the entire family tree, and then you can just mail back your daughters' contact information."

When I had not heard back from him, I gave him another call. He *had* received the family tree, but instead of sending me the information I needed, he wanted me to come to see his condominium with its swimming pool, and then, maybe he would give me his daughters' contact information.

I thought back to the wedding so many years ago, when he and Helen had married. And I realized that my mother had been right about him after all. The man *was* "a little refugee."

# BATHROOM HUMOR

If you've frequented men's rooms, you may have seen the helpful reminder just above the urinals:

Our aim is to please,
So please aim.

Most guys do their best, but fairly soon you might notice a few telltale drops on the floor. You might even say to yourself, "Nobody's perfect."

My friend, Walt is definitely *not* perfect. But he's well aware of his failings in this department.

That's why he has covered the entire floor area around his home toilet with paper towels. He's obviously someone who leaves nothing to chance.

I've never actually been to Walt's apartment, so what I'm about to tell you is merely hearsay – but from a highly reliable source. Theresa is what you would call "honest to a fault."

One evening, when Theresa was visiting Walt, she asked him about the paper towels. He explained his problem and asked her for advice. But it quickly became evident that Walt would not, or could not, make any adjustments to his routine.

Walt's aim is actually excellent, but not when he gets up in the middle of the night. Theresa suggested a nightlight, but Walt replied that any kind of light would wake him up. Perhaps he could urinate while sitting down, but evidently *that* he can do *only* when fully awake.

Then, there was the other problem, for which Walt also *had* found a very practical solution. Sometimes, during his nocturnal trips to the bathroom, he managed to urinate on the toilet seat. No problem. The next morning, he would just wipe it off with a towel.

Theresa, trusting soul that she is, told me all of this in the strictest of confidence. Obviously her trust was misplaced. I am, after all, a known prankster *and* gossip.

A few days later she got a priority mail package and called me immediately. She was furious! "You may have thought that was very funny, but it wasn't!"

Here's what I'd put into the package: a pile of paper towels, a face towel, a pink plastic water pistol, and a note.

"Why are you so mad?"

"Don't you remember how afraid I am of guns?"

"Theresa, you thought that was a *gun*?"

"Well, at first, yeah."

"OK, now read me the note."

"What note?"

"It's in the box. Maybe it's mixed in with the paper towels."

"Oh, I've got it."

"Theresa, go ahead and read it to me."

"OK, it says, 'If you just washed your face in Walt's bathroom and someone said you had to dry it with either some paper towels or a face towel, which one would you use?'"

"I'd shoot myself!"

# LITTLE THINGS CAN MEAN A LOT

Did you know that Americans work longer hours and have less vacation time than the citizens of virtually every other economically advanced country? If you don't believe me, you can look it up.

After graduating from Brooklyn College, I was resigned to having to work from nine to five for the rest of my life. And for most of the next five years I held a series of pretty crappy jobs that kept me stuck in an office all day. A couple of nights a week I went to NYU, where I studied economics.

One bitterly cold winter day I was sitting on a bench in Central Park eating my lunch. There was snow on the ground and only a few people scattered around. I had a bunch of walnuts with me that I would have for dessert, if you can call them that.

Did you know that you can crack a walnut by placing two of them between the heels of your hands and then pressing them together? I had cracked the first nut and had begun to eat it when a squirrel approached me. You know how, when squirrels beg for food, they kind of stand up on their hind legs, place a paw across their chest, and give you this kind of pleading look?

I had really been looking forward to eating those walnuts, but I'm a complete sucker when a poor squirrel begs for food. It was such a cold day and that squirrel probably had had nothing to eat. So I put one of the nuts on the ground. The squirrel snatched it quickly and dashed off with it.

Just as I got ready to crack another nut, the squirrel was back again. Well, you can probably figure out that by the time I was ready to return to the office, that squirrel had cleaned me out.

All afternoon I thought about how every winter, those poor squirrels living in the park had to exist on handouts. But then, I began to realize that those squirrels had a better deal than *I* did. Sure, I could buy all the nuts I needed, but *those* guys got to stay in the park all day. They did not have to go back to the office after lunch.

I had a friend who was extraordinarily lazy and extremely smart. Nadine managed to live quite well, but had no visible means of support – not that I'm criticizing. When I told her about my encounter with the squirrel, and how I wished that I could hang out in the park all day, she grew very thoughtful. Then she looked me straight in the eye and announced: "Steve, you should get a job teaching in a college."

"Are you nuts?" I exclaimed, completely unaware of my pun.

When Nadine finished laughing, she said, "Look, it makes perfect sense. College professors work about half the hours that a normal person works."

"*Really*? I remember all those compositions we had to write in freshman English. Poor Professor Park must have been up till two in the morning marking them."

"Steve, you know that only English profs get stuck marking compositions. None of the other profs has that kind of workload."

"Just look at the big expert! You dropped out of Brooklyn College four times during our freshman year."

"True, but I also got *readmitted* four times. Which, incidentally, the Registrar informed me, was a new school record."

"OK, what about making up exams? And marking them? *That* takes up a lot of time."

"Puuuuullllleeeeeeeeeeezzz!" she replied, heaping maximum scorn upon me. "They've been teaching the same courses for so many years, they could make up exams in their sleep. Or use old exams."

"What about marking exams?"

"How long does it take to mark a multiple-choice exam?

Fine. I would now play my trump card. "Who would hire me? I only have a master's degree. And at the rate I'm going, I won't have my PhD for years."

"There are sixty-five colleges in the New York area. (I wondered where she was getting her facts.) If you apply to all of them, I'll bet at least *one* college would hire you. Look — what do you have to lose?"

I knew that Nadine was completely right. And sure enough, that fall I was teaching economics at New York Institute of Technology. Coincidentally, it was located just a couple of blocks from Central Park.

They had me teaching five sections of the intro economics course three times a week. I had a fifteen-hour week! It was, by far, the easiest job I had ever had, and was certainly a lot better than sitting in an office all day, trying to look busy. And as things turned out, I actually enjoyed teaching.

After my first day, I knew I could never go back again to a real job. My life had changed. And all because of my encounter with a squirrel — and some great vocational counseling from Nadine.

Soon the leaves were turning and it was getting colder. It was the middle of the busy season for the squirrels, who were gathering food for the winter. Often I took long walks in Central Park, and I always carried plenty of walnuts.

# THE CITY UNIVERSITY OF NEW YORK MEDICAL SCHOOL QUICK WEIGHT LOSS DIET

Caroline is a yo-yo dieter. Name any diet – Scarsdale, Weight Watchers, Dr. Atkins, and even Dr. Romano's lettuce leaf diet – and she's tried it. But nothing worked for her. You know the story: she'd lose some weight, struggle to keep it off, and then gain it all back again – plus a few added pounds.

She worked at a large New York bank that had an excellent employees' cafeteria, with a very well stocked fruit and vegetable salad bar. Still, Caroline – and thousands of others just like her at the bank – just could not resist all the other wonderful dishes that were available. And then one day – a miracle! Ellie, who worked in her department, brought in copies of a diet she had found on the Internet – The City University of New York Medical School Quick Weight Loss Diet.

Ellie and Caroline decided to start a weight loss contest, and anyone who worked on their floor was eligible to join. Every day, each of the contestants would put a dollar into the office pool. By the end of the day, forty people on their floor had taken up the challenge. The person who lasted the longest on the diet would win all the money. Everyone who entered the contest had to keep putting in a dollar a day for as long as the contest lasted.

So even if you went off the diet, you still had to put your dollar a day into the pool. Whoever lasted the longest would not only lose a ton of weight, so to speak, but also win thousands of dollars. They were all on the honor system, but you could easily see who had dropped out by looking at what they were having for lunch, not to mention the pounds they were quickly regaining.

The diet was very strict. Every Friday, the menu for the following week would appear on a special website dedicated entirely to the diet. For example, one day's meals included half a grapefruit, a cup of coffee with two tea spoons of skim milk and an artificial sweetener, and one piece of whole wheat toast for breakfast; lunch was one pear, three ounces of low-fat cottage cheese, and an eight-ounce glass of tomato juice; dinner was four ounces of boiled salmon, four ounces of any kind of rice, and a celery stork; and a mid-evening snack was four ounces of skim milk and a rye crisp.

Ellie maintained a chart with the names of the initial participants, updating it each week by adding a star next to the names of those still in the running. The drop-outs would usually slink over to her desk when they thought no one was looking, and confess their failure. Ellie would usually console them by saying, "You're still a big winner. Look at all the weight you've lost." Of course, most of them quickly put those pounds right back where they had lost them.

After four weeks, Ellie, Caroline, and seventeen others were still going strong. Some of the drop-outs were not very happy about continuing to contribute their dollars, but a deal was a deal. Still, according to Ellie's informal record-keeping, the remaining contenders had collectively lost nearly 275 pounds.

Around the six-week mark, a few of the participants were growing a little testy. Bill, who had always been considered rather eccentric, would sometimes retire to the men's room, settle into a stall, and then howl for several minutes before dunking his head into the toilet. Somehow this procedure calmed him down. Still, others, who happened to be occupying adjacent stalls, found this behavior somewhat disconcerting. Eventually, personnel called him in for a nice, friendly chat.

At the eight-week mark, there were nine stalwarts still in the running. Ellie had dropped out, but she continued managing the list and the pool treasury, which had grown to $1,600. Caroline and Bill were going strong, and all nine of them were much slimmer than when they had started.

By now everyone who ate in the cafeteria knew about the pool, and management even arranged for the nine finalists to eat for free. But how much could they eat? Indeed, this was certainly not one of those all-you-can eat diets.

By the end of twelve weeks, there were just three survivors – Caroline, Bill, and Phil, an accountant who wore suspenders, had a pocket protector, and seemed to have no friends. Caroline was getting more and more nervous, and Bill was ready to jump out of his skin, but Phil was apparently quite calm, although it was a bit hard to tell.

And then it happened. And when it did, it happened more or less the way everyone had expected. At around 10 a.m., Bill noticed that the lunch menu that day had just three items – one piece of toast, an eight-ounce glass of vegetable juice, and three medium size plums. Bill was beside himself! He *detested* plums. Just *looking* at them, made him sick.

He became frantic! He had come this far, had eaten every one of the prescribed menu items, but now this, this, this *abomination!* If only he could substitute, say, half a cantaloupe for the plums, then he'd be able to stay on the diet.

"Hey, Ellie," he yelled across the office. "Can I substitute half a cantaloupe for the three plums today?"

"How should I know? Ask Caroline."

"Hey, Caroline, are we allowed to make any substitutions?"

"You got me, Bill. Maybe Phil knows." Bill took one look at Phil and knew the guy was clueless. Bill desperately needed that substitution, but who could he ask? There wasn't any contact info on the diet website. He went to the City University Medical School website, but he couldn't find any reference to the diet.

He found the school's phone number, and at around eleven am he managed to get connected to the Nutrition

Department of the Medical School. He tried to explain his dilemma to the department secretary, and even tried asking *her* if he could substitute the half cantaloupe for the three plums. She modestly replied that she wasn't really qualified to answer his question. And she wasn't sure who could help him. So she put him on hold. Big mistake! By now Bill was banging his fist on his desk. Finally, she came back on the line and said that the Chairwoman was at a meeting, but she would call him back in about an hour. Bill gave her his number and tried to explain that it was an emergency. He was not happy when she replied that this *was* a Medical School, and they had a lot of emergencies.

Bill waited at his desk for the phone to ring. By now word had spread and almost everyone on the floor was keeping an eye on him. In fact someone had even alerted security, and a couple of uniformed guards were discretely looking on.

And then, at exactly noon, his phone rang. All work stopped and all eyes focused on Bill. "Bill Johnson, here at the bank where banking is a relationship." It was the Chairwoman of the City University Medical School Nutrition Department. Someone had managed to turn the call into a floor-wide conference call. Everyone was listening in.

Bill: Thanks for calling back, professor.

Chairwoman: No problem, Mr. Johnson. How may I help you?

Bill: Look, I've been on your diet for twelve weeks

Chairwoman: Are you referring to the City University Medical School Diet?"

Bill: Yes! And if you could just tell me if I –

Chairwoman: Hold it right there!

Bill: I *can't!* And you're the only one who can help me. This is an emergency!

Chairwoman: Mr. Johnson. I want you to calm down and listen to me. We have been getting calls for months about this diet. Just this morning we've had more than a dozen!

Bill: "Professor, I'm truly sorry! It's just that I need an answer to a simple –

Chairwoman: *Listen…to…my…words*: There *is* no City University Medical School Diet.

Bill: Are you sure that you're with the City University Medical School?

Chairwoman: Yes! I am the Chairwoman of the Department of Nutrition of the City University Medical School. The diet you're referring to is a fraud. Do you understand what I'm telling you?

Bill: Yes, it's a fraud. I understand. But I need your help. Please, will you help me?

Chairwoman: I'll help you if I can, as long as you understand that the diet is a fraud, and that it has nothing to do with our school.

Bill: I *understand!* I *understand!* It's a fraud! OK, you're a nutritionist, right?

Chairwoman: Yes I am a nutritionist. I have a PhD in nutrition, I chair the Nutrition Department, and I also lecture on nutrition at the Graduate Center. And I have also published extensively –

Bill: OK, OK, so please tell me, I'm *begging* you!

Chairwoman: Tell you *what?*

Bill: For lunch today, can I substitute half a cantaloupe for the three plums?

# TEACHING AVOIDANCE

Long before the introduction of online courses, thousands of innovative professors found ways to minimize – if not completely eliminate – their contact with students. I would like to tell you about three pioneers in this field who were on the faculty of the Colonel Augustus Schlockman College, located next to the Long Island Railroad train yards in the Woodhaven section of Queens.

Although Colonel Schlockman never actually served in the military, he *did* provide the Zitnik family with a very large sum of money to help establish the college. Now, twenty years later, the college president and most of its administrators are Zitniks, as are nearly all the members of the Board of Trustees. The school's motto, "It's not *who* you know; but *what* you know,' is included in all official communications. And in its advertising, the college proudly proclaims having "the world's most dedicated faculty, always ready to go that extra mile for our students."

Before we get started, let me lay my cards on the table. While I do try to cover a decent amount of material in the courses I teach, I am certainly not above occasionally cutting corners. Like dismissing my evening class an hour early; or not showing up for most of my office hours. But you could hardly call me a slacker – at least relatively speaking.

The college's administrators were well aware of these minor transgressions, and they felt the need to draw the line somewhere. Schlockman College *did* have standards, however lax they might have been. So they decided to check up on all the professors who taught the late evening courses that were scheduled to run from 8:10 to 10:40.

The college had a long-time employee who most of us knew only as "the Romanian." Nobody knew his name, or whether he was even from Romania. He did have a thick accent, but he avoided conversation and always looked as if he was hiding something.

The Romanian was given the assignment of checking the rooms to make sure that we didn't dismiss our classes too early. He was quite good at his job. He would gently open each classroom door for just two or three seconds, and then shut it without making a sound.

There was just one drawback. It turned out that the Romanian *also* enjoyed going home early. So he usually came by around 9:15. Clearly, there was nobody checking up on *him*.

My class was in the next-to-last room before a stairway. I quickly figured out that after the Romanian glanced into my room, he checked the next room, and then went to another floor. I soon noticed a pattern. About ten seconds after my door opened and shut, I would hear chairs scraping the floor in the next room, and then voices out in the hall.

My neighboring colleague must have kept his eyes glued to the door. Or maybe he listened for the sound of the stairwell door closing behind the Romanian. I wondered if he stopped his lecture in mid-sentence to dismiss his class.

I never got to meet this mysterious fellow, or even to learn his name. Still, I admired his determination to do the absolute minimum amount of work. He had *my* vote for slacker of the year.

My students never caught on to what was happening. Nearly all of them came to school straight from work, struggling to get to their 5:30 classes. They were all as happy as I was to leave early.

What I would do, once I knew the coast was clear, was finish up whatever we were discussing, and then ask if there were additional questions. There never were. I was usually on the subway platform by 9:45.

Dr. Samuels was the faculty member with whom I was closest. During my first semester at Verrazano, he kindly taught me the ropes. He was a retired high school teacher who had a doctorate in education, and had been hired here to teach English. The only problem with him was that he was completely burned out after more than forty years of teaching.

Dr. Samuels would begin each class by erasing the blackboard. Then he would call the roll. After that he would write some stuff on the board and ask his students to copy it. Were there any questions? No? So then he would take the roll again, and the period was over. Another professor once observed that if Dr. Samuels leaned on the blackboard, his entire lesson would be recorded on the back his jacket.

Finally, we have Professor Cherniak, who taught money and banking. The college owed him big-time. As the human resources director of Third Capitol Bancorp, he had hired hundreds of Schlockman graduates – most of whom would have been otherwise unemployable. Miraculously, they managed to avoid running the bank into the ground. But it finally dawned on upper management that Bob Cherniak was a complete incompetent. He was offered an extremely generous early retirement package that he could not refuse.

And so, at the age of 46, he happily plunged into a second career at Schlockman College. His field of expertise was the Federal Reserve System. The Fed publishes more than one thousand weekly, monthly, quarterly, and annual press releases, reports, periodicals, studies, and other printed matter. Professor Cherniak made it his mission to supply his students with each one of them.

Every day, cartons of these materials would be delivered to the Business Department office. A student assistant using a hand truck needed three or four trips to bring them to Professor Cherniak's classroom. Instead of lecturing, the good professor would distribute whatever he found in the cartons. One day, a huge, heavily taped carton arrived from the post office. Later, when he was distributing its contents, some of the students began laughing; Professor Cherniak learned that he had been handing out the monthly report of the Southwestern Missouri Horse Traders Association. One student asked if this would be on the final exam. Then another one quipped, "Don't *bet* on it."

I remarked to one of Professor Cherniak's Business Department colleagues that he could have saved time by placing piles of publications on his desk and have the students file by and pick up one of each. "Yeah," she added, "and then he could have a huge garbage pail next to the desk."

You might think that some of the students would have complained to the Business Department Chairman – not that he would have done anything – but they were all delighted that they didn't have to buy any textbooks or take any tests. They understood the implicit course contract: Your grade was based solely on class attendance. Students who attended regularly got "As;" students who never came to class got "Fs;" and those in between got "Bs," "Cs," and "Ds." On his evaluation forms, his students always wrote that Professor Cherniak was a very fair grader.

I shared an office with Professor Cherniak and three other colleagues. Each of us had a four-drawer file cabinet. There were another dozen file cabinets that Professor Cherniak had appropriated. There were also hundreds of cartons stacked from the floor to the ceiling. Someone had taped a colorful sign on the wall:

The Professor Robert Cherniak Warehouse
(If we don't have it, the Fed didn't print it.)

One day, I got to meet his wife and daughter, who were waiting for him to finish "teaching" his last class.

"Can you believe this?" I asked as I cast my eyes over his empire. They burst out laughing.

"Dad was even worse at home."

"Really?"

"Would you believe that I actually had to call the fire marshal on my own husband? And that our home was declared a fire hazard?"

"Well," I said, "I guess your loss was our gain."

Woody Allen once said that "eighty percent of life is just showing up." At Schlockman College, three faculty members solved the existential question of how to live the other twenty percent: Be there without being there.

# Part III

## LOSS OF INNOCENCE

Can you remember your first date and your first kiss? Can you remember when you lost your innocence? Once lost, it's gone forever. These stories are largely about self-deception, heartbreak, and maybe just growing up.

# A SEAT ON THE SUBWAY

Subway crime is one of New York's favorite pastimes. Back in 1965, the Mayor finally decided to put a policeman on every train. Then, a few years later, they started running shorter trains at night. This pushed crime off the subways and back up in the streets and alleys where it belongs.

Most subway crimes are committed by teenagers against those least able to defend themselves – women, the elderly, or the isolated passenger in an empty car. What happened to me on a crowded subway train not only defied the very laws of probability, but it all took place unnoticed by over 100 fellow passengers. What happened was that I was molested by an indescribably beautiful young woman.

I was sitting there, your typically somnolent subway rider, vaguely reading the *Post's* sports page. It was about 5:30, the height of the rush-hour, and I was on my way to the dentist, whose office was way out in my old neighborhood. These visits were about the only time I went back.

She got on at 34th Street and stood about eight feet away from me. Everything was just right – the delicate nose, high cheek bones, unbelievably clear blue eyes, the kind of half-pouting mouth that always struck me as extremely sensual, all framed by straight, long brown hair. In those days, women still wore dresses. I could imagine the greetings she must have received on her way past construction sites, sidewalk domino games and other gathering places for New York's hot-blooded masculinity.

I hate to get caught staring at people, even when there's good reason to stare, so I forced myself to return to my paper. The next time I looked up, I thought I saw her eyes directed at me, but if she had been, she quickly looked away. Probably my imagination. I waited about two minutes and then looked up again. And again she quickly glanced away. But still, I wasn't sure. So I decided to try an old subway trick. I pretended to doze off. When I suddenly opened my eyes, I caught her again.

Now I'm not a bad-looking guy, but quite frankly, I don't get all that many stares on the subway, or out on the street for that matter, so you'd really have to convince me before I'd make a move. That's all I needed was to embarrass myself in a crowded train and then have to ride all the way out to Brooklyn whilst everybody sneered at me.

Just after we went over the bridge, she moved a little closer. I could have touched her by reaching through the tangle of people between us. It was just the two of us now, and I began to hope that maybe she really *did* want to meet me.

But then something terrible happened. A lady with a huge package got on at DeKalb Avenue, and we were cut off. There I was, just mustering my courage, when the fates decided I was unworthy. How many chances should he have? We send him the woman of his dreams and what does he do? He sits.

And *sits*. How could this happen! Should I get up? Sure, and make a fool of myself. Suddenly, the train lurched and the lady and her package went crashing into a clutch of people near the door. "Lady, Why doncha hang on so yuh wount hafta lean on otha people?" They made a little room for her near a pole and now, I couldn't believe my luck! There she was, no more than a foot away.

All I had to do was reach up and stroke her face, her hair. I wanted to ask her to sit on my lap. I wanted to hold her, kiss her hair, and tell her that I'd never leave her; that as soon as I saw her, I knew that she was the one. Maybe she was thinking the same thing, because she started to inch even closer, if that were possible. She was actually standing between my legs, holding onto a strap directly above me. I think if I were wearing shorts, I would have gone out of my mind.

So there I was, attempting to read the paper in a crowded subway car, while engaged in some kind of simulated sexual act. But this just couldn't be. It must have been the motion of the train. *That* was it – she couldn't help but rub against my leg. OK, so why was she standing there? She could have chosen a less compromising spot. No, it was clearly fate that placed her veritably between my legs.

Now was the time to spring into action. So if she was going to rub my leg, why shouldn't I rub hers? First I looked up at her, but still she looked away. Maybe it had to be impersonal. A lot of women like you to turn out the lights before they do anything, which must have been why she didn't want to meet eyes for longer than a second.

Somehow, I couldn't move my leg without rubbing against the guy sitting next to me. But she kept doing it, so I just sat there quietly going out of my mind. As I began to take leave of my senses, it occurred to me that I was actually being molested. This had to be a first in the history of the New York City subway system.

"Well, you see, officer, I was just sitting there when this beautiful woman came over and raped me."

"I see. And were there any other people present when the perpetrator had her way with you?"

"Oh, about a hundred or so."

"Would any of them step forward to verify your story?"

"Well, you know how it is, officer. When this kind of thing happens, everyone turns the other way."

"Yeah, I know what you mean, Mac. But your word against hers wouldn't stand up in court. I seen hundreds of cases like this one. Look, next time, buddy, get a couple of witnesses."

When a woman rapes you on a subway train, you're sometimes a little curious about why she picked you, what she saw in you. Were you just some random guy? Does she do it only to guys who are sitting down? How often does she do this sort of thing? Just a few friendly, inoffensive questions.

Of course now I'm really flipping out! This can't possibly be happening to me. Here is this woman all over me, and I'm still too shy to say two words to her. This can't continue. I'm getting desperate. I've got to have her. I'll do anything! I'll break my dentist's appointment! I'll give her my seat!

Could it be? Could that be all she wants? My seat? A guy with half a brain would have given her his seat in a second. What a great way of breaking the ice. But if she's going through this whole number just to get my seat, then she isn't interested in me. Who the hell does she think she is? Just because she's the most beautiful woman I ever saw, does she think she has some sort of divine right to get someone else's seat on the subway? Boy, I really resent her attitude. Here are all these really tired people, several of them with heavy packages, and *she* wants my seat. No, there are plenty of people in this car I'd give the seat to before her. Boy, that would really show *her*.

We reached the Prospect Park station, the first stop outside the tunnel. The late afternoon sunlight comes through the unwashed windows. I look up at her. She again looks away.

This charade has *got* to end–I have to get up the guts to talk to her. "Look, lady, you know you've been staring at me and rubbing against my leg. I don't want to sound crude, but if you were me, how would *you* interpret these actions?"

No, too indirect. How about, "I couldn't help noticing what you've been doing, and I wish you'd keep it up." No, no, too smug.

So what do I do for openers! It's absurd – we've practically gone to bed together, and I'm afraid to say anything. Because if I did, maybe she'd go away and I'd wake up.

What I needed was a plan of action. OK, the problem is that I'm afraid to embarrass myself if she snubs me. If only I could talk to her in private. Then I'd know what to say. Sure, I could tell her about my friend Arnold, how he followed a beautiful woman across Jersey, transferring buses four times along the way. He had two huge sample cases with him. Finally, she got off the last bus in some tiny town way out in South Jersey. She began walking along the deserted street. Arnold followed with his sample cases. Finally, she realized that this man had been following her. She started to run. Arnold trotted after her with his sample cases. She rushed into a big rooming-house, and as she fumbled for her keys in the vestibule, Arnold came clomping up the porch stairs.

"You've been following me! What do you *want?*"

Arnold was panting as he put down the cases. "Would you care to go out on a date?"

With that, she shoved a big ring in his face. "Sorry, I'm en*gaged!*"

And then she's inside, and the door slammed shut. Arnold pounded on the window. "At least, do you want to go for a cup of coffee?"

Guess not.

Now I knew what I had to do. I'd just tell her that story, and preface it by saying that this would explain everything. We were getting close to Kings Highway, which was my stop. Almost half the train would empty out here, so there was a good chance she'd be getting off. OK, if she got off at Kings Highway, I'd walk along with her and say, "Look, I've got to tell you this story so you'll understand everything." Somehow, that seemed like an excellent idea.

The train was pulling into the station. Out of the corner of my eye, I saw her take one last look at me as she started moving toward the door. I quickly followed. She seemed quite surprised to see me walking next to her. I started to say, "Look, I've got to tell you..." when she smiled sort of tentatively and said, "Steve?"

Then, in a flash, going back at least eight years–"Sharon?"

"Of course I'm Sharon. I thought that was you, but I wasn't positive. I didn't want to make a fool of myself if you had turned out to be someone else."

I put my arm around her and pulled her toward me. I hugged her and kissed her hair. We stood back, holding each other's arms. We were laughing. It was as if our lives had been planned to lead up to this moment.

"God, Sharon, how *are* you?"

"Great! Look, Steve, I'm engaged!" And with that, she shoved this big ring in my face.

# THE FIRST TIME

Can you remember the spring of 1955? If you were growing up in Brooklyn back then it would probably stand out in your memory. Eddie will never forget that spring. He was almost 16 and he was unbelievably horny.

It was pretty rough coming of age back in the fifties. You had to at least get engaged to get a "steady piece," and Eddie had never even had a date. But things were going to take a change for the better. They just had to.

Eddie was on his way to a party. He waved to Mr. Goldberg who was watering his lawn. There were kids playing hide-and-go-seek and still smaller kids playing stoop ball. Little girls were jumping rope and George, the ice cream man, was rolling down the block on his motor scooter.

The party was in some girl's basement. All the parties were in basements that parents had fixed up so their kids wouldn't mess up their houses. Eddie went in the side door, down the stairs, and found that the party was already in full swing. "Unchained Melody" was playing on the Victrola and there were several couples dancing.

You had to make your move between records or you'd never get to dance. Eddie set his sights on a really cute girl with a dirty blonde page boy and a white cashmere sweater. He was just a sucker for blondes.

She was dancing with Alan. No problem. As soon as the record ended, she disengaged from Alan. "Would you care to dance?"

"Sure," she smiled, "but the record didn't come on yet."

"So?" said Eddie, and he slowly pulled her toward him. She seemed to melt in his arms. They were cheek-to-cheek. He could smell her hair, her perfume. Still, the next record didn't come on.

"It's stuck!" said the girl who lived in the house. "Give it a knock." One of the boys hit the Victrola with his fist and the next record began. It was Nat King Cole singing: "They tried to tell us we're too young. Too young to really fall in love."

"I like your hair," she whispered.

"You do? That's funny."

"What's funny?" she asked.

"I like yours."

"Yeah?"

"Yeah, let's go for a walk," he said.

"OK, but first you've gotta to tell me something."

"Sure. What?"

"Your name."

"Eddie. What's yours?"

"Marsha."

"So can we go?"

"Why not?"'

They made their way over to the stairs. "Hey, Joanie! I'll see you tomorrow."

"OK. Marsha. Remember, ten o'clock in front of the Dubrows."

"Sure, Joanie."

"Wanna go over to the bay?"

"Sounds nice, Eddie."

He took her hand and they started walking. By the time they arrived at the bay, he had his arm around her. Here was a guy who had never been out on a date. He wondered if this counted as a date.

"It's really beautiful here," she said.

Eddie took this as a signal to make his move. He gently guided her face toward his. They kissed. She put her hand on the back of his neck. She moved her fingers into his hair. He

110

was feeling giddy. He was getting an erection. Now she was rubbing up against him. Could she feel it? But he was too far gone to worry about that.

They kept kissing. Finally, she said the words he never thought he would ever hear.

"Could we go someplace?"

Where could they go? His parents' apartment? They were probably sitting there watching "Your Show of Shows." The beach? That's it! Under the boardwalk. They started walking. He was so excited he could hardly contain himself. Every block or so they would stop to neck. Finally, they reached the boardwalk. The waves were breaking against the rocks. There was a three-quarters moon. Sea gulls swooped down over the water.

Eddie wanted to remember this moment forever. They climbed down the steps and took off their shoes. Eddie couldn't believe they were actually going to *do* it. They made their way under the boardwalk. Marsha put her hands on his shoulders and said to him. "Look. Eddie, I'm telling you right now. I'm not going to go all the way. All right?"

"Sure."

"If you're nice. I'll take you in my mouth, but you gotta be nice."

"I'll ... I'll ... I'll be nice!"

Eddie was nice.

All of that happened nearly thirty-five years ago. Even if they didn't go all the way, when you're a horny kid like Eddie, it was like really doing it for the first time. And no matter what happens, you can't ever get that feeling again. The feeling of doing it for the first time.

Eddie has gone through a lot of changes since that spring evening. He went to college, he married, then had a couple of kids. Changed jobs a few times, and like so many of his contemporaries, he got divorced. He lost his wife, he lost his hair, and he gained about fifty pounds. But most of all, he lost ever feeling again what he felt that night with Marsha under the boardwalk.

111

Now he goes to parties again, but they're no longer in some girl's basement. Now they're held in homes in Great Neck and Westchester or in the Hamptons. And now Eddie drives to these parties in his brand new Volvo. And now he knows that getting laid is no big deal.

Tonight there's a party in Scarsdale. Eddie takes the Major Deegan and then the Thruway up to Yonkers and then heads up Central Ave. How ugly everything is here. Just one neon sign after another. And no kids. Where are all the kids? Probably inside watching television like everyone else.

Eddie parks and rings the front bell. An overly made-up woman greets him and he hands her a bottle of scotch. She points him to the bar. He looks around. Same old tired broads. Ah well, who the hell is *he* to talk? Maybe he should get himself a hair transplant and drop a few pounds. Then maybe he could latch on to some younger broad.

"Wanna dance?" this dumpy woman with dyed blond hair asks him.

"Why not?"

"Come here often?" she asks with a smile.

"Sure. All the time."

"What I mean is do you live around here?"

"No. I live in Brooklyn," said Eddie.

"Brooklyn?"

"Sure, what's wrong with Brooklyn?" said Eddie getting a little annoyed. The one thing he couldn't stand was these smug suburban JAPS who thought their shit didn't stink.

"So what did you say your name was?"

"I didn't. My name's Eddie."

"Listen. Eddie. I left Brooklyn thirty years ago and I never looked back."

"Well. I stayed."

"I mean. I'm not putting it down or anything. It's just that it's changed."

"You mean you don't like black people?" asked Eddie.

"I like everybody. It's just that I got married and this is a great place to raise children. Do you have any?"

"Yeah. Two," said Eddie.

"Same here."

"Say, what's your name?"

"Oh. I'm sorry. My name is Marsha."

"Marsha? *Marsha*?"

"Yeah, something wrong with my name? I never had any complaints before," she said smiling.

"Uh...uh...where were you on the night of May 15th, 1955?"

"What is this? Twenty questions?"

"Did you live on East 19th Street and Avenue S?"

She stops dancing and stares at him. "Eddie?" He nods at her.

"Eddie, you're the same Eddie?"

He nods and opens his arms wide. She rushes into them. They embrace. He smells her hair. He smells her perfume. Then he whispers into her ear.

"How about a blow job?"

# BEING BONNIE

## 1

Almost everything I know about women I learned from Bonnie. Although she was just twenty-one – two years my junior – she already knew more than most people learn in a lifetime.

Bonnie was kind of pretty, but you still might not give her a second look. When my friend Eddie gave me her phone number, it came with the guaranty that she was great in the sack. That was all the introduction I needed, so I called and made a date with her.

I think she was even less impressed with me than I was with her. At the time, I was living in a tenement near the Bowery and planning to attend law school. Bonnie was working temp jobs and probably would be for the rest of her life. She had a ton of interests, but seemed to go from one enthusiasm to next. As Gertrude Stein had so aptly put it, "There's no there there."

I decided that even though I might get laid, it just wasn't worth the bother. But I was having a party in a couple of weeks, so I invited her. We could always use another girl.

My parties consisted mainly of my friends from high school and college, and whoever else they invited. Two of my oldest friends, Bob and Chuck, were the first to arrive. "Where are all the girls?"

"Bob, it's only 8 o'clock. I'd be amazed if any girls show up for at least half an hour. For some reason, girls hate to be the first ones in the door. Go figure."

"Well, now that *we're* here," said Chuck, the girls won't have to worry about that. So Hank, is that your bar over there?"

"Yeah, please guys, help yourselves."

Bob, Chuck, and I had played ball, hung out, and triple-dated since we were in high school. And we'd probably gone to more than a hundred parties. We had a longstanding pact that if one of us met a girl, the other two would not try to put the moves on her. And that deal had worked out quite well for all these years.

Bob had worked part-time while in college doing data entry, and he was now doing something in computers, which he claimed was the field of the future. After working as a copy writer at an advertising agency for about a year, Chuck went to Officers Training School, and was assigned to a destroyer based in Japan.

Soon my apartment began to fill up – with more guys. But at 8:30 on the dot, a couple of girls walked in and the party finally got started. A little later Bonnie showed up, and she immediately hit it off with Chuck. Later, when he and Bonnie started making out, I began to feel pangs of jealousy. *That* was pretty strange. I mean, I hadn't even been that attracted to her.

Well, I suppose the grass is always greener in somebody *else's* yard. And when they left together toward the end of the party, I had a full blown case of jealousy. Perhaps the one saving grace was the non-compete pact that Chuck, Bob, and I had observed all these years.

After the last guests left, I cleaned up and went to bed. It was almost 2 am, and tomorrow was a work day for most of my guests. Thankfully, I could sleep in, since I didn't have a regular job. But sleep did not come easy, as I kept going over what had happened – or rather, *not* happened, between Bonnie and me.

Just as it was getting light outside, I heard my phone. *Shit!*

116

"Hello?"

"Am I speaking to Henry Wilner?"

"Yes?"

"I am the mother of Ensign Charles Stickney."

"Good morning, Mrs. Stickney. What can I do for you?"

"Charles attended your party last night, did he not?"

"Yes, Mrs. Stickney."

"It's seven in the morning, and he has not yet come home. Is he with you?"

"No, he's not."

"I am worried sick over him. Can you please tell me where he is? If not, I will have to call the police."

I had to think fast. "Mrs. Stickney, you know how Chuck will occasionally have a drink?"

"Regretfully, I have observed this behavior."

"Well, he felt that it would be better if he did not try to go home on the subway. So my neighbor, David Bayes, agreed to put him up for the night."

"Please give me Mr. Bayes' phone number."

"I'm sorry, Mrs. Stickney, but David doesn't have a phone. If you'd like, I can walk over there in a few minutes and ask Chuck to call you. I'm sure he's fine."

"That would be satisfactory. And thank you for your help."

*Now* what? It's bad enough that I'm feeling so jealous, but now I have to be the mediator between Chuck and his mother. So I waited half an hour, called Bonnie, and asked her to put Chuck on. I told him that his mother was on the warpath, and he said he'll call her. I warned him to use a payphone and to stick to the cover story I had made up.

"Hank, my mom thinks I'm still a virgin."

"Well, I guess you're not anymore."

"Certainly not after last night! OK, thanks for covering for me. I owe you."

## 2

For the next week, Chuck was with Bonnie every night. I don't know how he explained things to his mother, but I was very thankful to be off the hook. The only problem was that I was painfully aware of what a big mistake I had made. But I had had my chance and I blew it.

The night before he shipped out, Chuck invited Bob and me to what he termed, "our last supper." We could not be sure when we would see each other again. The war in Vietnam was heating up, and Chuck's ship could be sent there. And there was a possibility that Bob and I might be drafted. Bob was probably safe, since he was the sole support of his family, and I was hoping for a student deferment when I began law school.

Chuck confessed that he was leaving without having done the one thing he had always wanted to do.

"You mean that stupid thing in a bar?"

"That's right, Bob. And it almost happened in some pub in Hawaii."

"You mean that thing with the stool?" I asked.

"Yeah! And would you believe, I actually got my chance?"

"So what happened?"

"Well, Bob, this other Naval officer and I got into a fight with three or four Marine assholes. And you guys both remember how I always wanted to smash a bar mirror with a stool. So I picked a stool, had a clear shot, and flung it right at the mirror."

"And missed?" asked Bob.

"I was so fuckin' drunk, I missed the mirror completely and hit a row of bottles lined up behind the bar."

"You know, Chuck: your mom's right. Just last week she told me you were an irredeemable alcoholic."

"Shut up, Hank! Oh, yeah! That reminds me, I wanted to update you guys on my social life." Bob and I were now all ears.

Chuck gave us a blow-by-blow account of his fling with Bonnie, and then said something that *really* got our attention.

They would write to each other, but who really knew when they'd see each other again.

"Now the three of us have this informal pact about girls, right?"

Bob and I just nodded.

"So let me make myself perfectly clear: Please do not have any compunctions about putting the make on Bonnie while I'm gone."

"How does she feel about *you?*"

"Who knows? So like I just told you, Hank, feel free to call her. And the same goes for you, Bob. Look, I'm going to be 8,000 miles away from here, and I don't expect to be back for at least another six months."

"This sounds completely crazy!" said Bob.

"I know, I know! The thing is, yeah, I like her and everything, but I don't have any monopoly on her. And I also don't have to remind you guys how hard it is to get laid. So why not spread the wealth? I mean, what are friends for?"

"You're actually serious?" I asked.

"You're damn straight I'm serious! We've been friends a long time. So please, I really mean this: I don't want to stand in your way. And besides, who knows if I'll ever see her again. Six months is a long time."

# 3

A couple of weeks later I got a call from Bonnie. She wanted to get together. "Sure! I'd love to. Would you like to have dinner?"

Maybe I did have a chance after all. And I certainly didn't have to feel guilty, considering what Chuck had said.

A couple of nights later, we went to a very cheap and homey restaurant in Little Italy. Before I could make my move, Bonnie told me that she had a confession to make.

"I'm not a priest."

"And I'm not a Catholic."

"In that case, I think it balances out."

"Are you ready, Hank?"

119

"Please confess."

Bonnie reached across the table and placed her hand on mine. I couldn't believe this was happening. Her hand felt warm and she looked into my eyes. She was smiling. Then she took a deep breath.

"Hank, I think I'm in love with your friend, Chuck."

I was stunned. I felt like everything that I had ever wanted was suddenly snatched away. In just a few seconds my mood plunged from the highest cloud to the lowest depth. She saw the look on my face, but didn't know what to make of it.

"I wanted you to know. And I wanted to thank you for inviting me to your party. If it weren't for you, Chuck and I never would have met."

Wow! She didn't have a clue that I had fallen for her. And why should she? I never gave her the slightest hint of how I felt. And now I was caught in the middle, considering what Chuck had told us. I wondered if Bob had already hit on her.

"Bonnie, you're welcome! I'm sorry that Chuck is so far away."

"Me too. But we're writing to each other, and I want to meet his closest friends. So tomorrow night, I'm having dinner with Bob."

"Great!"

"You guys are quite a crew! You must have gotten all the girls at college."

"Well, maybe not all of them."

# 4

A week later I called Bob to check in with him. He seemed troubled about something, but I knew better than to ask him outright. Soon he just blurted it out, "Hank, she's in love with me."

She? Oh no! "Bonnie?"

"Who else?"

"What about Chuck?"

"Well, she called me and said she wanted to get together because she wanted to get to know Chuck's friends."

120

"And then?"

"Do you need me to draw you a road map?"

"Bob, I had dinner with her about a week ago. She told me she was in love with Chuck."

"I know. She told me the same thing. But you remember what Chuck told us?"

"Sure. So then you put the make on her?"

"No, *she* made the first move."

"Wait a second, Bob. Let's see if I've got this right. She tells you she's in love with Chuck. And then she comes on to you?"

"Well I have to tell you, she so fuckin' seductive, I didn't really have any choice."

"I'm not blaming you, Bob. I'm just trying to understand this chick."

"She's nuts: pure and simple."

"So how do you feel about her?"

"Like I just told you: she's nuts!"

"Is that good?"

"Maybe for getting laid. But certainly not good for anything long-term."

"Wow! That's amazing! You know, I was really getting to like her."

"Please, Hank, don't let *me* stand in your way."

"Well, there is the small matter that she's in love with you."

"*And* Chuck."

"*What?*"

"She told me that she loved the two of us."

"*Holy shit!*"

"Exactly."

## 5

Every so often, Bonnie and I would get together. One afternoon, as we were walking along Second Avenue, she spotted a guy she knew. The three of us chatted for a couple of minutes, and later I asked how she knew him. She said she had lived with him last summer.

"Really? The two of you were so casual, it's hard for me to believe you were involved with him."

"*Involved?* Are you *kidding?* I lived with about ten different guys that summer. I was waiting for a sublet, and in the meantime, I needed places to stay."

"Did you know these guys before you moved in with them?"

"Maybe one or two. The others I met here and there."

I was amazed. And then I realized that perhaps nothing she would tell me could surprise me. Little did I know....

## 6

One day I got a call from her. "I have a new phone number, but it's good only during the day."

"Oh, did you get a new job?"

"No, I moved. I live on the upper Eastside."

I learned not to ask too many questions. Besides, it really wasn't any of my business. A few weeks later, I got together with Bob.

"Hank, I think she's really going off the deep end."

"Bonnie?"

"Who else?"

"What happened?"

"Well, did you know she moved back in with an old boyfriend? His name is Brad, and I think he works for an insurance company."

"Yeah?"

"Well, I go over there sometimes during the week – in the daytime. They're in this apartment on the top floor of a doorman building on Third Avenue in the seventies."

"So you see her when her boyfriend's at work."

"Well that's the idea. But yesterday, she wanted me to stay later."

"To meet him?"

"No, dummy! I guess she just couldn't let me go."

"So what happened?"

"You won't believe this! The apartment is on the 17th floor. I'm finally leaving – and this guy, Brad – is due back any minute. So we get into one of the elevators – there's another one right next to it – and she presses 16. And we're making out in the elevator.

"OK, we're in there three minutes, four minutes, maybe five minutes, making out like crazy. And then, suddenly, the door opens, and there's this kind of short guy standing there. Bonnie looks at him, and cool as a cucumber, she says to him, 'Brad, I want you to close the door and go up to the apartment. I'll be up in a minute.'"

"What did he do?"

"He hesitated for a few seconds, kind of shook his head, and then went upstairs to wait for her."

"That is unbelievable! She's got some pair of balls!"

"You're telling *me*! I think that was the most awkward moment of my life."

"It must have been just as awkward for that poor guy."

"Yeah, I was a lot more embarrassed for *him* than I was for *me*."

"Well yeah. But what's wrong with her? I mean, she put both of you guys into that situation. What was she thinking?"

"I really don't even want to know, Hank. Anyway, I'm probably going to bow out very soon."

"Say, just out of curiosity, do you think she and Chuck are still writing to each other?"

"Actually, they are. He never writes *me*, so the only news I get is secondhand through Bonnie."

"Is he OK?"

"Yeah, as far as I know."

## 7

One morning Bonnie pushed Brad too far. She told him that he was too possessive. And Brad must have finally felt that enough was enough. He told her to pack up her things and be gone when he returned from work.

I don't know if I was the first person she called – or the last. We piled her stuff into a couple of cabs and headed downtown. Now the woman I loved was actually living with me. The only problem was that she loved two of my closest friends. What was I *thinking*?

I knew that she certainly would have preferred to live with Bob, but that couldn't work. Aside from any reservations that Bob might have, the fact that he lived in a three-room apartment with his mother and younger brother was definitely a drawback. Bob's mother, a recent widow, was still very fragile. He was supporting her and his brother, who was finishing high school

A few days later, Bob told me he had broken off with Bonnie. "Man, she was draining my psychic energy. And besides, Hank, I know how you feel about her. So now, except for our nautical friend, you've got a clear shot. Good luck!"

## 8

I was definitely going into this with my eyes wide open. Given her history with guys, she would probably break my heart. But on the upside, I would now have what we used to call, "a steady piece." Even romantics need to get laid.

Bonnie put me off the first few nights, but we were sleeping in the same bed, and that was really nice. Still, when we finally did it, her post mortem was brutal. Did I have any idea what women liked? Couldn't I be more sensitive? And didn't I realize that women wanted to be made love to, and not just fucked?

It took me some time, but the lessons were a whole lot of fun. After about a week she paid me the highest compliment she would ever give me: "Hank, I think you'll do."

Whatever else, I'm a pretty good listener, and Bonnie loved to tell stories. I didn't mind that the stories usually involved other guys. Mercifully, she hardly ever mentioned Chuck – and never said a word about Bob.

Bonnie had grown up in a small suburb west of Chicago. Having nothing better to do after high school, she enlisted in the Waves. "Join the Navy and see the world." But after just a few weeks Bonnie had seen enough and desperately wanted out. When she applied for a discharge, she was reminded that she had a legal obligation to remain in the Navy for three years – not just three weeks. So she befriended a Jewish chaplain, who, of course, fell in love with her. Within a month, he had managed to help her get discharged. He never heard from her again.

Not yet eighteen, Bonnie realized she had very limited prospects. But a boring suburban life was not one of them. She moved in with a friend who was living in Chicago and quickly found temp work as a typist. Although she was extremely bright, college was never an option, perhaps because, as her teachers had often observed, "Bonnie never applies herself."

She didn't have a regular occupation, but one of the things she did do – why did this not surprise me? – was to work as a prostitute at business conventions. The astounding part about this work, was that nearly all the men she met wanted to talk to her even more than they wanted to sleep with her. She sensed that they were often very lonely, so she just let them talk. "I felt that I was much more a psychiatrist than a prostitute."

I asked her how she decided to live in New York. She smiled, hugged me, and said that she would save that story for another time.

On weekdays I studied for the Law Boards, and weekends I earned $5 an hour – great money in the early 1960s – working off the books for a company called "Budget Movers." That kind of work either gets you into great shape, or it kills you. Somehow, I survived.

Bonnie worked sporadically, but she never gave me a penny of what she earned. I figured that maybe she was saving up for another apartment, which was OK with me. Because, even though I loved her, I knew that I'd never be able to hold on to her. And I doubted that any guy ever would.

I often wondered if she and Chuck were still corresponding. But that seemed less and less likely. How could he keep up with Bonnie's changing addresses? And then, completely out of the blue, a letter arrived – addressed to *me!*'

Dear Hank,
It's been awhile. I heard from Bob that Bonnie moved in with you. Good luck! I think the two of you will be great for each other.
I have some really exciting news. Would you believe that next week I'm getting married? Oh, I know the two questions you're too polite to ask.
"Yes" to both of them. Hoshimi (starlight) is indeed Japanese, and yes, she *is* with child. If you're wondering what it's like to be with her, do you remember the scene in *South Pacific* when they sang "Happy, happy, happy, happy talk?"
As you can imagine, my mom is less than pleased, but she and my dad will be here for the wedding. I wish you and Bob could be here too, but hopefully the next time we get together, you guys will meet my new family.
Your amigo,
Lt. Charles J. Stickney

There was no point in showing the letter to Bonnie, because it might have really upset her. At least that's what I told myself.
Often Bonnie and I would go for walks through Little Italy, the Village, Chinatown, and other lower Manhattan neighborhoods. Sometimes she'd stop to talk to seemingly random people, but they almost always turned out to be very friendly. She would tell me that I needed to be open to new experiences. Right, I thought. Bonnie's all the new experience I can handle right now.
One evening, after we had made love, she decided to tell me why she moved to New York. She had gotten pregnant, but she had no intention of marrying the father. In fact, she had met someone else, and they were soon engaged. They made arrangements to come to New York.

126

He would come first, and move into his friends' large apartment, and then she would soon follow. The apartment was in *The Apthorp,* an ornate old building that occupied a square block on the upper Westside. Her fiancé's friends, a brother and sister in their mid-twenties, had grown up in the apartment. Their parents, who had moved to Hawaii, were still paying the rent.

Then she started to cry. I put my arms around her and could feel her shaking. I held her tighter and kissed her cheeks, her forehead, her eyes, again and again and again. Finally, after several minutes, she was able to stop crying.

"Are you OK?"

"I'm sorry, Hank. Please, could you just hold me? I'll tell you the rest of the story tomorrow."

## 9

The next day she seemed fine. I wasn't sure if or when she would continue the story. But a couple of nights later, she said that she wanted to tell me what had happened. We were lying in bed with our arms around each other. I was braced for another crying jag, but I was also very anxious to hear the rest of the story.

Her fiancé's name was Frank. They had packed up his car and a U-Haul and he would drive to New York. Bonnie would come by bus a few days later. She still had some last minute things to do. A few hours after Frank left, Bonnie heard on the news about a heavy snowstorm somewhere in Pennsylvania. But she didn't worry too much because he would still be in Ohio by dark, when he planned to stop at a motel. He had said that he didn't feel comfortable pulling that big U-Haul at night.

I could almost sense what was coming next. Again the tears started to flow. But she was determined to finish the story.

I stroked her hair. She took a deep breath and continued. "I got a phone call at eleven that night from a Pennsylvania State trooper. There had been a terrible accident on Route 80.

127

Frank's car and the U-Haul had jack-knifed and skidded off the highway. He was killed instantly.

The tears were streaming down her cheeks. She stopped to gather herself, and then, after a few minutes, she went on. "I didn't know what to do. I was eight months pregnant, the love of my life was suddenly taken from me, and I had no place to live."

"So what did you do?"

"I decided that I would come to New York. Frank had told me so much about the brother and sister we would be staying with, that I felt as though I practically knew them. They were very kind. They actually begged me to come to New York and stay with them.

"I loved Frank more than anyone in my life. He *was* my life. He made me laugh. He could read my moods. Even when I was mad at him, all he had to do was smile and I just melted. And when he touched me...."

I waited until it was clear that she would not continue, "That is all so sad. To suddenly lose someone like that.... So what did you do?"

"I really had no other place to go. All I had was a bus ticket to New York, so I came two days later. When I got to their apartment, they took me in their arms and just held me. Later they told me that I was now their only connection to Frank, and that they would love me just as they loved him."

"They sound like wonderful people."

"They are."

"So you stayed with them until the baby was born?"

"Well, it gets a little more complicated."

I had a premonition: "Wait! Don't tell me..."

She nodded. "That's right! The brother."

"But you were so depressed."

"I was. I barely got out of bed for the whole time that I stayed with them. The last four weeks before I gave birth... well, it had become a very difficult pregnancy. The only times I left the apartment were to go to their doctor. He was very

128

worried about me, but in the end I did give birth to a very healthy little baby girl."

"And the brother?"

"Well, you guessed it, Hank. He had fallen in love with me. In fact he even proposed. If I married him, the three of us could raise the baby together."

"But you didn't love him."

"Oh, he was very sweet, but I was not at all attracted to him. His sister was also very nice – I mean, look, the two of them had been extremely kind to me.

"And besides, I was in mourning. In fact, I suppose I'm *still* mourning Frank. He was such an unbelievable guy."

"So what happened after you had the baby?"

"Well, I knew that I'd never be able to take care of her. At least not at that stage of my life. So without telling the brother and sister, I gave her up for adoption."

"What did you say when you told them? They must have been very upset."

"Actually, I never told them. While I was in the hospital, I met this young doctor. So instead of going back to the apartment, I moved in with him."

"*My God!*"

"I know, Hank. But I just couldn't face them. Especially the brother."

"So you just left them hanging?"

"No, I did send them a note thanking them for their kindness. But I didn't say anything about the baby, or where I was living."

At that moment I realized that it would end with us, and probably in the not too distant future. I still loved her, but deep down I knew that she could never love me back. So I decided to just try to enjoy things while they lasted.

In a few weeks I'd be taking the Law Boards. I spent most of my time studying, and occasionally Bonnie would quiz me. I kidded her that *she* was the one who should be taking the exam.

On a gray winter morning I walked over to New York University. Bonnie was still asleep when I left. I kissed her forehead and heard her murmur without waking. Once the proctor commanded us to open the seal with our Number 2 pencils and begin the exam, I had put her completely out of my mind.

When we finally staggered out of the exam hours later, a bunch of us decided to go for pizza. None of us had met before, but the shared experience of going through this ordeal made us instant friends. As we took our seats around a large table, a woman sat down next to me and introduced herself. I don't think I had ever met anyone so attractive. She was really smart, very funny, and I loved how she would touch my arm for emphasis when she was making a point. I felt as though I could sit there for hours talking to her, looking at her, and wanting to put my arm around her so we could snuggle.

Should I tell her that I'm living with someone? Or should I do what Bonnie probably would have done? Leave with her, go back to her place, and hop into bed?

I felt completely torn. No matter what I did, it seemed I would have regrets. I wished that I didn't have to make a decision; that somehow everything would become very clear, and that the right choice would be made for me.

And then it was time to go. My new friends would quickly fade away, because it was time to return to our real lives. We all stood up, and as we were leaving, she handed me a slip of paper, looked at me with her beautiful big blue yes, and mouthed the words, "Call me."

Everyone else left, and the two of us were left standing there. I knew that if I just opened my arms, she would step right into them. But I didn't. And then, just as she was about to walk away – to walk out of my life – I touched her cheek. She smiled, and said, "I'll talk to you soon." And then I watched her walk down the street. I kept hoping that she would glance back. But she didn't. I felt a tremendous impulse to run after her. But I just stood there. And then, after she disappeared around the corner, I put her number in my pocket. It was time to go home.

# 10

I half-expected Bonnie to still be sleeping, even though it was mid-afternoon. But she was out somewhere. When I opened the closet to hang up my jacket, I saw that all her clothes were gone. Then I noticed that there were empty spaces on the book shelves, and that she had even taken her tooth brush. In the kitchen, instead of finding a note on the table, I saw the strip of pictures we had taken just a week ago in a photo booth near Times Square.

I would never see her again. She must have met someone else. I mean, isn't that the story of her life? In the photos, she was sitting on my lap and we were smiling at the camera. Bonnie probably already knew where she would be living and when she would move.

Suddenly, everything became very clear to me. I began to laugh. Now that I realized what had happened, it really was quite funny. I wished that I could see Bonnie just one more time to congratulate her. And to apologize for so greatly underestimating her. Chuck, Bob, and I had been actors in a play that Bonnie had been writing for years. The play would go on, but she had arranged for each of us to take his bow and leave the stage.

I was still smiling as I reached into my pocket, walked into the bedroom, and picked up the phone.

# KABUKI

## 1

When my sister, Laila, invited me to a Kabuki play, all I could say was something like, "You're going to be in a *what?*" And now, all these years later, all I can tell you is that Kabuki is a very formally acted and stylized Japanese drama, conveyed through song and dance. It seems based on stuff that happened maybe three hundred years ago. Think of it as a 17$^{th}$ century Japanese "avant-garde" musical drama. It was not – if you'll pardon the pun – exactly my cup of tea.

But hey, it was free and it was OK if I brought a date. The woman I brought actually knew Barry Manilow in high school. Sadly, I know a lot more about *him* than I can remember about *her.* Except that she was very nice.

The play's directors were Japanese, and spoke and understood virtually no English, so communication with the cast – most of whom were professional actors – was almost entirely through pantomime. I never understood how Laila, who played the second samurai, had managed to get a part, considering that she had never studied acting, nor had much experience except for one or two parts with her community theater company.

The play was held in a small theater on 42$^{nd}$ street between 9$^{th}$ and 10$^{th}$ Avenues. Most of the people in the audience were friends of the actors. There were a few Japanese people in the cast, but most were – as they might have jokingly described themselves – *gringos* and *gringas.*

While we waited in the lobby for my sister to change into street clothes, I saw a woman who looked just like Julie Christie, who had just starred in "Doctor Zhivago." My date said, "You know, it's bad enough that you have to stare at her, but must you make it so obvious?"

I apologized for being so rude, but not before I noted that the woman was talking to the third samurai, who played opposite Laila. She *had* to know him. When she came out, the three of us went for a snack, and I could see that Laila was very taken with my date. In those days there was still some hope that I would settle down with a nice girl.

The next morning, I called Laila, and when I told her that I needed to reach "Julie Christie," she was very cool to the idea. "I thought you were with a very lovely woman. What's wrong with *her*?"

"Nothing! She's nice. But she's no Julie Christie."

Very reluctantly, my sister said she would see what she could do. "But I really don't like this."

What's not to like, I thought to myself. All I need is a phone number.

A few days later, Laila called. "I've got some good news and some bad news." The good news was that the woman I wanted to meet had just separated from her husband. And the bad news? The third samurai, who did indeed know her, had taken a liking to me. I would need to call him to get her number.

It was terribly awkward, but I did manage to give him my oh-so-sincere, "While it's so flattering that you're attracted to me, as luck would have it, I don't happen to be gay at this time," speech. From there I improvised with something like, "So if we can just get past that, could you just give me the phone number of the most beautiful woman I have ever seen?" He graciously gave me the number, along with a pleasant, "And if you should happen to change your mind…." I thanked him and said that if I ever changed my mind and decided to join the other team – not in those exact words, of course – he would be the first to know.

That evening, when I called, she was amazingly friendly, even animated. We made a date for the next weekend, and I was so inspired, I wrote a poem to her and rushed out to put it in the mail.

She lived about a half mile from me on the Lower Eastside, and we arranged to meet at the Philippine Garden restaurant, a place we both knew. Everything seemed to be going quite well. She talked excitedly about her dream to be on Broadway and I talked about finishing graduate school and then changing the world.

She hadn't mentioned the poem, so there was no point bringing it up. I guess it was the standard type of thing a guy would write if he believed in love at first sight. We walked back to her building, and I can still remember standing in the hallway outside her apartment door and asking if we could see each other again.

"No," she said. "We really don't have much in common." She was an actress and I wasn't remotely connected to the theater. But there was more. She grew up in Oklahoma and was part Cherokee. The Cherokees were considered a very good looking people, and, like Nancy, they had high cheek bones and blue eyes. Oddly, so did I. But I'm not even a small part Cherokee. There *are* no Jewish Indians, but considering how she had just made me feel, perhaps I could have qualified for membership in the Shmohawks, a legendary tribe of Jewish Indians. (If you're part of the 99 percent who knows no Yiddish, shmo – sometimes spelled schmo – means a dull, stupid, or boring person.)

A few weeks later, a married couple I had introduced, invited me to a cast party for *Mame*, which starred Angela Lansbury. They were obligatory guests because they lived below the hostess, an actress who was in the play. I figured, maybe I could meet another actress.

The party was on the second floor of a four-story, elegant building on Riverside Drive. Richard and Judy lived just off the lobby, and from their door we could see the grand staircase. As guests were buzzed in and would proceed up the stairs,

Richard, who was an excellent pianist, would serenade them with his grand version of, "There's no business like show business." We watched them preen as they climbed the stairs. We had been laughing so hard, we were almost reluctant to go to the party ourselves.

I noticed that almost everyone was greeting everyone else with hugs and saying, "I almost didn't recognize you in street clothes." So I tried that line on a few women who just looked at me like I was a schmuck. Then a guy walked over and threw his arms around me, using the same line I had been using. He did look somewhat familiar. Seeing my puzzled look, he decided to help me out. He was the third samurai.

## 2

About twenty years later, I was bullshitting in front of my house in Brooklyn with a neighbor, when an ancient truck with wooden sides pulled up. Two women were in the front, one in her twenties, and the other, maybe old enough to be her grandmother. The older woman rolled down the window and announced: "Hi! We're Indians! Once a year we come around to your neighborhood with our lawn furniture, all of it made by Indians."

The back of the truck was filled with wooden chairs and benches. The women exited the truck and placed a couple of benches on the lawn. "Let's try them out!"

David and the older woman sat on one of the benches, while the younger woman and I sat on the other. They *were* very comfortable.

"What tribe are you with?" I asked the older woman.

"We're Iroquois. We were the first to run into battle."

"Really? I'm Indian, too." David gave me a strange look.

"What tribe?" she asked. I thought maybe she was just being polite.

"I'm part Cherokee."

She stared at me for several seconds, and then she smiled.

"Yes! I can see you are!" And then she turned to the younger woman and said to her, "Just look at those high cheekbones and those blue eyes!"

# THE LADIES' MAN

Like all the other urban cowboys and cowgirls, I'm out there every weekend lookin' for love in all the wrong places. My wrong place of choice is "The Living Room," which could pass for a bar in any college town. Except that the students must have stayed on years past graduation.

I've met all kinds of women in The Living Room, but somehow none of them panned out. Now don't get me wrong. I really *do* want to meet someone special, and maybe even settle down... eventually. But right now I'm a boy who just wants to have fun. Still, I've always maintained that if some girl really knocked my socks off, I'd blow this scene in a New York minute.

I think the clock just started ticking. There is a woman standing a couple of feet away from me. I think I'm in love. There is no way to describe how beautiful she is. And she's smiling at me.

"Hi, I'm Riva." She extends her hand. I want to kneel down, reach into my pocket, and place a ring on her finger. Instead we shake hands.

"I'm Steve." We stand there. I'm ready to tell her that I promise to give up everything for her. Which happens to be quite a lot. But before I can tell her, she asks, "Would you happen to know Bill Murphy?"

Bill Murphy! Shit! The guy's even better looking than me. Well, I wasn't gonna *lie* to her. So I said, "Yeah. Bill Murphy.

He's about six foot one, good build. From a distance you could mistake him for me. Oh – you thought *I* was Bill Murphy?"

"No, silly!" And she kind of gives my arm a little push. I love how she said that. "No, I would never mistake you for Bill Murphy. The two of you are like night and day. And I don't mean that in a derogatory way."

"So you *know* Bill."

"I wouldn't say I *know* him. I met him here last week. He asked for my phone number, but I wasn't sure about him, so we agreed to meet here again tonight."

"So you're asking me for a recommendation?" She nodded.

"He's OK. He comes in here a lot."

"And you do too?"

"Well, yeah. This is the hottest place on the Eastside. I'm in here maybe two or three times a week. It's a nice place to hang. You can relax in here."

"That's very nice. Is there anything else you can tell me about Bill Murphy?"

"Like what?"

"Well, I kind of got the impression that he was, well, that he was sort of a ladies' man?"

"Bill? Oh I don't know about that."

"What about *you*, Steve. Would you call *your*self a ladies' man?"

"Past tense."

"You mean you *were* a ladies' man? So when did you *stop?*"

"Oh, about five minutes ago."

"Are you trying to flatter me?"

"If it's working, yes.."

"I'd say it was successful, for a first try anyway."

"Wow! The only thing is – I'm serious. I've never met anyone like you."

"Thank you, but you don't know me from a hole in the wall."

"Trust me. I would have no problem distinguishing between you and a hole in the wall."

She smiled, touching me on the arm. I really liked the way she did that.

Just then, guess who joined us? That's right, good ole Bill Murphy. "Sorry, Riva, I just got out of work. Steve, thanks for keeping Riva company."

As he began to steer her to a booth she smiled and said, "Steve, it was really nice meeting you." I thought Bill was giving me a dirty look, but I just shrugged. Maybe I'd see her again.

It must have been a couple of weeks later when I saw her again. The only problem was that I saw Bill, too. I had heard the two of them were "an item." Was I jealous? You can bet on it. But like she said, "You don't know me from a hole in the wall." I might have felt even worse, but in fairness, Bill *had* met her first. If she had dumped me for him, that would have been an entirely different story.

I was still coming to The Living Room maybe two or three nights a week, but I didn't see them anymore. In fact, I even stopped looking. After all, there were plenty of attractive chicks and I'm pretty good looking if I do say so myself. It's really not hard to meet someone. Forget about rehearsing pick-up lines. Just say anything. If she's interested, she'll talk. If she isn't, the greatest pick-up line in the world won't help. One night on a subway platform, my friend Bob spotted this really attractive woman. "Can you tell me anything about macrobiotic cooking?" he asked. She pulled a macrobiotic cookbook out of her bag. A year later they got married.

So I wasn't exactly waiting for Riva. But then, one night, there she was. A week later we had made a date for that Saturday night. A couple of nights before our date I ran into my buddy, Jeff, when I stopped by the Living Room. "Hey, Steve, there was this chick in here a few minutes ago. She was asking about you."

"Riva?"

"Yeah, real good looker? She wanted to know if you were – are you ready for this? – a ladies' man."

"What did you tell her?"

"*Shit* yeah! Biggest stud on the Eastside."

"You *told* her that?"

"Man, I. was just playin' with you. I told her you were the best. I told her you go out of your way to help old ladies across the street. I told her you were an *old* ladies' man."

"I'm not sure which would be better. So she left?"

"Yeah, maybe ten minutes ago."

"Thanks. I'll catch you later." So what was *that* all about? Was she checking me out? Maybe having second thoughts about seeing me? Well, in another forty-eight hours I'd know one way or the other.

Finally, the moment of truth had arrived. I was five minutes early so I walked to the corner and back to her building.

I brought flowers with me. Her doorman grinned while I waited for her. "What lovely flowers. For me?" She rushed back upstairs to put them in water. Then she was back again and when we got outside, she took my arm. As we walked down Second Ave., I knew I was with the most beautiful woman in New York.

It was like a dream. At first, she didn't even let me come upstairs. Then it was just for a cup of coffee. And then it was all night.

I told her how I felt about her. She said I was very sweet, but that she still had her doubts about me. After all, I had been with so many women. How could she feel confident that I would always remain faithful? I had to agree that she had a point, not that I didn't keep trying to persuade her that I was a changed man.

We had been seeing each other for about six weeks when she asked me if I would like to meet her parents. Wow, things were really moving along. And then, when I least expected it, something happened. Or maybe, something *didn't* happen. I called Riva one night and ended up leaving a message. When she hadn't called back by the next day, I started to worry. Maybe something happened to her. Maybe she met someone else. I called her that night. Again, no one home. I thought of staking out her house. I thought of calling the police. Finally, around midnight, she called.

"Riva, where *were* you?"

"Didn't I tell you? I was out of town for a couple of days."

"No, I had no idea. I was afraid something happened to you."

"Now Steve, don't be an alarmist. I'm sure I told you I had to go to Cleveland on Monday and Tuesday."

"Cleveland? For your job?"

"Of course for my job. Do you think I would *know* someone in Cleveland?" I'm still sure she hadn't said anything about the trip, but at least I was feeling a little relieved.

"So are we still on for this weekend?"

"Steve, my mother just came down with a cold, and she doesn't want to give it to us. So we can't go this weekend."

"Well if *that's* out, why don't we do something else?"

"I don't know, Steve. Right now I'm pretty tired. I didn't get much sleep the last couple of nights."

"OK. I'll call you later in the week." I knew right that second that it was over. I don't know why she couldn't just come out and say it. So I let things slide. When I called her and got her machine, I left a message. She never returned my call.

Now I'm back at The Living Room almost every night. And I'm doing OK. Really. I won't lie to you and say I've forgotten Riva. In fact I caught a glimpse of her just the other night. She was in here. In fact she happened to be talking to Jeff. Later he told me she was interested in some guy. She wanted to know if he was "a ladies' man."

# LISTENING TO THE RAIN

We're lying in bed in a cottage way out in the country. The early spring rain has been falling for hours. The windows are open just an inch or two and we can hear the rain on the leaves and the bushes and upon the roof.

The sweet damp air smells of grass and trees. The crickets have taken shelter from the rain. The night has just one sound and it pours down steadily.

We lie quietly, barely touching. Once we knew each other so well, but that was long ago. How had we suddenly decided, on impulse really, to come out here after so many years?

Do you remember? Remember those times so long ago? The ocean. You wanted to find sea shells. Purple ones. You told me how those tiny sea creatures built their homes. So I bought you a book on shells. Remember?

You had never seen the ocean till I took you there. How could you have known so much? I grew up only a few miles from the ocean. We'd walk there when we were boys to play football on the beach. We'd play tackle because you couldn't get hurt in all that sand.

I tried to do things with you for the first time. Even if I had done them before, it was the first time for you. And that pleased me. It made me so happy to see you smile.

Remember when we went to the botanical gardens? You told me the names of almost everything, even though it was your first time. Then, when you thought no one was looking, you lit your pipe and we got a little high.

145

It's funny how we always did things like that in the city. The flea markets, the zoo. Remember that horse who came over to us at the children's zoo? We gave him lettuce and an apple. Later you said that that horse had to live on handouts. I wanted to laugh and cry at the same time.

There's one day that really stands out. We had walked along the beach that afternoon. Later we said the words that only lovers are supposed to say. We've said them many times since then, but I wonder if we really believed them. Except that evening. At that band concert right on the ocean.

Yes, I know that you remember. The sea gulls. All of them in a line. Gliding in time to the music. Rising, floating, soaring higher and higher, and then swooping down on a roof as the music came to a cymbal-crashing end.

John Phillip Sousa in the twilight. Another march across the sky. This time another formation. An airborne parade in our honor. At the end of the piece we applauded as the gulls touched down upon another roof.

And so it went that night. But nothing after that could ever be the same. We drew closer as we learned more about each other, but nothing could ever be as it was that night. Perhaps we were only meant to be good friends, but like those seagulls, we tried to soar with the music.

Do you ever go back? I guess you can't get up on that roof anymore; that roof where we watched our first thunderstorm. Wasn't that something? There we were safe and dry at the top of the stairs and inches away the rain was pouring down. Then the sky would light up and seconds later the thunder would come crashing down. We'd hear the sounds echoing down the street, bouncing off the buildings, like a demented drummer with a great sound system, turned loose in the sky.

# PEGGY ANN

## 1

Anyone who got to know her would tell you that there was nothing truly remarkable about Peggy Ann Mackey. She *did* have those laughing blue eyes, that turned-up nose, and although she was already in her late twenties, she still had that trim, typically school-girlish figure. Just no uniform. Still, if you looked really closely, you'd guess that maybe Peggy Ann Mackey was Swedish. Swedish along the lines of a Liv Ullmann, rather than those fleshy-faced, voluptuous beauties who might have advertised saunas or Erik cigars on television.

One night, about three weeks into the fall semester, just as I was about to enter the classroom –

"Professor Slavin?"

I usually go to class a few minutes early to put an outline on the board, and my students quickly get to know that it's best to let me get this over with before they bother me with any of their nonsense. I particularly dislike those self-centered individuals who think that their personal questions are somehow more important than my outline.

"Would you be terribly upset" – I like to cut them off before they can finish their questions – "if I finish this first, before we get to your question?"

She must have sensed this about me immediately, because when I stopped my hand on the doorknob and looked at her, she took a step back. She carried her books, schoolgirl fashion, flat against her chest, and she looked really apologetic. That deflated me a bit, enough to ask if I could help her.

"Dean O'Connor let me register late. I'm in your class." Then she shifted her books and opened her handbag, evidently looking for her bursar's receipt.

"That's OK. I trust you. You don't have to show me anything." Then I flashed my big Irish grin.

You see, I'm not really Irish. But once, many Christmases ago, I managed to talk my way into a job loading freight for Railway Express. The guy who interviewed me actually asked if I *was* Irish.

"Well," I told him, "when my ancestors came here, the trip took so long that they couldn't remember where it was that they came from."

"That's good Irish blarney, Slavin – you're hired!"

I really should have told you that I was teaching at St. Francis College in downtown Brooklyn. A school that educated successive generations of Irish immigrants and the children of Irish immigrants. The President once told me that even today most of the students were the first ones in their families to go to college.

Brother Michael, who had just taken over as President, wanted every full-time faculty member to teach at least one course at night. The idea was to make the evening students feel that they were really a part of the school. Most of us were quite happy with this arrangement since the evening students were invariably more serious and highly motivated than their compatriots during the day. And they were generally several years older.

Peggy Ann Mackey – I still didn't know her name then – and I were standing in the hallway. Several students had walked into the room during our short conversation. I realized they were staring at me in a peculiar way. Now, one thing I never do – and this is a very firm rule – is get involved with any of my students. The *women*, I mean. Never. There is something degrading to the professor who uses his position to help him get physically and emotionally closer to a young woman that he

148

might not have otherwise accomplished. It's the longer version of getting her drunk and quickly taking advantage of her vulnerabilities.

I held the door open for her and we entered the room. "Please see me after class," I said and walked directly to my desk, put down my notes, and immediately started on my outline.

My lecture that evening was on the origins and structure of the Federal Reserve System, but I managed more of my usual quota of amusing anecdotes and witticism. And when the period ended, there she was, along with a couple of other students. I took care of them first.

"Do you have another class, Ms. Mackey?" I asked as I entered her name on the class list.

"Yes, Mr. Slavin. I have accounting with Professor Walters."

"I won't keep you then. Just make sure you catch up on all the work. Get notes from someone in class and maybe we can talk on Wednesday night."

"Great! I've already borrowed someone's notes. See you Wednesday."

I watched her walk down the hall. Well, she definitely wasn't a flirt. Sometimes you'd have these young women who stare at you. What do you do? At a party I'd stare back. But here I try to be careful not to encourage them. Oh, not that I have to worry about that so often. But I suppose I had been kind of hoping that Peggy Ann would have stared at me.

Even then, when I think about it, I was already starting to fall in love with her. Of course, all of us, eventually, must have been at least a little in love with Peggy Ann Mackey. I know that sounds a little ridiculous maybe, but that's the kind of woman she was. Yes, even that first night we were standing outside the classroom, I would have loved to take her by the hand and say, "Let's go for a walk."

We would have walked right out of the school. All those bewildered students passing us on the way to my class. "Professor Slavin, are you all right?" Didn't they understand that I had feelings too? Didn't they want to take her hand and walk down to the promenade where we could see the skyline? I'd have my arm around her. She'd murmur softly and snuggle closer.

Later that night, we'd lie in bed all talked-out, listening to the foghorns echoing in the harbor. The sounds of the city floating far off. We'd hold each other through the night.

"Professor Slavin? No outline tonight?" Oh, no! The next class had come into the room. Quickly I erased the board. What would we be talking about? Oh, yes, the degrees of competition under oligopoly. Just what I wanted to be doing tonight.

## 2

Maybe people fantasize because nothing ever happens. A psychologist once told me that most of what people think has really taken place has happened only in their minds. He might well be right, but what later happened certainly wasn't a fantasy – or at least it didn't seem so at the time.

The semester had wound down toward finals and before long it would be Christmas. There was a large Christmas tree in the lobby and virtually every wall of the school was covered in decorations. By this time, Peggy Ann was just another student in my macroeconomics course. She seldom said much in class (most of my students said very little) but she was doing well enough on my exams to earn an A. Evidently she was bright enough to make up all the work she missed.

Because the last evening of the course came out just before Christmas Eve, my announcement that the final exam would be one week early was met with loud and enthusiastic applause. It's not my holiday, but I was glad to watch their faces when I made the announcement. I watched Peggy Ann's face. She seemed extremely happy. Of course, she was still Ms. Mackey at the time.

I knew that after the final I'd never see her again, but there wasn't too much I could do about it. There was no way I could ever get involved with one of my students – not that she was

150

breaking down my door. And yet, something told me that maybe, maybe somehow, something was meant to be. And who was I to argue with fate?

After the course ended she would no longer be my student. Then it would be OK. That's right, it would be just fine. With me, that is. But she never even tried to talk to me since that first night, and of course she had no idea how I felt.

On the night of the exam, everyone was there on time. I was used to students drifting in ten or fifteen minutes late, but they were all there poring over their notes and chatting away nervously. Peggy Ann was sitting in the first row, something she had never done before.

After I gave out the exam, I sat at my desk and began marking some papers from my day courses. Every so often I'd look up, not that I really expected anyone to be cheating, especially in an evening course. Once or twice I thought I caught her looking at me. I remembered what my psychologist friend had told me about fantasies and promptly dismissed the notion.

One by one the students turned in their papers. Some of them shook my hand and said they enjoyed the course. They all smiled and wished me a Merry Christmas. There were still several students left in the room when Peggy Ann stood up. Slowly, she picked up her things. She handed me her paper and our eyes met. I knew that if I didn't say something – anything – she would walk out the door and out of my life.

If she said she enjoyed the course, I could say that I enjoyed having her and Merry Christmas! That's right. Merry Christmas, and I think I'm in love with you. Could you imagine me saying that? And those other students sitting there?

We both started to talk – "I really..." We stopped and smiled. "I really..." This time we just broke up. I couldn't believe this was really happening. I couldn't believe that she really felt the same way I did.

"Professor Slavin, could I talk with you after the exam?"

*Could* she? She could talk to me for the rest of my life.

"I'll tell you what: why don't we go for coffee after class? OK?"

"Are you sure it's no bother?"

Bother? It just happens to be my greatest desire.

"Somehow," I told her, "I'll make the sacrifice."

"Great! I'll be back in a couple of minutes. I just have to make a phone call." She left her coat and books on her seat and left the room.

A phone call? A husband? No ring. A boyfriend? Probably just telling whoever it was who was going to pick her up that she wouldn't be needing a ride. Actually, I did have my car parked a block away, so I could even offer to drive her home. Then I'd see where she lives. Maybe she'd invite me in. Maybe.

Soon she was back and the last straggler handed in his paper. He must have dimly perceived what was happening because all he asked was where the grades would be posted. Then we were alone. Now I would actually live out my fantasy.

"Have you ever been to the promenade?" I couldn't actually believe I was saying this.

"Is that that walk along the water? All the way down by Remsen Street?"

"Right. You know, it's really nice there now. I used to live in the neighborhood and I'd spend hours there. But it's pretty cold now because it's right on the water."

"I've got a warm coat."

Unbelievable. It was really going to happen.

We went down to my office and I put away my papers and grabbed my coat. When we were outside I wanted to take her hand, but that would come later. A lot would come later. Right now it was great to *be* with her. And she really looked lovely today.

"Professor Slavin, I wanted to ask you some stuff about jobs. Is that OK?"

Ask me anything. Ask me if I'll marry you. Ask me when I first knew that I was in love with you.

"Anything. Go ahead. You can ask me anything."

She smiled. I wanted to put my arm around her. I wanted to stop walking right there in the middle of Montague Street and just hug her.

"Well, I work for this bank. They pay for my school. I mean, otherwise I couldn't afford to come here."

"And they told you they'll promote you when you got your degree."

She smiled again. "Right. How'd you know?"

"I'm very perceptive."

"*Are* you?" It was more of a statement than a question. I think she was finally starting to flirt. Or was she just teasing?

"That's me. I've been everywhere, done everything, and know everything. That's why they hired me at St. Frances."

Again we laughed.

"By the way," I said, "you know the term is over. So I think we can call each other by our real names. Mine is Steve."

"Steve." she said as if she were trying it out. "Do you like to be called Steve or Steven?"

"Steven – but only by people I like."

"Then I guess I better call you Steve."

"Of course, Ms. Mackey."

"Oh, I suppose you may call me Peggy Ann."

"Thank you very much, Peggy Ann." I bowed. She curtseyed.

"Is that really your name?"

"It is now. I was born with Margaret, but when I was twenty-one I had it changed."

"I think Margaret is too formal."

"Well, you know these Irish families. Everyone's a nun or a priest or a saint. My Mom thought it was quite appropriate."

"Did they send you to parochial school?"

"You'd better believe it, Steven. My mom is really happy I'm coming here. She thinks there is still hope."

"*Is* there?"

"I don't know. What do you think? You're the expert."

"Not on this subject."

"You aren't? Aren't you Irish?"

"I wasn't when I got up this morning. No, I'm Jewish. Russian-Jewish."

"But the name."

"Courtesy of an Irish immigration official who couldn't understand what my grandparents were saying."

"Still, you *look* Irish."

"Well, one of us has to, Peggy Ann."

"Is that how you got the job at St. Francis?"

"No, but that was how I got the job at Railway Express." I told her the story of that Christmas so many years ago. Boy, did I need that job! The Christmas of 1963. "And where were you in 1963?"

"In 1963? In 1963 I was in the fourth grade at St. Brendan's."

"You mean on Avenue T?"

"How did you know that?"

"I told you, Peggy Ann, I know everything." And as I said this we stopped walking. We stood there looking at each other. Ten seconds. Twenty seconds. Very slowly, imperceptibly, we began to embrace. I could feel her fingers lightly touch my arms. She put her head on my chest. My arms went around her.

People must have been walking by. But we just stood there. Just holding each other. Who knows how long? Slowly I became conscious that this was the happiest moment of my life. No matter what happened after this, no matter what, this moment – these few moments – would never change. It was there, fixed in time, something that no one could ever take away.

"Hey. Steven, how about that cup of coffee?"


### 3

It's been almost a year and once again the halls and offices of St. Francis are decked out in tinsel and mistletoe and a huge tree stands in the lobby. I've already made my announcements about finals being held a bit earlier and I'm looking forward to the end of the term. And I'm thinking of Peggy Ann.

I try to reconstruct everything that happened just a year ago, but all I can do is wonder. I wonder how much of it was real and how much merely took place in my mind. But whatever did happen, happened that same night as we walked along the promenade.

We held hands as we walked. Peggy Ann talked about growing up in Brooklyn and never really leaving. We had actually lived a just a few blocks from each other, but we could have been in different time zones. And yet, here we were and now everything was going to be fine.

"Can you tell me the names of the three bridges? The three big Brooklyn bridges you can see from here?"

"You know, Steven, I'm not exactly a tourist."

"Go ahead, then, Ms. Mackey."

"Brooklyn, Manhattan, and Williamsburgh."

"Wrong!"

"*Wrong?*"

"Wrong, Ms. Mackey."

"Well, why don't you set me straight, Professor?"

"Very well, Ms. Mackey. Or do you prefer Miss Mackey?"

"Either will do, Professor Slavin."

"Very well, Ms. Mackey." We stopped walking again. We were leaning on the iron railing and looking out over the harbor. The lights of the skyline were twinkling in the cold air. Foghorns echoed across the harbor. I stepped behind her and put my arms around her. She reached up and placed her hands on my wrists. We stood there like that. Then she said: "You *tricked* me!"

"I didn't."

"There are only *two* bridges you can see from here."

"Three."

"OK. I said the Brooklyn Bridge."

"That's one."

"The Manhattan Bridge."

"That's two."

"But Steven, you said three."

"Right."

155

"Well, you can't see the Williamsburgh from here."

"I agree."

"So you tricked me. You can see only two bridges."

"Uh-uh."

"No?"

"No — I *did* say three bridges. And you can see them from here."

"I don't think so, Steven."

"Look all the way back there; all the way over to your left."

"By those lights back there?"

"Yes — the blue ones."

"Is that the Verrazano?"

"Uh-huh."

"You *did* trick me."

"No, you tricked yourself, Peggy Ann."

"That's right! You see, Steven, the term's over and you're still teaching me. Once a professor, always a professor. Hey, yuh know, I'm getting cold."

"I'll tell you what. I'm parked a few blocks from here. Would you like me to drive you home?"

"Great! It turns out, this coat isn't as warm as I thought it was."

"So what do you think of the promenade?"

"Steven, it's really nice. If only it weren't so cold tonight. I could have stayed here for hours."

"Me too."

"You're not tired of it?"

"No. I never seem to get tired of it. I used to come out here in the summer and read. Then I'd come back at night and watch the sunset. Me and about twenty-thousand other people. But if you wanted to stay tonight, I would have stayed there for hours. I really like to hold you."

"Sure, tell me about it."

"You don't believe me?"

"Tell me another one, Steven. Do you happen to have a bridge for sale, too?"

"Sure, and for you I'll even knock a few dollars off the price." I had my arm around her as we left the promenade.

"Yeah, right."

"I suppose you don't believe anything I say."

"Well, maybe some things. But not what you just said about staying there for hours in the cold."

"No? Well, I'll tell you what. I'll just have to work on it. Convincing you, that is."

"I'm from Missouri. In case you don't happen to know, that's the "*Show me state.*"

"I thought you were from Brooklyn."

"Maybe you should have been an actor – or a comedian. That's the feeling I got when I watched you up there in front of the class. Like you were performing or something."

"I hate to admit it, but remember that first night when you came to my class?"

"Sure."

"Well, I was showing off."

"Really?"

"Well, a little, anyway. I'm usually much more boring."

"Well, you do seem a bit on the conservative side, like you're holding back something. But you're really interesting. In fact, you're my image of a college professor. Except you don't wear tweeds – or smoke a pipe."

"I used to smoke a pipe. But I gave it up when I was fifteen."

"Fifteen! That's a long time ago."

"Thanks a lot."

"Come on. Steven, you don't look a day over sixty."

"Thanks again."

"Don't mention it."

"I won't ... Oh, there's my car, the one that hasn't seen a car wash in ten years."

"The blue one?"

"Yes, under all the dirt, I think it's blue."

We got in and drove through downtown Brooklyn and drove onto the expressway at Atlantic Avenue. Peggy Ann lived

157

way out in Brooklyn, not far from where we grew up. I always believed that it was my fate to marry a girl from Brooklyn – someone who would understand me.

I parked in front of her house. "I'd invite you in, but my Mom's probably asleep. She's been sick for the last year or so. I moved back home to help her out."

"I'll tell you what: let's exchange phone numbers and we can talk tomorrow. You know what I'd really like to do?"

"What?"

"I'd really like to do exactly what we did tonight."

"That's very nice, Steven, but I don't think I could take another exam like that one."

"Does that mean that the only way you'd be willing to go to the promenade with me is to take an exam first?"

"Let's talk about it tomorrow, OK? I really have to get in." As she walked to her door, she turned and waved. I waited until she was inside.

While I was driving home I thought of how unbelievably lucky I was. How many people ever got to feel this way? I remembered my first date. It had been a complete disaster. I was fifteen years old. In fact, that's when I took up pipe-smoking. To be more sophisticated.

How many times did I feel this good? Maybe once or twice when I was a teenager and I thought I was in love. Dion and the Belmonts – Teenager in Love. I can still remember the words: "Each day I ask all the stars up above. Why must I be a teenager in love." That's me – a forty-two-year-old teenager in love.

## 4

Peggy Ann Mackey. Where are you today? And whatever happened to my teenage love? I called her the next evening, but her mother told me she was working late. And I didn't want to call too late that night, so I waited till the next evening. Still no Peggy Ann. So this time I left a message and she called me back a couple of days later.

Already I was getting depressed. They say that you can't stay on a real high for very long, but I sure was a long way down. She could have called sooner if she'd wanted to. If she really cared.

By now I began to wonder if it would ever really happen. She was going away that weekend and would call me when she got back. I waited. I actually counted the hours. No call. Nothing. I knew it was hopeless, so I decided to call her one more time.

"Peggy Ann, may I ask you a question?"

"Sure."

"OK. Just answer me yes or no. Would you like to go out with me?"

She hesitated. So I knew. "Look," I told her, "I guess I'm backing you into a corner, so I'll tell you what: if you really want to see me, give me a call. OK?"

"OK."

It took me about a month to really get the message. I knew then that most of it had taken place in my head. Peggy Ann Mackey existed only in my fantasies. I don't know if it's possible for one person to fall in love, and not the other. I don't know how much I imagined and how much had really happened on those cold winter sidewalks just a year ago. But when I walk passed that spot on the sidewalk of Montague Street where we stopped and held each other, I know that it all really happened. And that's something that I will always be able to keep.

# Part IV

## WRITERS ANONYMOUS

It's understandable that certain groups of people prefer to be anonymous – alcoholics, overeaters, drug addicts, gamblers – and even clutterers. But why are so many writers anonymous?

Some writers certainly do prefer to be completely unknown. If you're a ghostwriter, then your living depends on someone else getting the credit for your writing. This is true for speech writers, many coauthors, and, of course, ghostwriters.

At the other end of the spectrum are the legions of unknown writers dreaming of getting recognition – or even fame – for their work. In fact, most would be very happy just to get published. Still, they persist. But nobody knows their names.

# THE MANAGED TEXTBOOK

When I began writing my doctoral dissertation, I applied for dozens of full-time teaching jobs, but all I could find were a couple of part-time jobs that barely kept me alive. A few chairmen told me to come back when I had my degree in hand.

Then I saw an ad for an economic researcher in *The New York Times*. It was a freelance job with one of the City's oldest and most venerable publishing houses, Appleton-Century-Croft. But sadly, the company had fallen upon hard times, and had become primarily a textbook mill. During my interview, Doreen, the editor with whom I would be working, explained that they now were publishing what were euphemistically referred to as "managed texts." Fairly well known professors at major universities would be the nominal authors, but the writing and research would be done by hired hands, such as me.

My job would be to find background articles in financial periodicals, update statistical tables, and suggest new topics. One day, I asked Doreen about a photograph she had on her desk. There she was with a huge stack of pages she had torn out of a book. She was grinning at the camera, while merrily tearing out still another page.

She explained that it was quite OK to recycle material from old texts the company had published. "Who's going to sue for plagiarism – the authors?" We both laughed. Then I asked why all their books were ghostwritten.

"Because economists can't write."

"Hey, I'm an economist and *I* can write! Or at least I'll *be* an economist when I get my PhD."

"Then you can't write! Trust me, Nora: we don't even let our 'authors' write the acknowledgments for their *own* books."

"*Why*? How bad can they possibly be?"

"*Bad*! You want to see *bad*? I'll show you bad!" She stood up and reached for a book from the shelf of textbooks above her desk.

"Here: just look at this acknowledgment."

As I started reading, I must have been shaking my head in disbelief. I heard Doreen giggling. This poor soul had written something like this: Writing this book was like coaching a football team. Doreen Spencer was my captain and quarterback. My running backs were so-and-so and so-and-so. He went on fill his entire roster, position-by-position.

"Nora, *that* is why we can't let our 'authors' write even one word. I have never met an economist who could write."

That afternoon she asked me to check the outline of the book we were working on to make sure it was up to snuff. You teach the introductory course, right?"

"Yeah, I've been teaching it for a couple of years."

"I need you to make sure that this outline includes most of the same topics that are covered in the other standard texts."

That evening I read through the outline and sensed something very familiar about it – maybe a little *too* familiar. So I put it side-by-side with the table of contents of the bestselling introductory text. And *voilà*! All the odd-numbered chapters covered identical topics.

Then I checked the outline against the table of contents of the second bestselling text and – you *guessed* it: all the topics in the even-numbered chapters were also identical. Whoever had written the outline had taken quite a shortcut. Worse still, since we would be plagiarizing the books of other publishers, we could be sued.

When I brought in the outline along with the two texts and showed them to Doreen, she was just amazed. After a few minutes she looked at me and said, "Nora, I need you to write a new outline. We're already behind schedule."

A few days later, when I brought in the new outline, Doreen had it photocopied. While she was waiting for the copies, she called up a couple of her ghostwriters and asked them to come in to pick up their assignments. Then she turned to me. Nora, can you write chapters 7 through 9?"

"No problem."

A month later I delivered the chapters. After glancing at them, she asked me to write another three chapters. When I mentioned my economics background she replied, 'No, you're *not* an economist. Economists can't write! And since you can, then you can't possibly be an economist. Nora, you are a writer!"

Yeah, I thought to myself, "Not just a writer, but a *ghost* writer!"

Then she asked if I could I come to the office tomorrow afternoon to meet someone very special? She wouldn't tell me who it was, but just that it would be a big surprise.

That evening, another ghostwriter called to ask if I knew who we would be meeting. But it was all a big secret.

The next afternoon, Carol, Frank, and I were sitting around in Doreen's office. None of us knew for sure who we were going to meet, but we agreed that it must be someone who didn't work for Appleton-Century-Croft. Or maybe someone very high up in the company who wanted to meet us because of the great job we were doing. As outside contractors, we were not privy to much of the office gossip; so we really had very little to go on.

And then Doreen walked in and announced that today we would be meeting with our book's author, Professor Jackson.

"So how come *he's* the author?" asked Carol.

"Well," we needed someone from a prestigious school with a large economics enrollment. Someone with an Ivy League background, a person whose name sounds familiar to other economics professors. Personally, I had never heard of

165

him before he was signed. And just between you, me, and the lamp post, the man can't write his way out of a paper bag."

This sounded nuts to me. "Doreen, why did he agree to become the author?"

"Three reasons: First, he is being paid very well. Second, he gets to show how important he is when he's promoting the book. And third, it's great for his academic reputation."

"And he actually agreed to not write a word of the book?" asked Frank.

"Well, let's just say that the man is well aware of his limitations."

"What about his *ethical* limitations?"

"Now Carol, we don't want to get into *that* kind of discussion right now," answered Doreen.

"So, he's really OK with not doing any of the writing of a book that has *his* name on the cover?"

"Carol, he seems to be. After all, he *is* getting the big bucks."

"Just for a *name*?" I asked.

"Well, he's here today to give us some guidance."

"*Guidance!*" Frank blurted out.

"You know: he'll tell us about a few things he'd like us to put in the book. And speaking of the devil…"

Professor Jackson knocked on the open door and then strode into the room, greeted Doreen, nodded to the rest of us, and sat down.

"Carol, Frank, and Nora, I'd like you to meet Professor Jackson. Professor Jackson, this is Carol, Frank, and Nora." Each of us stood up and very solemnly shook hands with Professor Jackson.

The good professor was as academic as you can get, complete with tweed jacket, elbow patches, a pipe, and even an ascot. He was from one of the Big Ten schools where he was a full professor.

We sat there in awkward silence for about thirty seconds. I noticed that he wouldn't or couldn't make eye contact with the rest of us, as Frank, Carol, and I exchanged glances.

166

Then Professor Jackson pulled out his pipe, filled it with tobacco from his pouch, lit the pipe, and began to draw on it to keep it lit. In those days smoking was still legal almost everywhere, but it would have been nice if he had asked us if it was OK to smoke. Well, I thought, nobody's perfect.

Finally, Doreen explained that Professor Jackson had been anxious to meet with us so we could talk about his book. And that he would be very happy to provide whatever guidance we needed.

We glanced at each other, and I noticed Frank trying not to smile. In fact, I began to grow afraid that we might all burst out laughing.

OK, what could we ask him? Professor Jackson, how do you feel about meeting the *real* authors of *Jackson's Economics*? How much are they paying you? Do you have any ethical concerns about this enterprise?

No one spoke. The silence grew increasingly awkward. Finally, Professor Jackson put aside his pipe, began to clear his throat, and with all eyes upon him, he spoke. Each of his words was very carefully enunciated. "Equity ... and ... efficiency."

The four of us looked at him, waiting for him to continue. Surely he had more to say. But he *had* no more. Wait! He looked at each of us and then he said once more, "Equity ... and ...efficiency." And then, perhaps because we might be hearing-impaired, or maybe because his words were so profound that they bore still more repeating, he said it two more times.

We sat there dumbfounded. The good professor smiled at us. We scratched our heads, looked at each other, looked at Doreen, and then looked back at Professor Jackson.

"Any questions?" asked Doreen.

We shook our heads no.

I mean, what was there to ask? Clearly, Professor Jackson had managed to distill the entire contents of a two-semester book into just three words. Surely no one had ever managed to come anywhere close to having done this.

Again there was a long silence. The professor sat back, relit his pipe, and was soon puffing away. He was at peace. He would look back at this moment as perhaps the peak of his illustrious academic career. And who knows, maybe he could get still another book out of those three magic words.

Then Doreen said, "Professor Jackson, I want to thank you so much for taking time out of your very busy day to meet with us."

"And thank *you* Doreen, and thank all of you for your help in writing this book. Together, I believe we can write what may turn out to be the greatest introductory economics text... well, the greatest introductory economics text since Samuelson. And I truly believe that I could not have done this without you. So just remember, ... 'Equity and efficiency.'"

Then he stood, shook hands again with each of us, and walked out of our lives.

# SAM THE MAN

## 1

Everybody has a story. But if you're a big celebrity, then a lot of people will want to read it. The only problem is that very few celebrities can write. OK, in fairness, *most* people can't write. So when a big publisher wants to do a celebrity autobiography, then a ghostwriter is hired to do the actual writing.

I am a ghostwriter. That's why even though my books have sold in the millions, nobody knows my name. After all, I'm just a ghost.

I'd love to tell you about some of the autobiographies I written, but if I did, I'd never get work in this town ever again. But I'm going to make an exception. The subject of this autobiography couldn't care less, the editor probably won't care, and I've finally left the profession.

The story I'm about to tell you took place relatively early in my career. Another writer told me about an ambitious young editor who was looking for someone to ghostwrite an autobiography of a professional basketball player. Hey, why *not?*

The next day I was sitting with Terrence in his cramped little office talking about my subject, Sam the Man. Sam was one of the most interesting players in the National Basketball Association. An excellent shooting guard – he held the record for consecutive three-point baskets in one game – and he also happened to be quite outspoken. Because he played in New York, he was quoted a lot more often than he might have been in, say Oklahoma City. But as Terrance explained, Sam does not speak the Queen's English.

"That's OK, neither do I."

"No, I mean he *really* does not speak the Queen's English. You'll need to omit more than a few of the fucks and sucks – if you get my drift."

"Will Sam mind if I do?"

"It's hard to tell. I'm not sure if he can read."

"So I'm ghostwriting the autobiography of a man who may be illiterate?"

"Well, maybe. If he could write, then we wouldn't need a ghostwriter."

"And I would be out of a job."

"Exactly."

"Will I get a share of the royalties?"

"No, but we will pay you quite a nice sum for your work."

"Is there anything else I need to know about Sam?"

"No, not right now. We'll set up a few interviews and you can record them. And we've hired a researcher to provide plenty of background information."

"Here's the first installment to get you started. And here's your contract. Please read it, sign it, and get it back to me within a day or two."

I left his office, and when I got down to the street, I glanced at the contract. Shit! I would be making more money than I had earned in the last the two years. Oh happy day!

A week later I met with Sam the Man for our first session. I asked him questions and he would sometimes answer with a simple yes or no. But if the question interested him, he sometimes rambled on for 10 or 15 minutes. He was actually a pretty interesting guy.

He liked to talk about his sex life, and it certainly was an extensive one. Sometimes he'd ask me about mine, but I told him his was much more interesting, and that the book was about his life and not mine. He fully agreed and then would recount still another sexual exploit. As I remember, sex with four women on his king-size water bed was his all-time record.

But as he noted, "Listen man, yuh gotta get em tuh take off them heels first, if follow what I'm sayin."

"I hear yuh, Sam."

A few days after I delivered the first set of chapters, Terrence called to talk about them. "I loved the sex scenes," he told me. "But remember, we don't want to say too much about the drugs. The National Basketball Association has some sort of policy against players discussing their drug habits."

"Even pot? I mean, look, it's the seventies. Everybody smokes."

"You know that, I know that, Sam knows that, and the NBA Commissioner knows that, but it would be better to tone it down a little."

"Won't Sam mind?"

"What he doesn't know won't hurt him. Besides, we haven't yet established whether or not he can read."

"No problem. Any other restrictions I should know about?"

"Well, there is one delicate issue. You know that Sam's a nudist, right?"

"Yeah, but he hasn't brought it up."

"OK, Roger. When he does, we need to handle it very carefully. The Commissioner will come down on him if it's too overt."

"One other question, Terrence. How do I handle his grammar, or lack thereof?"

"Well, in general, we want to capture the flavor and meaning of what Sam says, but we do want the book to be readable. "

"I'll do what I can."

"Great! Talk to you soon."

## 2

One of the first things you learn when studying grammar in elementary school is that a double negative is a big no-no. Still, you can make the case that it's a legitimate way to provide emphasis. For example, you may remember the Big Bopper and his 1958 hit song, "Chantilly Lace," and one of its lines, "Honey, I ain't got nooooooooo money." That sounds a lot better than, "Honey, I haven't got any money."

But when Sam the Man said, "Nobody don't care for nobody no more," I had to draw the line. How much emphasis do we need?

"Come-*on*, Sam! A quadruple negative?"

"Say *what*!"

"You have four negatives in the same sentence. Even two negatives would be grammatically incorrect."

"What exactly is you sayin?"

"You are violating the basic laws of grammar."

"So put me in jail."

"Sam, if there were a grammatical jail, you'd be in for life."

"Hey, as long as the food's good and I can play ball, what can be bad?"

Well, I thought, you can't argue with that.

When I mentioned the grammatical issue to Terrence, he seemed unperturbed. "Keep in mind, Roger, that Sam is a very emphatic guy."

"Is that a euphemism for being illiterate?"

He just smiled.

"Look, Terrence. Even ghostwriters have a little pride."

"As do editors. Believe me, I never would have signed this guy if I didn't believe that this would be a bestseller."

"Don't you feel like we're both prostituting ourselves?"

"Roger, do you remember what the great Samuel Johnson had to say on the subject?"

"Vaguely. But I'm sure you do. Why don't you refresh my memory?"

"OK, this was also attributed to Winston Churchill, so take your pick. At a dinner party, Johnson asks the haughty woman seated next to him if she would sleep with him for one million pounds. 'Of course I would,' she replies.

"Then he asks her if she would sleep with him for ten pounds. 'Do you take me for a prostitute?' she replies indignantly.

'We've already established that,' replied Johnson. 'Now we're just haggling over price.'"

"Terrence, I'm glad to see that you feel just as shitty about *you*rself as I do about *my*self."

"That's right! Ghostwriters, editors, and even publishers – we're all in bed together. And we do it for the money."

As I got into the elevator, I had concluded that almost everyone will sell out: the only question is, "At what price?"

### 3

Late one afternoon Terrence called. "Roger, I want you to watch the six o'clock news."

"Which channel?"

"It doesn't matter."

"Is it Sam the Man?"

"Who else?"

"What did he do?"

"Roger, you won't believe it if I told you. You need to see this for yourself. Then give me a call. I'm still at the office."

A few minutes later, I turned on the news. The third item was all about Sam the Man. The Knicks had a game with the Utah Jazz that evening in Salt Lake City. But Sam would not be playing. He had been suspended indefinitely. Then they cut to a commercial.

What could he have done? A flagrant foul? Hit a ref? Drugs? Some kind of sex scandal?

It was soon cleared up. A reporter was interviewing people outside the basketball arena. "I can't believe he *said* that!" "What a hateful thing to say!" "All we can do is pray for him and hope that God forgives him."

Sam must have said something pretty awful to have made all these people so upset. Then the news anchor came back on and said he would play the film clip. And there's Sam screaming, "Those goddam bleep Mormons! They can all kiss my bleep. The next Mormon I see, I'm gonna tell him he can bleep my bleep!"

I couldn't believe what I was seeing and hearing. Maybe Sam wasn't the sharpest knife in the drawer, but still, how could he visit Utah and then go around insulting the Mormons? I mean, there are more Mormons in Utah than there are Jews in Jerusalem.

I called Terrence. "Can you believe it?" he asked. "How dumb can he *be*! "

"Will this affect our project?"

"It's hard to say. I just got off the phone with his agent. Sam will be issuing an apology within the hour."

"I hope he'll be able to read it."

"Maybe he can memorize it."

"So he'll be on the eleven o'clock news?"

"If they don't lynch him before that."

Sam lived to be on the eleven o'clock news. He made a very brief statement apologizing for his hateful words, and said that he was truly sorry. But I thought I detected some puzzlement not just in his expression, but even in his body language.

There had to be more than a hundred reporters shouting questions at him. He answered each one calmly, but he still appeared somewhat perplexed. And then, a reporter said to him. "I cannot understand how you could come to our state and insult what is practically our official religion."

"Religion? I ain't never insulted no religion!"

Another reporter yelled, "Did you or did you not insult the Mormons?"

"Oh them guys? Yeah, I had some choice words tuh say tuh them. Yuh wanna hear some more?"

His manager pulled on his arm as another reporter yelled, "Are you bleeping crazy? Don't you know that most of the people in Utah are Mormons."

"Well, yeah. Everybody know *that*!"

"So you do know that most people here hold to the Mormon faith."

"Say *what*?"

"Most people in Utah are members of the Mormon faith."

Sam was completely astounded. His mouth hung wide open. Then he said, "You telling me that the Mormon is a religion?"

"Of course!" yelled one of the reporters. "What did *you* think it was?"

"Hey man, I thought the Mormon was a nick-name for the people of Utah. Yuh know. Like the nickname for all of the cats up in Canada? Those guys are all Canucks.... Wait, I got another one! Those folks in Idaho? I saw that basketball movie about them. They called Hoosiers, right?"

Terrence phoned me the next morning. "Great news, Roger! Sam's interview was a tremendous hit. We're going to wind up this project by the end of next week and immediately go into production. We want to ride this publicity wave and have the book in the stores in exactly six weeks."

"That's *nuts!*"

"Of course it's nuts. But it's also good business. Yuh gotta strike while the iron's hot! So I need you to write up the rest of what you've got and get it to me by the end of the week. And then, by the middle of next week, I'll need a closing chapter. Can you *do* it?"

"Do I have a choice?"

"Of course not! But my boss approved a twenty-five percent bonus if you meet both deadlines."

"OK, Terrence. I better get off the phone and start writing."

## 4

Sam, whose basketball career would have ended soon anyway, agreed to speed up his retirement. He announced to the reporters covering the Knicks that he would play his last NBA game stark naked. The commissioner announced that if Sam played a game naked, that would indeed be his last game.

Sam wanted his farewell game to be in his home arena, Madison Square Garden. The day before the game he received a three-word message from the commissioner: "Don't do it."

Terrence and I were pretty sure he would, but with Sam you never could be sure just *what* he would do.

Half an hour before the tip-off, the Garden was packed to the rafters. The question on everyone's lips was, "Would he or wouldn't he?" Not even his coach and teammates had a clue.

When he emerged from the locker room in his sweat suit and began the shoot around with his teammates, every eye in the arena followed his every move. After the National Anthem, he took his place on the bench with the other players who were not in the starting five. And then, exactly seven minutes into the game, he reported to the scorer's table, and a few seconds later his name was announced.

The fans went wild! They knew exactly what was coming. Off came the sweat suit. All Sam had on was a jock strap. Pandemonium! Everyone in the arena was standing and screaming. There were so many flash bulbs going off, it seemed like the fireworks on the Fourth of July.

When he strolled onto the court most of the players were laughing, and even one of the referees. A couple of players came over and slapped hands with Sam. Before one of the Knicks could inbound the ball, several whistles were blown as a whole bunch of cops rushed down to the court to place Sam under arrest. He said something to a police captain who smiled and ordered Sam released.

The referee handed the ball to one of the Knicks. He inbounded the ball to Sam. Sam dribbled across midcourt and then pulled up about thirty feet from the basket. No one was guarding him. He glanced at the basket, and got set to shoot.

The crowd hushed as he got off the shot. The ball seemed to hang in the air forever. And then, as it finally began its descent, time slowed even more as we all counted off the seconds in our minds – *one* Mississippi, *two* Mississippi, *three* Mississippi, *four* Mississippi, and then…. *Swish*! The crowd went totally nuts! Some fans were jumping up and down, some were crying, and everyone was screaming. Sam looked like Rocky when he won the heavyweight championship. It took almost ten minutes until order was restored. And as the police escorted

Sam out of the Garden, they were smiling and waving to the crowd. Even after he had left the arena, the crowd was still chanting, "Sam the Man! Sam the Man! Sam the Man!"

Two days later Sam's autobiography was in all the bookstores, and it became an instant bestseller. He was interviewed by everyone from Howard Cosell to Barbara Walters. He had become a national hero. The Democrats *and* the Republicans wanted to nominate him to run for the Senate. There was even talk about an appointment to the president's cabinet.

How did I feel about all of this? I liked Sam the Man. The word may be overused, but he certainly was "authentic." He was interesting, he was funny, and in his own way, he was smart – even if he *did* occasionally use quadruple negatives.

Did anyone actually believe that Sam wrote the book? I doubt that anyone is that dumb. I'd like to believe that I told a credible story of an individual who does not come along every day. Sam the Man was unique. And, as everyone knows, writers like me are a dime a dozen.

My name was in the Acknowledgements. Someone wrote, "And I'd like to thank my good friend, Roger Grayson, for his many helpful suggestions." Better yet, when my last payment came, it was double what I had expected.

Terrence, largely on the strength of his success with Sam's autobiography, was promoted to editorial director. I called him a couple of times to congratulate him, but he never returned my calls.

# THE COLLEGE MAN

## 1

When you're hot you're hot! After my last book came out, I was sizzling. In fact I was a little burned out. My plan was to take a couple of months off, and if I'm not pushing the metaphor too far, just cool out.

Then one day I got a call from a man who told me he was the attorney of a woman whose name I knew. She was a major socialite who was often in the news. Mrs. Covington would like to meet me.

A few months ago, I would have jumped at the chance, but a few months ago I was just another starving writer. Still, it wouldn't hurt to meet her. Would tomorrow at four be satisfactory?

## 2

She lived on Fifth Avenue in the seventies in what was still called a prewar building. I told the doorman my name, and that I was there to visit Mrs. Covington. He told me to get off the elevator at ten.

"What's the apartment number?"

He smiled and said, "Just get off at ten and you'll be in her apartment."

"You mean she has the whole *floor*?"

"Actually she has *three* floors – ten, eleven, and twelve. But she receives guests on ten."

179

When I stepped off the elevator, the attorney introduced himself and then showed me around. There were paintings by a few of the Impressionists and at least three Picassos. He smiled when he saw my expression and said, "Yes, they *are* originals."

Then he ushered me into a forty-foot living room with a spectacular view of Central Park. When I sat on the couch, I sank about a foot into the pillow.

Mrs. Covington then made her grand entrance. She must have been pushing eighty, and you could see that she had had some "work" done. Still, she looked pretty good. I stood and she walked over to me, shook hands, and took a seat next to me on the couch. Her attorney sat just across from us.

"May I call you Roger?"

"Of course!"

"Roger, I'm Suzanne. And of course you've already met Bart. I am a great admirer of your work. I read a few chapters in your book about that basketball player. You are a very talented writer."

"How did you know I wrote the book? It was supposed to be an autobiography."

Bart answered for her. "Well, Roger, when Suzanne asked me to find out who actually wrote the book, I placed a call to your editor. Not only did he tell me your name, but he highly recommended you."

"Well, that was very nice of him. He had sworn *me* to secrecy and then he volunteered my name?"

"Roger, I then followed up by googling your name and the title of the book, and guess what?"

"Wow! I'll never work in *this* town again."

"Now that you mentioned it, Roger, I have a proposition for you," said Suzanne.

"Don't tell me: You used to play in the National Basketball Association and you'd like me to ghostwrite *your* autobiography."

"Amusing, but no. Actually, I'd like you to write my husband's biography."

"Your husband?"

"I really should explain what I'm doing – and *why* I want to do it. But first, are you ready for the one-minute story of *my* life?"

"I doubt very much that your life story could be told in less than a thousand nights, but I'm all ears."

"Roger, if someone ever *did* write my life story, perhaps it could be called, 'The Wife of Bath.' My first husband, Mr. Covington, was extremely rich, and fifty years my senior. He died when I was still in my twenties and left me a huge fortune. I entered my second, and longest marriage, entirely for love. We were together for forty-two years.

I went into a depression after Michael's death, and didn't fully recover for several years. And then I met Harry. Harry is my age, and he's the sweetest man I've ever known. He had been what you might have called an academic nomad – going from one college teaching job to the next."

"If you don't mind my asking, did Harry come from a privileged background?"

"Hardly. When we married, which was eight years ago, he didn't even have a bank account. My friends and relatives all said he was a 'fortune hunter.'"

"*Was* he?"

"I didn't care then – and I still don't. Harry makes me laugh – and he's completely devoted. He calls me dear and sweetie, and he's always there when I need him."

"Why do you want someone to write his biography?"

"Harry is a storyteller. The only problem is that his stories are almost random. They're about things that happened to him over the years. I would love to have all of them together in a book."

"So what you're proposing can be considered something that a vanity press would publish."

"I suppose. But I would consider this more of a book for a vanity *reader*."

"I don't know. With all due respect, it just doesn't sound like the type of project I'd be that interested in."

"Roger," said Bart. "You're an excellent writer. You were able to take the words, the thoughts, and, really the life of that basketball player, and make them into a first-rate autobiography. If there's anyone who can take Harry's stories and shape them into a biography, you're the one."

Then it was Mrs. Covington's turn. It was the old two-on-one offense – *and* they also had the home court advantage. "Roger, this book means a great deal to me. Still, I can understand your reluctance. So I can think of only one reason why you might even consider taking on this job."

"Mrs. Covington, I really can't think of *any*. I wish I could. I can see how much this means to you."

As I prepared to be dismissed, I saw her nod at her attorney.

"Roger, Mrs. Covington is prepared to give you one *million* reasons to help you change your mind."

I looked at him, and then at her. They were perfectly serious. I looked again at each of them, and asked, "When do I start?"

### 3

The next morning there was a different doorman on duty. When I gave him my name, he said that I was expected and pointed me to the elevator. A butler met me when I got off at ten and took me directly to the living room.

Harry was waiting for me. He was quite large, probably about eighty pounds overweight. "Please don't bother getting up," I said as we shook hands. "I'm Roger and you must be Harry."

"Right you are!" he answered with a big smile. I could see immediately what Mrs. Covington liked so much about him. He really seemed genuinely nice.

"So you're a writer."

"Yes, and I understand you're a retired college professor."

"I was also an administrator."

"Really?"

"Well, actually just once."

"Where was that?"

"A small college in Boston. Newburyport College."

"Never heard of it."

"I was the Dean of Faculty."

"That sounds like a very important job."

"Oh, it *was*! I had a lot of responsibilities."

"Did you like your job?"

"Well, there *were* some problems."

"Like what?"

"Well, the college used to take out ads in all the newspapers. The ads were aimed at veterans."

"Yes?"

"The ads said, shake the money tree."

"Was that because the veterans would get government loans?"

"That's right! But very few of them ever graduated."

"That's terrible. So they got stuck with large debts."

"Well that wasn't the only thing. One night an accounting professor gave back an exam."

"Yes?"

"Everyone in the class failed."

"So what happened?"

"All the men sitting in the first row took out guns and placed them on their desks."

"Really?"

"Yes!"

"That must have been so frightening!"

"I guess."

"So then what happened?"

"I think the professor gave them another exam."

"Yeah?"

"Yeah, that was it."

"OK, you were the Dean of Faculty, right?"

"Yes."

"So what did you *do* about this?"

"Nothing."

He just sat there with a benign smile on his face. I now realized that poor Harry was definitely not the brightest candle in the menorah. But Mrs. Covington was right: her husband *did* tell some interesting stories.

## 4

A couple of days later I returned for our next session. When Harry entered the living room, I noticed that he was walking very slowly. I realized everything about him was kind of slow. It took him awhile to get settled in an overly stuffed easy chair.

"Harry, could you tell me something about your educational background?"

"Where should I start?"

"How about college?"

"I went to Northeastern."

"That's in Boston?"

"Yes."

"I noticed that you have a pretty strong Boston accent."

"Really?"

"Yes. Did you grow up in Boston?"

"No."

"So where *did* you grow up?"

"Winthrop."

"Isn't that near Boston?"

"Yes, it borders on Boston."

"So that must explain your Boston accent."

"I guess."

"Did you go to college right after high school?"

"No, I went into the Navy."

"Did you see the world?"

"What do you mean?"

"You know, 'Join the Navy and see the world?'"

"No, I never left the United States."

"Did you use the GI Bill of Rights to pay for Northeastern?"

"Yes. I never could have afforded it without the Bill."

"Did the GI Bill also help you pay for graduate school?"

"Yes."

"Where did you go?"

"NYU."

"New York University is a very good school. What did you study?"

"Business."

"Did you get a Masters of Business Administration?"

"Yes. And then I went back to Northeastern and got a Masters of Education."

"So you have two advanced degrees."

"Yes."

"Were you planning a career in college teaching?"

"I guess."

"So how many years did you teach?"

There was a long pause. I thought maybe he had fallen asleep, but his eyes were open and he was smiling. After about twenty seconds he came up with the answer: "I guess over thirty years."

"And you taught business."

Another pause. "Yes."

"What courses did you teach?"

"Everything."

Yeah, right! "Can you give me an example of a course you taught?"

"You mean, like a subject?"

"Exactly."

"Oh, why didn't you ask? I taught a lot of different subjects."

I was beginning to get the idea that just maybe this would be the hardest million dollars I would ever earn. Still, I pressed on, knowing this might be the *only* million dollars I would ever earn.

"I'll tell you what: Why don't I ask if you taught a specific course, and then you just answer yes or no. OK?"

He smiled. I guess that was my signal to start down the list.

"Did you teach accounting?"

Long pause. "Yes."

"Did you teach that course at several different colleges?"

Very long pause. "Yes."

"Did you teach accounting at Newberryport College?"

"No, I was an administrator. I was the Dean of Faculty."

"OK, so where *did* you teach accounting?"

"A lot of colleges."

"Can you name one?"

"Yes."

I waited. He smiled. I waited some more. He kept smiling. After a while I realized that I would need to rephrase the question.

"Can you tell me the name of a college where you taught?"

"I taught at a lot of colleges."

*Shit!* Was this guy playing me? No, no, I was just getting a little paranoid. "Did you teach at Harvard?"

"No."

"Did you ever teach at a community college?"

"Yes."

"Did you ever teach at any community college in the Boston area?"

"Yes."

Wow, now we were getting somewhere. "How about Massachusetts Bay Community College?"

"Yes."

"Did you teach accounting there?"

"Yes."

"What else did you teach there?"

"A lot of different courses."

"Like what?"

"Everything."

*Shit!* He got me again!

## 5

At our next session I tried to get more of an overview of Harry's career. "Where did you get your first teaching job?"

"You mean at which college?"

"Yes."

"I sent my resume to a lot of colleges. I didn't hear back from most of them – and the rest sent rejection letters."

"I can certainly relate to that. After all, I'm a writer."

"Really? I didn't know that writers also had that problem."

"That's OK. So then what happened?"

"The day before the beginning of the fall semester I got a call from the Business Department Chairwoman at Hartford Community College."

"In Connecticut?"

"Yes."

"And she actually offered you a job over the phone?"

"Yes, she had a sudden vacancy."

"Were you living in Hartford?"

"No, but I wasn't too far from there."

"Did you teach accounting?

"Yes, I taught about four sections of introductory accounting."

"How did it go?"

"Great! I knew right away that I was cut out to teach in college."

"How long did you teach there?"

Long pause. "Only that semester."

"Was it just a temporary position?"

"No, I think it was supposed to be permanent."

"So why did you leave?"

Long pause. "The chairwoman thought she was God.'

"Where did you teach next?"

"Next? Let me see." After about thirty seconds: "At the University of Hartford."

"When did you start teaching there?"

"Well, I collected unemployment insurance benefits for six months, so it must have been about six months later."

"So at least you didn't have to move. How long were you at the University of Hartford?"

"I taught there for five years."

187

"Really? Was that the longest you ever taught at the same school?"

"No, the longest was at Empire State."

"When was that?"

"That was my last teaching job."

"OK, we'll get back to that later. Tell me why you left the University of Hartford."

"Well, it was complicated."

"How was it complicated?"

"They wanted me to finish graduate school."

"Well, you already had a Master's in Business Administration, right?"

"Yes, but they wanted me to get a Doctorate."

"And if you did?"

"Then I would get tenure."

"So I guess *that* didn't work out."

"What do you mean?"

"Well you didn't complete your Doctorate."

"Yes, but they never gave me a chance."

"That's *terrible!*"

"Yeah, they broke their word."

"Tell me what happened."

He took a little time to gather himself. I could see that this was very difficult for him, and I felt bad about asking Harry to dredge up such unpleasant memories.

"They told me I had five years, right? So for five years I took the train from Hartford to New York, and took courses at night at NYU."

"That's a pretty long ride."

"You're telling *me!*"

"How many courses were you able to complete?"

"Just three. In three others I had incompletes."

"So you really hadn't gotten all that far toward your doctorate."

"I guess not."

"So then they fired you?"

"Yeah, but when you think about it, they really broke their word."

# 6

I felt we were making a lot of headway. Each time we'd get together, Harry would tell me about his time at another college. Mrs. Covington told me that she loved what I had written and was amazed to find that even *she* had never heard some of the stories that Harry had told me.

And then I had a terrible thought. What if Harry ran out of material? But the solution came to me very quickly. I'm a writer. If I had to, maybe I could come up with my own stories. Who would ever know? Harry?

It turned out that Harry had been looking forward to our sessions. Whether it made him feel important or he was just lonely, he was always glad to see me. Occasionally we just kind of hung out, and there were times when I actually told *him* stories. Eventually I came to realize that we were *both* storytellers, but his wife was paying *me* for writing down *his* stories.

Harry's next teaching position was at Schenectady Community College in upstate New York. There he taught introductory statistics and business math.

"So why did you leave *that* job?"

Harry thought this over for a while. Then he broke into a wide grin and began to chuckle. I waited till he was ready to explain.

"This was really funny. Several students in my business math classes complained to my chairman, and then to the Dean of Students that I had given them inaccurate information."

"What *kind* of inaccurate information?"

"Well, a new shopping mall had been built just outside of Schenectady. In fact it was the largest shopping mall in the state."

"How large *was* this mall?"

"I'm pretty good with numbers, so I can tell you exactly how big it was. This mall was 3.6 million acres."

189

"Are you *sure*?"

"What do you mean?"

"Well, maybe it was 3.6 million square feet?"

"Why do you say that?"

"I know that Central Park is about 840 acres. Are you saying that this shopping mall was what, more than a thousand times as big as Central Park?"

"I don't know."

"What did the dean do?"

"Would you believe he actually agreed with the students? He insisted that it was much smaller than 3.6 million acres. You know, if there had been any justice, *he* would have been the one who was fired!"

"Well, why don't we go on to the next college?"

"OK."

"So where did you teach after Schenectady Community College?"

"Let me see. Oh yes! I remember, because I didn't have to move. I got a job at the College of St Rose in Albany."

"That's a four-year college?"

"Yes. And it has a beautiful campus."

"How long were you there?"

"One year."

"Do you remember why you left?"

"Boy do I remember! It never would have happened anywhere but in a Catholic College."

"I don't understand."

"Right in the middle of the semester, the Pope died. So the president of the college announced that on the day the Pope was buried, classes would be optional."

"OK. So what happened?"

"Nothing."

"Nothing? Then why did they let you go?"

"Beats *me!*"

"Maybe if you tell me exactly what happened, we can figure this out."

"OK. The day after the Pope was buried, the Academic Vice President called me into his office. And he asked me whether or not I held classes the day before."

"*Did* you?"

"No! And I know I was within my rights! Because classes were optional."

"So what was the problem?"

"Well the Academic Vice President was very angry. He said that almost all of my students came to my classes that day."

"Why would they come to your classes if you weren't holding them?"

"That's what the Academic Vice President asked *me*. I said that since classes were optional, I decided not to hold them."

"So what was the problem?"

"He told me that I should have informed my students in advance that I wasn't holding classes instead of just not showing up. Can you *believe* that?"

"But if you *knew* you weren't going to be hold your classes, why *didn't* you tell your students in advance?"

Long pause. "Well *think* about it! If classes were optional for *me*, then classes are optional for them *too*, right? So I wanted to let them make their own decisions."

By now I strongly doubted that Mrs. Covington would continue to enjoy these stories. Clearly this poor soul was not exactly the sharpest knife in the drawer. Who would make himself the victim of his own self-imposed misfortune? Who did he think he was – Rodney Dangerfield?

## 7

Next up was Worchester Community College in Massachusetts. This was another school that Harry had really liked. The only problem was the students. Harry felt very strongly about open enrollment schools, and he thought WCC would have been a fine school if not for the students.

I reminded him that without students, he would not have had most of those jobs. He agreed, but he felt that *these* students were particularly bad.

"Some of my students even though they knew more than I did."

"Can you tell me what happened?"

"A bunch of my students complained about me to the chairman."

"Were you a tough grader?"

"No, if anything, I was too easy."

"Then what were they complaining about?"

"Mainly about how I marked exams."

"Really?"

"They brought their exam papers to the chairman and told him that I marked several answers wrong, when they were right."

"What did the chairman say?"

"He sided with the students."

"Really?"

"Yes. He even claimed he showed the exam papers to other professors in the department and that they also agreed with the students. Can you *believe* that?"

"It *is* hard to believe."

"So he let you go?"

"Yeah, he thought he was God."

## 8

I have a good friend who has taught comparative literature at Queens College since the late 1960s. She described that decade and the one that followed as "the golden age of academia." Thousands of colleges introduced open enrollment and financial aid was vastly expanded. Many schools desperately needed instructors. I began to understand now how Harry had managed to find so many jobs.

It was finally time to learn what had happened at Empire State College – Harry's last teaching job. Part of the State University of New York, the school had a student body composed entirely of adults. Virtually all received substantial life experience credits and worked with individual instructors taking independent study courses.

So the students, the classes, and the entire environment were very different from every other school where he had taught. Harry had finally found his academic home.

The hours were longer, and there was a substantial amount of clerical work. But Harry didn't mind. Everyone called him Professor, and he felt very good about himself.

And then the trouble started. A new Academic Dean was hired, and Harry's status was changed from employee to contract worker. Not long after, his paychecks stopped coming. As someone who had always lived from paycheck to paycheck, Harry quickly took notice. He asked his chairwoman to speak to the head of Payroll. She felt so badly about his not being paid that she lent him several hundred dollars.

A few days later she called him into her office and told him that Payroll had sent him a form a few months ago. He was supposed to fill in his Social Security number and sign the form.

"I *did* that!"

"Harry, they even sent you a second form – and a third one!"

"I know. I filled *those* out too!"

"Harry, what did you *do* with those forms?"

"I still have all them of them. I can show them to you."

"Harry, do you understand *why* Payroll asked you to fill out those forms?"

"Beats me."

"The Internal Revenue Service requires contractors to get a Social Security number before they can pay people who do work for them."

"I happen to know that. After all, I have been teaching business for thirty years."

"So why didn't you send back those forms?"

"No one asked me to. So what am I supposed to be – a mind-reader?"

I saw how upset he was and even imagined seeing steam coming out of his ears. It took a few minutes for him to regain his composure.

When he was ready to continue, I said, "Surely they didn't let you go because of that."

"Well, no, but I'm sure they counted that against me."

"What happened next?"

"I guess it was my naps."

"Could you explain that?"

"I like to take a nap every day after lunch."

"Nothing wrong with that!"

"Well, twice a month, the dean who ran our center would hold a meeting right after lunch."

"And you would fall asleep there?"

"I think what they really objected to was my snoring."

"So they fired you for *that*?"

"Well, not right away. But I'm sure they put that into my record."

"So they finally let you go after six years?"

"That's correct."

"Did they give you a reason?"

"Yes. They were required to give a reason in writing."

"What *was* it?"

"Are you *ready*? They said I didn't know the subjects that I was teaching." Then he smiled, while shaking his head in disbelief.

"Did you have good relations with your students?"

"Of course! At Empire State, almost all our courses were one-on-one. So I got to know a lot of them."

"Did your students come to your defense?"

"Are you *kidding*? I know for a fact that many of them were in on it."

"I don't understand."

"Nearly all my students signed a petition asking that I be fired."

"For what reason?"

*"Incompetence!"*

"Wow!"

"I know! I couldn't believe it either! Look, I know I'm not perfect, and maybe I didn't do all my paperwork, but how can anyone question my competence?"

I just took my head. I mean, what could I say?

*** 

When I received my last payment, I couldn't believe my eyes. Mrs. Covington had made me a multi-millionaire. She said she loved every word of the book. She thanked me for writing such a faithful biography of her husband. I deposited the check immediately and counted the days until it cleared.

# WAITING FOR GOLDBAR

## 1

If you were in town last spring, you may have seen one of the flyers announcing the unveiling of a recently discovered Madonna and child. The unveiling was to take place on April 1st at high noon on the steps of the Metropolitan Museum of Art.

And sure enough, in front of a huge crowd, a large oil painting of Madonna and Child was unveiled. The crowd gasped, and then quickly broke into great cheers. There were the two of them in radiant color – the singer, Madonna, and the cooking diva, Julia Child.

The mastermind of this historical event was my friend, Arnie Goldbar, perhaps the City's greatest punster. It was *he* who thought up the pun, convinced an artist friend to paint it, and then managed to lure thousands of onlookers to the unveiling. "And," he pointed out, "I got them there on April Fool's day!"

Arnie's day job was actually in public relations. While he was truly a PR genius, he was also extraordinarily lazy. Indeed, despite his great originality and creativity, Arnie was invariably dismissed from every job he ever held.

When he was hired by the New York State Department of Labor, I predicted not only *why* he would get fired, but *when*. "How can you possibly make that prediction?" he asked. "The job doesn't even start till Monday."

197

"Arnie! I *know* you! Guaranteed, you will be late on Monday morning."

On Monday evening, Arnie called me. "I just wanted to let you know that you were wrong. Remember what you predicted?"

"Yeah, that you would be late on your first day."

"Do you remember your *exact* prediction?"

"Of course! "I said, "You will be late on Monday morning."

"I wasn't!"

"I don't believe it!"

"Well, you were wrong! I didn't get there till after lunch."

Within a couple of weeks, he was getting almost daily warnings from his boss about his chronic lateness. But Arnie was quite confident that he had solved the problem by constructing a colorful bar graph. Anyone could spot the trend: His daily lateness over the two-week period had declined almost steadily, and was now barely over two hours.

"So, Arnie," I asked, "how did your boss respond to your chart?"

"He *loved* it!"

"Really?"

"Yeah, he liked the colors."

"What about all your tardies?"

"Now *those* he didn't like so much."

Arnie, of course, continued to come in late, and he kept making charts for his boss. Finally, one day his boss warned him that if he was late one more time, he would be fired.

The next morning, he was an hour late.

"What did your boss say to you?"

"Luckily I had just made another chart for him. And even though I was late that day, I still got to the office fifteen minutes earlier than the day before."

"So what did he say?"

"I told you, Steve. He liked my chart."

"What were his exact words?"

"Well, his exact words were, 'Coming in late right after I gave you that warning was like spitting in my face!'"

That afternoon Arnie was fired. But he never saw it coming. After all, his daily lateness had fallen to a record low. And whatever anyone else might say, the daily lateness charts don't lie.

## 2

Did Arnie have a favorite PR pun? Yes! It's the one he did for the Vegetarian Party's fundraising dinner. He and his wife, both officials of the party, had been separated for many years. And yet, they would be sitting together at the dinner.

Before we go any further, do you remember the old aphorism, "Politics makes strange bedfellows"? Well here's the headline Arnie came up with for the press release he wrote for the dinner: "Politics mates estranged bedfellows."

The best PR job Arnie had ever had was working in the Mayor's Office for the Handicapped. Years later, when he was being interviewed on a public access TV show, he fondly recalled those days.

Interviewer: Tell us, Arnie, what was the greatest PR coup you ever pulled off?

Arnie: There is no question that it was the time when the Mayor's Office for the Handicapped fired this poor woman who happened to be a quadriplegic. They gave her virtually no notice.

Interviewer: That's awful! So what did you do?

Arnie: Well, they claimed it was because of budget cuts, but in those years, with all the federal grants pouring in, the city had more money than it knew what to do with. The bottom line was that the poor woman was out of work.

Interviewer: OK, so you were doing PR for that agency. Firing that woman sounds like pretty bad public relations.

Arnie: It *was!*

Interviewer: So wasn't your job to make the Mayor's Office for the Handicapped look good?

Arnie: Of course! But there was no way the agency could look good firing a handicapped woman.

Interviewer: So how did you handle it?

Arnie: Well, I decided to run with the story. I mean, wasn't this the greatest human interest story of all time? So I called every radio and TV station in the city. And when the access-a-ride van brought her home at six pm, there were reporters and cameras set up on her front lawn, on the sidewalk, and all up and down her block

Interviewer: So she must have been on the evening news.

Arnie: Would you believe that she was on every channel that night and the next day?

Interviewer: Arnie, that's wonderful! So did she end up getting her job back?

Arnie: No, but she got some great publicity.

## 3

For a while Arnie had a beautiful girlfriend named Marla, who had just finished chiropractic school. They lived in a studio apartment in Brooklyn Heights with a great view of the Brooklyn Queens Expressway. While thinking about how he could help Marla start up her practice, Arnie had one of his greatest PR inspirations. "Let's set up the 'Bad Back Hotline!'"

They would use the phone number 223-2225. Check it out on your phone by matching the letters B-A-D-B-A-C-K with each of these numbers. And what have you got? You've got the BAD BACK hotline!

They managed to get that number from the phone company, but since the exchange, 223, was not in Brooklyn Heights, they would have to pay fifty cents for each forwarded call.

I can still remember the recording he made: "You've reached the Bad Back Hotline. You don't need to suffer from back pain any longer. Just leave your name and number and one of our doctors will get right back to you."

Now all that was needed was to publicize the Bad Back Hotline and a flood of people would be calling BADBACK.

Since Arnie was the PR guru, he would handle the logistics. He drew up a plan, which called for designing a flyer with a picture of a person doubled over in pain, then get flyers printed up and distributed wherever people with bad backs congregated.

But it never happened. Arnie always had great ideas, but as a world class procrastinator, he almost always put off acting upon them. And so, one day, Marla moved out. The Bad Back Hotline never got a call, except, perhaps, the one from me.

## 4

Over the years Arnie found it increasingly difficult to find a job. Then he got lucky. His old friend, Sammy, along with a couple of partners, had managed to scrape together enough money to start what they planned to be a bagel bakery and restaurant. They took out a lease on a rather large store on 7<sup>th</sup> Avenue, the main shopping drag of Park Slope, a gentrified neighborhood in Brooklyn. Arnie would do their PR.

It took him just one day to think up the name for their store-restaurant – *We ain't just bagels!* He convinced the three partners that it was the perfect name for their enterprise. The name had attitude, it was edgy, and it let potential customers know that they could buy a whole lot more than just bagels. And best of all, the name was ungrammatical, just like most of Brooklyn once was.

As the store's grand opening approached, Arnie had another great idea. Why not invite the press, the TV and radio stations, and all the local politicians? The lure would be a free sit-down meal *and* a big bag of bagels to take home. Just imagine all the free publicity this would generate!

Arnie knew that the idea of giving away free meals went all the way back to the early 1900s when a man named Nathan Handwerker opened a Coney Island hot dog eatery called *Nathan's*. To create the impression that his hot dogs were made of top quality meat, he invited the interns at nearby Coney Island Hospital to have free meals – as long as they wore their hospital whites. And his ads, which anticipated Arnie's own advertising copy, proclaimed that Nathan's hot dogs were so wonderful that many doctors ate there.

The day of the grand opening finally arrived. It would be an invitation-only affair, and the inside and outside of the store were festooned with red, white, and blue ribbons, banners, and balloons, all of which proclaimed, *We ain't just bagels!*

The invitations called for a noon opening, and because of the huge crowds expected for the free meals, the festivities would go on all day. Among the guests would be Brooklyn Borough President Marty Markowitz, a man who was rumored to be even fonder of speaking than of eating. Indeed, he had gone to great lengths to promote Brooklyn's many promising new eateries. Who knew? He might even be induced to make a speech.

Surprisingly, no one had shown up before the stroke of noon. But, of course, who likes to be the first person to arrive?

Around 12:30 the owners began to get a little nervous. And by one o'clock, it had become very clear that something must have gone terribly wrong. Who had been in charge of sending out the invitations? *Arnie!*

"Where the hell *is* he?" demanded Sammy. "Somebody, call him!"

A minute later Sammy was told that Arnie's answering machine had picked up.

"OK," said Sammy. "I want two guys to go over to his apartment. And take along a sledge hammer. If he doesn't answer, I want you to break down his door!"

"Are you *serious*?"

"You're damn *straight* I'm serious! I want you to bring him back here. I need some answers, and I need them right away."

An hour later the two guys returned with Arnie. As he stumbled into the store Sammy yelled, "What the hell *happened!*"

"I overslept."

"I don't give a shit about your *sleep!* What happened with the invitations?"

"Nothing. I mailed them."

"You *mailed* them? *When* did you mail them?"

"Well I intended to send them out at the beginning of the week. But then things got delayed."

"How *long* did they get delayed?"

"Well, till Friday. I *did* get to the Central Post Office just before they closed at 8 pm."

"You *schmuck*! You mean to tell me that you didn't mail out the invitations for a Sunday opening until Friday night?"

"Well, technically it was Friday evening."

"I don't give a technical *shit* if it was Friday night or Friday evening! You sent out the invitations the day before the event?"

"Well, technically it was *two* days before the event. From Friday to Sunday is actually *two* days."

"Get *out* of here! And don't *ever* come back!"

## 5

Arnie looks back fondly on his days with *We ain't just bagels!* Deep down, he felt that the business really had had a great chance to succeed, especially with the creative ideas he'd offered. It still saddens him that his old friend, Sammy, no longer talks to him. But long ago, Arnie had decided to forgive Sammy. Some people just couldn't get past certain disappointments. And going bankrupt *was* a pretty big disappointment.

Still, to be completely honest, Arnie realized that there was certainly enough blame to go around. And that the fact that he and Sammy were no longer friends was not entirely Sammy's fault. "You know," he once told me in a moment of great candor, "there are times when I do realize that just maybe I played some small role in the demise of *We ain't just bagels!*"

# NOTES FROM JEANNIE KAPLAN

## 1

The promenade in Brooklyn Heights provides a fantastic view of New York harbor. You can see the Statue of Liberty, the Brooklyn Bridge, the Staten Island Ferry, and, of course, the New York skyline. I was sitting on a bench with my legs stretched out and my face tilted up toward the sun. It was the first warm day of March, and I had just run back and forth a few times across the bridge. In the 1970s, it had not yet been discovered by tourists.

My eyes were closed, but I heard someone sit down near me.

"Did you go to Brooklyn College? I went there from 1958 to 1967. It took me that long because I changed majors six times. I graduated as a sociology major with minors in political science, history, and English."

Without bothering to open my eyes I muttered, "Maybe a little too much information."

She laughed. And that's what got me – the sound of it. It was sincere, self-deprecating, and pleasant.

I opened my eyes. She was fairly attractive, but what really caught my attention was her hair. It reminded me of Angela Davis's hair. In case you don't remember her, she was an extremely attractive black activist with a huge Afro. The woman sitting next to me had what would soon be termed a *Jewfro*.

"Jeannie Kaplan," she said as she extended her hand.

"Howie Greenberg. And yeah, I *did* go to Brooklyn."

"When did you graduate?"

"1957... No wait a minute: that's when I graduated from Madison. No, I graduated from Brooklyn in 1961."

"Yeah, so you *do* look familiar from college."

"I can't say that *you* do."

"No, probably not. I looked different then. Long straight hair – and I was always in the library studying. From the time I was in elementary school, if I came home with a 98, my mother asked me why I didn't get 99. And if I got a 99, she wanted to know why I didn't get 100."

"What if you got 100?"

"Then she'd find something else."

From what appeared to be a huge carpet bag, she pulled a pad of yellow legal size paper, wrote her phone number down, handed it to me, and then told me to write down my number. Glancing at her, I saw that she was perfectly serious, so I wrote my number.

Then she stood up and said, "I've got to run now. I'm already late for my therapist appointment. My parents pay for it, which makes me feel guilty, but then he and I have another thing to talk about."

I watched her as she rushed off down the promenade. She waved to a woman who waved back at her. Then she sat down again to begin another conversation.

I didn't call her and she didn't call me. Then, one weekday afternoon, I was running on the bridge and I saw her walking toward me. As we passed, I asked her to wait for me on the Brooklyn end of the bridge.

I reached the Manhattan side – and ran back to Brooklyn. I passed a couple of dozen people walking home from work. As I approached the end of the bridge I didn't see Jeannie, but there was a smiling guy in a business suit. He was holding a yellow, legal size sheet of paper.

The note was almost a page long. It was an explanation of why she did not have the time to wait for me, but she definitely wanted to talk to me. Why did that not surprise me?

A week later I invited her to a party. I was having about ten friends over. She said she'd try to come if she didn't have too much work to do.

As the last couple was leaving, they handed me a note someone had pushed under my door. I laughed when I saw the yellow paper. Jeannie needed four pages to explain why she couldn't spare the time to attend my party. It probably took her over an hour to write the note.

I decided to invite her to dinner. We would meet at a restaurant on Montague Street the next evening.

When I got to the restaurant, she was already there. "I hate being late," she confided, "so I set my clocks and my watch half an hour early. I've actually been sitting here for thirty-seven minutes."

"So you must know what you'd like to order."

"Well, I was looking at the menu, but I couldn't decide whether to have a chef salad or a hamburger and fries."

"Didn't you have the same problem picking a major?"

"I told you, didn't I, that I had seven different majors at Brooklyn?"

"Yes, you certainly did."

The waitress came over and asked if we were ready to order. Jeannie had her face buried in the menu.

"Jeannie, why don't we start out with a plate of cold appetizers? And we'll have more time to figure out what we want for entrees."

"OK, I sometimes have trouble making decisions."

The waitress, who was obviously used to this, said, "Plenty of time," and walked away. I asked Jeannie what she did for a living.

"I write term papers."

"I don't understand."

"I work for a term paper service. They pay me $1.50 a page."

"Isn't that illegal – not to mention unethical?"

"Well, to get around that, the company labels its service 'research.'"

"And you make a living doing this?"

"To be completely truthful, my parents help me. They pay my rent. Did I tell you that they also pay for my therapist?"

"Actually you did."

"I mean they *should* – after the way they screwed me up!"

It was hard for me to respond to that. If I agreed, that would imply that I thought she *was* screwed up. And if I didn't, then I was contradicting her. I just smiled.

"So how did you get into the term paper writing business?"

"It was easy. I knew someone who was working for the company. They actually advertise in *The Kingsman.*"

"Really? The college allows them to put ads in the student newspaper?"

"I think they have to. It's a first amendment issue – freedom of speech."

"Yeah, and freedom to cheat."

"Pease don't say that! I feel guilty enough taking money to do this."

"So you're good at it?"

"Well, having gone through seven different majors, I'm pretty versatile."

The waitress came back with the appetizers. "Are you folks ready to order?"

I looked at Jeannie. Again, her face was buried in the menu. "Jeannie, why don't we share a chef's salad and a hamburger and fries?"

"Sounds good to me!"

After the waitress left, I asked if s Jeannie if she had any long term plans.

"I was hoping to go to grad school, but my father put his foot down. He said – and these were his exact words – 'Young lady: with *your* academic track record, by the time you finish, you'll be an *old* lady!"

"That's pretty harsh."

"*Tell* me about it!"

## 2

It turned out that Jeannie and I had a mutual friend. Harry was a research librarian at the Brooklyn Heights branch of the Brooklyn Public Library. One day, I saw her talking to him. When I walked over she began to introduce us, and then started laughing when she quickly realized that Harry and I already knew each other.

She proclaimed Harry "a great resource for term paper writing." But today was special. Jeannie had a new assignment. She would be writing an entire Master's thesis. The pay was fantastic: $5 a page!

Harry and I just looked at each other. Obviously he felt the same way I did about her work. Later, after Jeannie went back to her cluttered table to go through the books Harry had given her, he confided how conflicted he felt about helping her.

"I try to rationalize by thinking that as a researcher, I need to be nonjudgmental. And that Jeannie is my friend. But on the other hand, I feel dirty. I'm complicit in facilitating this fraud. I've even consulted with my supervisor."

"Yeah?"

"She's as conflicted as *I* am. She said she would support me either way."

## 3

One day, Harry and I went for a long walk and ended up in front of the Grand Army Plaza Library. The main branch of the Brooklyn Public Library, it's situated at the north end of Prospect Park, about two and a half miles from Brooklyn Heights.

There was a large crowd on the library steps. Everyone was watching a group of amazingly talented break dancers. And standing near the front was Jeannie. We decided to creep up from behind and surprise her. When we got just a few feet from her, we began to cough loudly. Before even turning around, she managed to inform us that "It took me only forty-three minutes to walk here."

# 4

Jeannie's progress in writing the thesis was very slow. It took her several months until she finally handed in the last chapter. The company was so pleased with her work that they even gave her a two-hundred-dollar performance bonus. She said it was the hardest job she ever accepted.

Harry and I took her out to dinner to celebrate. Then we went to Capulets on Montague, the semi-hip neighborhood bar, where we continued our celebration.

"So, Jeannie Kaplan, MA, what will you do for an encore?"

"Howie, you're not going to believe this!"

"I think we're ready to believe anything," said Harry.

"OK, but this will test your faith."

"I'll drink to that," I declared.

"We all raised our glasses."

"To *faith*!" we shouted. In fact, for Harry and for me, it would be a leap too far.

"Are you guys ready?" We nodded.

"I got a call today from some guy with a thick Indian accent. At first I thought it was my friend Chuck, who does great accents. But this guy was really from India."

"Oh no! Don't tell me he wanted you to write another Master's thesis?"

"Close, Howie, but no cigar."

We sat there, waiting for her to tell us. But it became clear that she wanted us to guess. Harry and looked at each other. We both just shrugged.

"Come on, you're both smart guys. Figure it out!"

We sat there trying to do just that. Then Harry began to smile. We looked at him expectantly.

"Don't *tell* me!

Jeannie started laughing. Soon she was pounding the bar with her fists.

Then Harry went on. "That poor Indian guy. He was looking for someone to write his doctoral dissertation!"

"*Bingo!*" shouted Jeannie.

"How fucking sad," I observed.

"Sad? It's pathetic!" said Harry.

"So what did you say to the poor guy?"

"Well, Harry, I didn't know *what* to say. So finally I asked him how much the job paid."

"*What?*" we both screamed.

"Look, I felt terrible for the guy. I was just trying to be polite. I wanted to let him down easy. You know, show him that I took him seriously."

"Just out of curiosity, how much *would* they have paid you?" I asked.

"Ten dollars a page."

Harry and I burst out laughing. Ten dollars a page to write a doctoral dissertation. Un-fucking-believable!

But she was no longer smiling. Then, with a shrug, she said, "I simply couldn't afford to turn down such a great rate of pay."

Harry and I were suddenly stone sober. We tried talking her out of it, but she was bound and determined to take on what would clearly be a fool's errand. Besides being highly unethical, it would be virtually impossible to do. No department with a doctoral program would accept such a dissertation. As grad school dropouts ourselves, Harry and I could bear witness to just how high the bar was set. And then there was the high likelihood of getting caught.

Finally, she had heard quite enough. Without a word, she stood up and left the bar.

For weeks Harry and I checked with each other, but neither of us had heard from her. We stopped seeing her around the neighborhood, and she no longer came to the library. Finally, I tried calling her, but her phone had been disconnected. There was no way to reach her.

## 5

About a year later a team of investigative reports from *The New York Times* uncovered a cheating scandal involving hundreds of colleges and universities. The largest offender was a term paper mill. About a year later, a team of investigative reporters from *The Times* uncovered Academic Research Associates, which hired people to write term papers, college application essays, and even graduate theses. The story made the first page of *The Times*. And there was Jeannie's photo. She was actually smiling.

It turned out that the dissertation she had researched and written had been accepted by the sociology department of an Ivy League University. But the student who had "written" it was utterly incapable of defending his own dissertation. In fact, he could not answer even one question.

It was quickly discovered that Jeannie was the *real* author. This posed a terrible dilemma for the university. A department had accepted a dissertation that was not written by one of its doctoral candidates. This student had not written his Master's thesis or any of his term papers. The university's administrators clearly needed to resolve this dilemma as quickly as possible. So they wisely asked the Sociology Department to come up with a solution.

Within hours, the department announced that its members were so impressed with Jeannie's scholarly work that she would be offered a full scholarship. Since the dissertation she had researched and written had already been accepted, and she had accumulated such an impressive array of undergraduate courses, she would need just a few more courses to earn her Ph.D.

# JUST IN CASE

## 1

A rather tall woman about my age was standing at the other end of the subway car talking to another woman. She had a stack of newspapers under her arm.

A minute later she was talking to a couple of guys in business suits. Soon she had moved on to someone else. She seemed to be trying to sell her newspapers.

As she got closer, I realized just how attractive she was. Her long blonde hair hung straight down, which meant she was probably what was then called a "hippie chic." She was even wearing "granny glasses."

When she reached me I smiled at her. She smiled back. I wanted to ask her to just forget about those newspapers she was selling and sit down next to me. But then she began her pitch. "Just in case you haven't seen the latest issue of the Socialist Workers' paper, it's got a great article about capitalist exploitation of workers in the South Bronx."

She wasn't wearing a wedding band or an engagement ring. So maybe I had a chance. I just kept smiling and not saying anything; she kept going about the greatness of the article.

Meanwhile, the absurdity of her pitch began to make me start laughing to myself. She noticed my mood change and stopped smiling. "OK mister, what's so funny?"

"Let me see if I can explain. First, the Social Workers' paper may be really fantastic, but come *on* now, what are the chances that I am at all familiar with it – let alone that I had read that article?"

I could see that she was *really* getting angry. "Look, mister, if you don't want to support the American worker, just *say* so. But there's no need to make fun of our paper. Especially since you've never read it."

"No, that's not it at all! This may be the greatest issue of the greatest newspaper in the world, but let's face it: what are the chances that anyone you approach has even heard of it, let alone read this particular issue?"

"I'm sorry, but if you're not interested in our paper, please stop wasting my time."

"Look, I apologize. Obviously you really believe it's a great paper, and I wasn't trying to make fun of you – *or* your paper. I just couldn't get past the absurdity of your premise."

"Well then, just... have a nice day." And with that, this lovely and very earnest woman walked out of my life.

Later that day, when I told my friend, Bob, what had happened, he called me an idiot. "Steve, you should have bought her entire stack of papers!"

"Now you tell me?"

## 2

A few years later, a group of writers I knew launched a literary magazine, Box 749 – named for the post office box they had been assigned. While the list of contributors in the first issue was almost identical to the list of editors, the level of writing was quite good. I especially liked an article written by Patricia, which was a rebuttal to a piece by Norman Mailer in *Playboy*. In it, he revealed his fantasy of having sex with a woman on a pool table, and then watching her slide down into a pocket.

Patricia's friend, Gail, who wrote the small banks column for *The American Banker* – "The nation's only daily newspaper" – was also infuriated with Mailer. But her editors would have been less than pleased if *she* had cited Patricia's article in her column. So the two of them schemed about what they could do to let Mailer know just what a male chauvinist pig he was.

Something about the plan they concocted sounded vaguely familiar. Gail typed a letter to Mailer on American Banker stationery and enclosed Patricia's article. He never replied.

Sometime later, it dawned on me why their strategy sounded so familiar. Gail's letter had begun, "Just in case you haven't already seen this article...."

# TRUE CONFESSION: I NEVER DATED
## O.J. SIMPSON

Telling a joke is a good way to begin a speech. I'm not so sure how well that works with a short story, but I hope this one sets the right mood.

A very pale older man is sitting by the pool in a senior citizens development in South Florida.

"So you're new here."

He looked up at the sun-bronzed older woman.

"How could you tell?"

"You're pale as a ghost," she replied.

"Yeah, I just got out of prison."

"Really? What were you in for, if you don't mind my asking?"

"I murdered my wife."

"So then you're single?"

When O.J. Simpson gets out of prison, he won't have any trouble getting dates. After all, not only will he be single, but he'll still be a big celebrity.

If this all sounds like sour grapes, that's because it is. I don't mean to complain, but I really did get the short end of the stick. I'm nice, but I'm not famous. Nor am I rich.

When people meet for the first time, one will often ask the other, "So what do you do?" I always reply, "I'm a philosopher." And then they'll usually ask, "From that you can make a living?"

I actually do. But I do it the hard way. Like most other philosophers with Ph.Ds, I can't find a teaching job. So instead, I write books. Just a few years ago I made publishing history by completing the first philosophical trifecta – "Philosophy for Dummies," "Philosophy for Idiots," and "Philosophy for Imbeciles."

What kind of philosopher *am* I? I'm a moral philosopher. Can I sum that up in just a few words? Do the right thing.

If you know right from wrong, then that should be easy. But what *is* right and wrong? *Oy*, don't get me started! Look, if you really want to learn about moral philosophy, then read my magisterial, "The History of Moral Philosophy: the Last Three Thousand Years."

There's only one problem. It hasn't been published yet. I've even talked to my editors with the Dummies, Idiots, and Imbeciles series, but they reasonably pointed out that it would be quite a hard sell even in *their* market.

Writing books is horribly isolating. Hanging out with other writers would not just be fun, but might also offer some networking opportunities. So when I heard about the American Association of Authors, I Googled them. The only entrance requirements were to write nonfiction books, and to earn at least half your income from royalties. So if you could afford the annual dues, which were $100 a year, then you were in.

After joining, I found that nearly all of us were "midlist authors." Our books, while never bestsellers, usually go from printing to printing, selling a few thousand copies a year. Having done the math, I've estimated that my one millionth book will be sold shortly before mid-century.

Of all the members of the AA of A, I may have received the most rejections for a single book proposal. Over a ten-year period, not one person showed any discernible interest in "The History of Moral Philosophy." Thousands of agents and editors agreed that this was just not a viable project. And yet, it still had not dawned on me why I kept failing.

Einstein defined insanity as "doing the same thing over and over again and expecting different results." My training in logic led me to the conclusion that doing something differently just might lead to a different result. Like actually getting a contract for "The History of Moral Philosophy".

The AA of A held monthly lectures as well as an annual conference. The speakers were agents, editors, and relatively successful authors. The main topic was getting published. None of the speakers ever uttered a sentence that did not include the word, "platform."

I quickly learned that in publishing, this word does not mean something you stand on to give a speech. Its definition is much broader. The closest synonym might be megaphone. Examples of platforms are blogs, columns and opinion pieces in newspapers, newsletters, and magazines, radio and TV appearances, and talks to groups of people who might buy books.

But what if you don't *have* a platform? Then build one. What if you don't want to be bothered building a platform, or if you just can't build one?

I learned that several AA of A members partnered with people who *did* have platforms. These folks were either well-known experts in their fields or else, celebrities. What the experts and celebrities had in common was that they couldn't write.

So my coauthor just needs to be a celebrity. She or he doesn't have to know anything about moral philosophy, and certainly doesn't need to be able to write.

I began to think about the O.J. Simpson murder case, and of all the books it engendered. One of them, in particular, caught my attention.

If you're up on your trivia, then you might know the name Paula Barbieri. She had been dating Simpson for two years and was his girlfriend at the time of Nichole Simpson's murder. Barbieri was an actress who had appeared in several low-budget movies, and at the time, had no known literary credits. But that did not stop Little Brown from giving her a three-million-dollar advance for *The Other Woman: My Years With O.J.* Its main revelation was that O.J. was a far better football player than a lover.

Well, it doesn't take an Einstein to figure out my next move. I'm going to make an offer that even Ms. Barbieri can't refuse. Just imagine her delight when she's asked to be the coauthor of "The History of Moral Philosophy."

But what if she turns me down? And let's face it: her name won't sell that many books, even if it *did* once command a three-million-dollar advance.

And then, suddenly, it struck me who should be my coauthor. Can you guess who *that* would be?

That's *right!* O.J. himself! After all, who in the world has a greater firsthand knowledge of the difference between right and wrong?

# Part V

## BEFORE BROOKLYN GOT HOT

Today Brooklyn is hot: it's the new Manhattan. But not so long ago, Brooklyn was a place where you grew up. Those of us who came of age in the 1950s and 1960s look back and say that it was the best time and the best place to be.

In recent years, Brooklyn has finally been "discovered." Neighborhoods like Williamsburg, Bushwick, Crown Heights, and Red were swamped with hip twenty something's seeking affordable apartments and trendy restaurants and clubs.

I'm sure all these folks are leading interesting lives. So let them write their own stories. These are stories of Brooklyn before it got hot.

# FIRST DATE

I was nearly sixteen when my parents let me go out on my first date. All things considered, I was surprised when they consented. He was eighteen and actually had a car. OK, it was his *father's* car, but I was still impressed.

Back in the mid-sixties, almost no New York City teenagers drove cars. I imagined that the police routinely pulled them over and asked to see their licenses. So even before we left my apartment, I knew that this was going to be a memorable evening.

My friend Trudy fixed us up, but it wasn't exactly a blind date. We had seen each other at her friend's party, although we had never actually met. He *did* call me to make the date, but I doubt if our conversation lasted more than two or three minutes.

We sat in the living room while my father stated the basic ground rules and asked the standard questions. It was *his* first time too.

"Do you go to college?"

"Yes sir! I go to Pace."

"Pace?"

"Sir, I'm studying accounting."

"Can't you do that at Brooklyn College? It's a much better school, and besides – it's free."

"Well, to tell the truth ..." My father and I exchanged a look. He always believed that a person who began a sentence with that phrase could never be trusted.

My date went on to explain that his father wanted him to learn accounting, join his firm, and eventually run it.

The interrogation continued for another few minutes, and then we took the elevator down to the lobby.

"Boy, your dad's a pretty serious guy."

"Well I'm his only daughter. I guess he worries."

"I didn't meet your mom."

"She's visiting her parents in Florida. I know she would have wanted to meet you."

As we exited the building, he pointed across the street, "There's my car."

"Is that a Cadillac?"

"It sure is! 1966."

"But this is only 1965."

"Yeah, but they're already out. My dad buys a new one every two years."

"Wow, I'm impressed!"

"Just between you and me, I'm not so crazy about accounting. But my dad's paying for my school and for some extra tutoring. Still, I'm barely getting by."

"What's the problem?"

"Well, for starters, I didn't know that accounting had anything to do with numbers. I had to take intermediate algebra three times. I was lucky I graduated."

We drove to Flatbush Avenue and headed toward the Brooklyn Paramount. But about half-way there, he turned off into a side street.

"I think we should have stayed on Flatbush."

"I know, but there's too much traffic. I know a shortcut."
It was a Saturday night, and a lot of people were headed for downtown Brooklyn, which had about half a dozen huge movie theaters.

I could tell we were in Bedford Stuyvesant, because all the people were Negroes. I started to get nervous.

"Don't worry," he said, reassuringly. I know exactly where we're going."

I didn't like the tone of his voice, but I didn't say anything. It was almost completely dark. Then we pulled into a dead-end street.

"I think we're lost!" I said.

"No we're not. He pulled up, leaving the motor running."

There was no one around. I couldn't believe this was happening. But I thought to myself that he wouldn't dare try anything, if only because my friend Trudy knew him.

I waited for him to say something. Finally he did.

"*Put* out or *get* out!"

He said these words almost conversationally. Like, could you pass the salt?

I summoned up all my courage and said very firmly, "Take me home immediately!"

He laughed.

I opened the door and got out of the car.

He then backed up and then turned the corner.

I had no idea where I was. And all I had with me were my house keys. Not even a dime for a phone call.

I walked for blocks and finally found a small deli that was open. I asked the man if I could use his phone.

"Sure," he said. I called my father and the man gave me the address of the store. I told the man what had happened and he said that if I were his daughter, he would have the guy castrated.

It took my father about twenty minutes to get to the deli. I looked around in the meanwhile. There's one thing that I still remember – a poster of a beautiful woman. She was smiling and wearing a tiara.

She was Miss Rheingold, 1965. Wow, I thought to myself. A negro Miss Rheingold! Which was amazing because every beauty contest winner from Miss America all the way down to Miss Subways was white. Boy, I thought, when I'm legally allowed to drink, my first beer will be a Rheingold!

I asked the man about the poster. He started laughing. Soon he was pounding the counter with his fist. "My dear," he finally explained, "the woman on the poster is the *Negro* Miss

225

Rheingold. The company has two separate contests. Now between you and me, I think the Negro Miss Rheingold is a lot prettier."

He saw my puzzled look, and realized that I wasn't able to grasp the fact that there were actually *two* Miss Rheingolds. He handed me a copy of the Sunday Daily News, which was, by far, New York's best-selling paper.

There was a full-page ballot, with photos of six beautiful young Negro women. He saw me staring at the photos and began laughing again. Then I remembered seeing the same full-page spread a couple of weeks ago, but with six *white* women. Of course! I lived in a *white* neighborhood. There were just a handful of Negro students who went to my high school.

When my father arrived, he thanked the man, and, at my insistence, he bought a copy of the Sunday Daily News and several boxes of cookies. The man told my father that he had a very brave daughter.

Two evenings later, there was a somber meeting in our living room. There were five of us – me, my parents, and the parents of my "date." My mother asked me to tell them what had happened. They heard the entire story, even including Miss Rheingold.

His parents were deeply and sincerely apologetic. But they did not say what, if anything, they would do.

After they left, the three of us talked over everything. On the one hand, despite this having been such a terrifying experience for me, it could have been much worse. I had done exactly what I should have done. My parents and I agreed that I needed to tell Trudy, and that everyone we knew must to be warned about this predator.

Over the next few months I thought less and less about what had happened. I heard that he had dropped out of school, and someone said that he enlisted in the army. And then, a few months later, Trudy handed me a copy of the Kingsway Courier – our neighborhood newspaper. There, on the front page was a picture of him in his uniform. He was smiling.

Above the picture was this headline: "Local Boy Killed in Vietnam."

# GETTING EVEN

## 1

Are you old enough to remember when there was just one telephone company? AT&T, also somewhat affectionately called "Ma Bell," controlled all long distance and local phone calls. Ma Bell charged a lot for long distance calls, but phone service was quite reliable. And while there were rumors that the company was anti-Semitic, that was just how things were in those days. Most large corporations hired few, if any Jews.

One June morning two students from Lafayette High School took the subway to downtown Brooklyn, where they had interviews scheduled with the phone company. They hoped to get summer jobs as switchboard operators.

Camille Tiberio and Barbara Goldstein had been buddies since elementary school, so it would be great if they both got hired. They were there all day, taking a written exam, a physical, and having individual interviews.

At 4 pm, all ten of the girls who had gone through this process were sent to a small room where they would be told if they had summer jobs. A women they had never seen before walked into the room. Consulting her clipboard, she read off the list of girls who were hired. Nine names were called.

Barbara approached the woman. "Excuse me, m'am, but I didn't hear my name called."

"What's your name?"

"Barbara Goldstein."

"Sorry, it's not on my list."

"Can you at least tell me why I wasn't hired?" asked Barbara.

"Sure. It says right here that you failed the physical."

"My *God*! What's *wrong* with me! Please *tell* me!"

"Look, honey, I ain't no doctor. It just says here you didn't pass the urine test."

Camille overheard this exchange. "Hey everybody! Listen up!" She had everyone's attention.

"I'm Camille, and this is Barbara. All of you are witnesses, OK?"

They all nodded.

"Young lady, I don't know what you're trying to do, but it's not going to work. And if you don't button your lip this second, you're not going to be hired either."

"Well actually, you might be right if you don't hire me. You see, when we were given those bottles to pee into? Well, I couldn't pee. So Barbara poured some of her pee into my bottle."

All the girls were laughing. It wasn't hard to figure out what had happened.

"OK, Miss whatever-your-name-is: here's what you're going to do. You are going to put Barbara's name on the list. Or, if you prefer, take mine off. I'll leave that up to you. But just remember, we've got eight witnesses."

"I can't do that! I don't make the hiring decisions."

"No?" said Camille. "Then who does? Let's go to see that person right now. And that, lady, that's *your* decision."

"All *right* already! I can get into a lot of trouble for doing this."

"Yeah lady, but you can get into a whole lot more if you don't," said Camille.

## 2

Barbara and Camille worked for the phone company that summer, and the next one as well. When they started Brooklyn College in the fall, they laughed when they were told they needed to take a physical. "Camille, do you want me to help you study for the urine test?"

When they graduated, they both became teachers. For Camille, this would be for just a year or two. She had just gotten married, and once she started having kids, she'd let Anthony do all the breadwinning.

Barbara also had dreams. A math major as an undergraduate, she decided to go for her MA. Numbers were her thing, and even though there were very few women in her classes, she felt perfectly at home. When she got her MA, she would quit her junior high school position as soon as she could find a job teaching math at the college level.

Luck was with her; she got the first job she applied for. It was at a college she had never heard of. In fact, almost no one had heard of the American Institute of International Studies. It had opened just a year before and its classes were held in what had once been a clothing factory near the old Brooklyn Navy Yard.

When Barbara walked into her first class, she thought she was at a session of the United Nations General Assembly. About 90 percent of the students were foreigners; many of whom spoke almost no English. Still, somehow they could work out the problems she assigned. After all, wasn't mathematics a universal language?

She was not much older than her students, but their backgrounds and hers were amazingly different. She grew up in Bensonhurst, a Brooklyn working class neighborhood that was predominately Italian, but with a large Jewish minority. In fact, Sandy Koufax had lived just a block away. But long before she and Camille entered Lafayette, the Dodgers had deserted Brooklyn, and he had retired from baseball.

Her students came from many different countries in Africa, Asia, South America, and a few were from Europe. In most cases, their parents made great sacrifices to send them to this outstanding American college. Evidently they were quite impressed with the name of the school.

Most of the faculty members seemed nice enough, but she soon learned that many of them did not even have BAs, let alone graduate degrees. The administrators all seemed to be friends of the president. His father, who had made his fortune in the ladies' garment industry, put up the money to start the college. The building, which he still owned, had previously housed one of his "sweat shops." Still, she *was* teaching in a college.

### 3

One day, a friend told Barbara that he had a stolen telephone credit card number. He asked her if she wanted it. "Sure. I hate the phone company."

"Why do you hate it? Because they charge so much for long distance calls?"

"Actually I have a couple of other reasons. First, I used to work for them. They treated us like shit. And the men, most of them just high school graduates – if *that* much – got paid about twice as much as the women."

"So why else do you hate them?"

"Because they're fucking anti-Semites!"

"Barbara, I think I detect a hole in your logic."

"You mean, if they're anti-Semitic, how come they hired *me*?"

"Well yeah."

Barbara told him what had happened when she and Camille applied for summer jobs, how they took the infamous urine test, and how they both ended up working for the phone company.

"Hey, Barbara, I was aware that they can test your urine for diabetes and for kidney stones. But I never suspected that they could test it for Jewishness."

"Very funny! So while I was working there, of the hundreds of people I met, I don't remember one person who was Jewish. Oh, wait a second! There was another girl – Sheila Morse."

"That doesn't sound Jewish."

"It was changed from Moscowitz."

"She told you that?"

"Yeah, in the strictest of confidence. So now I have to kill you."

"Well before you do, Barbara, let me give you that stolen credit card number."

"Fine. And could you tell me how it works?"

"OK, I'll write down the number for you."

"516 741 9528 127K. Wow, that's long! Thirteen numbers and a letter!"

"Barbara, do you recognize the first three digits?"

"Sure, 516 is the area code for Long Island."

"The next seven digits are a phone number."

"Right! And the last three digits, 127?"

"That's the phone company's internal credit card code for the 516 area code. In other words, if the credit card number begins with 516, it has to end with 127."

"Doesn't this credit card number belong to someone?"

"Yeah, Barbara, it's actually a real person's number."

"Won't they be billed for all those calls?"

"Of course. But when they tell the phone company what happened, they won't be charged."

"Then won't the phone company go after the people making the phony credit card calls?"

"Yes, they will. So you'll need to take a couple of very simple precautions. First, use only pay phones. If you use your home phone, the telephone company will immediately track you down. And warn the people you call about what you're doing, so they don't give your name to anyone from the phone company.

"That's easy. How do I make the calls? And go slowly; I want to write this down."

You put a dime in the phone. You'll get a dial tone. Dial '0', and then the area code and number you're trying to reach. When the operator comes on, tell her that you're making a credit card call. She'll say, 'Credit card number?' And you'll say 'My number is 516 741 9528 127K.'"

"That's *it*?"

"That's it! She'll check to make sure it's a valid number, and then your call goes through. And you'll even get your dime back."

"That's fantastic! How many people did you give this number to?"

"Just a select few."

"How long is it good for?"

"Till end of the year."

"How can I thank you?"

"Do you want me to spell it out for you?"

"What, and ruin such a beautiful friendship?"

## 4

Getting that credit card number opened up all kinds of possibilities. Sure, she could make hundreds of calls to people she knew all over the country, and even in foreign countries. But that wasn't enough. She hated those anti-Semitic bastards. She needed to do a lot more.

A new semester was starting. Barbara knew what she would do. After calling the roll of her first class, she wrote the credit card number on the board. None of the students seemed to recognize what it was. Barbara just gazed out at the class. Let me start by asking you a couple of questions. First, does anyone here work for the phone company?"

"Do you mean in *this* country?" asked a young man with a thick African accent. "Everyone giggled."

"Yes."

No hands were raised.

"Now for my second question: Did any of your professors ever tell you that you would learn so much from him that his class will pay for itself?"

Many of them smiled and nodded. "Please, everyone, copy down the number I wrote on the board." She watched as everyone copied it.

"Using this number, each of you will pay for this course in less than one day!"

Now everyone was smiling.

"I'm going to tell you how it's done. You need to write down all the steps. "

Barbara never saw a class take such meticulous notes. Then she told them that they could call all over the world with that number. Just remember to use a pay phone, and to tell the people you call not to give your name to anyone from the phone company. "In our next class, you can tell us where you called."

Barbara repeated this performance in each of her other classes. When she left for the day she couldn't wait to tell Camille. They laughed and laughed as Barbara told her friend how she had obtained the number, how she had made all those free calls, and how she had given the number to her students.

"Barbara, I love you! So I will definitely come to visit you in jail."

## 5

Two days later, she met all her classes again. In each class, students talked about the calls they had made. Barbara kept a running tally of countries that had been called. As it approached sixty, one student, who apparently was saving the best for last, now told *his* story.

"I am from a very small village in India. We are all so poor that there is just one phone in the entire village. You can imagine how shocked my parents were when they were called to the phone. Neither of them had ever spoken on a phone before. Nor had any of my nine younger brothers and sisters."

"So you talked to *all* of them?" asked a student.

"Why shouldn't I? Was it not a free call?" Everyone laughed.

"How long were you on the phone?" another student asked.

"Five hours!"

"Did anyone make a longer call?" asked Barbara.

Apparently, no one had.

"Ashook! I think you hold the record!"

He smiled, and clearly, he was quite proud of himself. He added that his mother had grown alarmed that the call would be very costly. But he had assured her that he could afford it.

"And then my mother said, 'Then please explain something. If you can afford to call us from America and to talk to us for five hours, then your father and I are puzzled. Why are *we* sending *you* money?'"

Everyone laughed. Some of them had had similar conversations.

Barbara estimated that her students were costing the phone company hundreds of thousands of dollars a month. Was that enough? For the phone company, it was not even pocket change. And she realized that in another few months this credit card number would no longer be valid. She needed to figure out another number that could be used for the next year. She would have to work fast.

The first thing she needed to figure out was how the operator determined if a credit card number was valid. In stores where Barbara paid by credit card, they kept a couple of books at the cash register – one for MasterCard and one for Visa. Each book had tens of thousands of stolen credit card numbers. The clerk checked your credit card number against these numbers – a process which took more than a minute. But when Barbara dictated the telephone credit card number to the operator, it took her just a few seconds to determine whether or not the card was valid. How did she do it?

It took Barbara some time, and then – *Eureka!* I've *got* it! The operator was using a gyp sheet. If it took her only five seconds to determine whether or not the credit card number was valid, she could not possibly be going through a book of stolen credit card numbers.

Barbara figured that the letter must be the key. OK, she thought, let's test the letter first. So she went to a phone booth. By now she had memorized the credit card number: 516 741 9528 127K. She gave the same thirteen numbers to the operator, but she changed the letter to S. Five seconds later the operator said, "I'm sorry. That is an invalid credit card number."

Barbara apologized and hung up. So the letter *was* a key variable. She figured that the letter would change on January 1$^{st}$. But the thirteen-digit number would still be good, because the first ten numbers were someone's area code and phone number.

On New Year's Day, Barbara headed to a phone booth in a nearby building. She would use the old trial-and-error method. She dialed the number of a friend who lived in California. When the operator came on, she gave the thirteen-digit credit card number followed by K. In about five seconds the operator said that that was an invalid credit card number.

OK, she knew now that the company had switched over to a new letter. She dialed her friend again, and when the operator asked for her credit card number, she used A. But it was an invalid credit card number. And so was B, C, D, E, F, G, H, I, and J. She took a break and then went back to work. Half an hour later, she tried V. And seven seconds after she gave her credit card number to the operator, she heard her friend's phone ringing. When her friend said "Hello?" Barbara screamed, "Happy New Year!"

## 6

This year Barbara decided to *really* get back at those anti-Semites. She was friendly with some members of the Jewish Defense League, and it didn't take much persuading on her part to get them to give the number out to all *their* friends and families. Reach out and touch somebody? They'd reach out all right!

Barbara and her friends in the Jewish Defense League would marvel that there were two million Jews in New York, and yet if all the Jewish employees of the phone company could all meet in one room, they would not even make a *minyan* (a prayer group of at least ten Jewish men). Why not? Perhaps because so few Jews could pass the urine test.

Several months later Barbara spent a Sunday afternoon with Camille, her husband, Anthony, and their baby girl, Marie. They had a present for her – a book of quotations. All were attributed to President John Kennedy. Pointing at one of them, Camille told Barbara, "This quote could be your 'get out of jail free card.' When they try to lock you up, just tell them that you were following the advice of our late president."

The quotation read, "Don't get mad. Get even."

# A TALE OF TWO SAMMYS

## 1

When we were maybe eight or nine years old, we would happily spread stories about people we knew from the neighborhood. It didn't matter whether or not they were actually true, just as long as we thought they were funny. Their names would become punch lines to jokes, or sometimes serve as insults or put-downs we would apply to each other.

Every kid on our block knew "the crazy lady" and "the drunken super." The poor crazy lady would walk by almost scowling to herself. Once she rushed by and looked even more worried than usual. There were fire engines in front of her building and lots of black smoke billowing out. I felt bad for her, and maybe just began to realize that I'd feel the same way if *my* building caught fire. Maybe she had a really crappy life, and that's why she always looked so unhappy.

"The drunken super" was a hopeless alcoholic. Often in the evening we would hear him singing at the top of his lungs. In those days, apartment house furnaces were fueled by coal. One afternoon, when we heard shoveling sounds coming from his basement, my friend Bob guessed that the drunken super must be shoveling his bottles of liquor.

Then there was "Sarge," a nice looking guy with slicked back hair. He had been in an army sergeant in World War II, and the story we heard was that the experience left him shell-shocked. He lived on the first floor of our apartment house and would sometimes sit by the window. He always wore a tank top khaki-colored undershirt, and he was usually quite affable. But then, sometimes we'd hear him yelling at somebody, and everybody knew that Sarge lived alone.

Still, the oddest person on the block was Sammy. We heard that he was a genius – with an IQ over 200. But he could not, or would not, speak. His father had died suddenly when Sammy was just a toddler, and that was when he stopped talking.

Sammy lived in a private house in the middle of the block. He was usually outside in the late afternoon, but his mother kept the driveway gate locked, so no one could get in, and Sammy couldn't get out. They also had a big black German Shepard who would bark if any kid tried climbing over the gate.

We'd say hello to Sammy and he would nod or wave. If we were playing stick ball or punch ball and the ball bounced into Sammy's driveway, he'd return it to us. When George, the ice cream man, came around on his motor scooter, we would buy ice cream for Sammy. But he never told us whether he liked chocolate or vanilla, a cone or a pop, or anything else.

We wondered if the label of "genius" could actually be true if he never, in fact, spoke a word. In fact, some of the kids down the block called him a retard. Still, he was really sweet, and who knows what was going on in his head?

Then there was the other Sammy. A guy in his early twenties, he sometimes hung out in front of his house. He was a little strange looking. He had what looked like one continuous eye brow, he was kind of stooped over, and he seemed a little depressed. No one ever saw him smile. Sometimes after we walked by him, we'd speculate about whether someday they would have to come to take him away.

Then one day we all found out the truth about Sammy. His mother told her best friend that when Sammy was an infant, one of his testicles never descended. Why she decided to disclose this very personal information, no one knows. But she supposedly said to her friend, "I'm telling you this in the strictest of confidence. I know I can trust you: you're my best friend."

Within ten minutes this startling piece of news had travelled all the way up and down Kings Highway, and by nightfall, there was no one in the entire neighborhood who had not heard that poor Sammy had just one ball.

Kids being kids, when we'd walk by his house, who could resist holding up one finger. Not that we ever did when he was outside. But surely he knew that we knew. And if anything, he looked even sadder.

## 2

Well, time passes, and kids grow up. We were now in our late twenties, and Bob, Larry and I got together for our monthly boys' night out.

"Did you hear what happened to Sammy?" asked Bob.

As Larry and I looked at him questioningly, we each raised an index finger.

"No, not *that* Sammy! I meant the other Sammy."

"Oh no!" said Larry. Did something happen to him? Did he die?"

"He was such a sweet guy," I added.

"I guess you guys didn't hear the news" said Bob.

"News? What news?" we both blurted out.

"OK, first things first. A couple of years ago Sammy snapped out of it. Just like that, he started talking, and he became completely normal – at least for him."

"So he wasn't really retarded after all," I said.

"Retarded? *Retarded!* The guy turned out to be a fucking genius!"

"Yeah," said Larry, "remember they used to say he had a 200 IQ?"

"200?" asked Bob. "Try 300!"

"What are you leading up to, Bob?" I asked.

"Are you guys ready for this? Sammy invented some kind of sex pill. It's supposed to be ten times as powerful as Viagra.
"

"Hey, I gotta get some of those pills," said Larry.

"Actually, they're already on the market."

241

"And they work as advertised?" I asked.

"Guys, let me put it this way. You remember the other Sammy?"

Immediately, Larry and I both raised our index fingers.

"Well, I heard that even *he* has a smile on his face."

# I COULDA BEEN A CONTENDER!

You might remember the line that Marlon Brando uttered in the movie classic, "On the Waterfront." His character had been a promising young boxer, who no longer boxed.

So let me clear one thing up. No, I was not a boxer. Far from it: I was a poet.

Yeah, that *is* kind of a stretch, so maybe I should explain. In the 1970s, almost everyone I knew was writing poetry – or at least trying to. One poor guy I met handed me his card. On it, just below his name and contact information, was a single word – poet.

I was so embarrassed for him, I didn't have the heart to say anything. It turns out that just one of his poems was ever published, and that was in an anthology that accepted a single poem from anyone who would buy the anthology.

When I began to write poems, I would show them to my girlfriend, a sculptress named Kathy. A couple of times, she made fun of them by making up parodies, and then pretending to be giving dramatic readings:

It's night-time!

I'm all alone!

No one likes me!

I'm so unhappy!

Then she would laugh almost uncontrollably. When she did, I think I really loved her. She was quite beautiful, if half nuts.

Kathy had a friend with the unusual name of Julie La Moe. Julie was an artist, and she lived somewhere in the Village. I ran into her once at a party, and when she introduced herself, I told her that I was Kathy's boyfriend.

"What do you do, Steve?"

I told her that I taught economics and went to graduate school.

After a little more encouragement, I confessed that I wrote some poetry.

"Really? I knew you had to be doing something artistic, if you're seeing Kathy. She is such a *fine* sculptress."

That was certainly true. She designed table bases for a furniture maker who placed a piece of glass on each of them and sold them for four or five thousand dollars. He paid Kathy $85 a week, and, magnanimously, took care of her taxes as well.

Kathy used to date his son, who worked in the showroom and painted there in his spare time. One day, someone came into their store and asked the father if he could buy one of the paintings. Actually, he was interested mainly in just the lower left-hand quadrant. Without consulting his son, he sawed the painting into quarters, and sold off the requested piece.

About a week after Julie and I had run into each other, Kathy, with a big smile, told me that she had been talking to Julie LaMoe. "Julie said that she had run into a friend of mine. Someone she called, 'Steve, the poet.' I told her I didn't know any 'Steve, the poet.'"

We were both laughing. "Then she described you and I said, 'Oh, you mean Steve, *the economist!*'"

A few months after we broke up, I went to an open poetry reading in Dumbo, then an up-and-coming neighborhood on the Brooklyn waterfront. Everyone said they like my poems. And so, for the first time, I sent them out to literary magazines listed in "Writers' Market." A tiny magazine in Mount Vernon, Iowa, took one from the first batch I sent.

By this time Kathy had a new boyfriend, Bruce, a flutist, who played for a living in Grand Central Station. When I told her that one of my poems was published, she managed just a very unenthusiastic, "Really?" That was the last time we talked for several years.

Most of my poems were connected to New York, and increasingly to Brooklyn, where I was born and had grown up. After living in Manhattan for about six years, I had moved to Brooklyn Heights, and often ran on the Brooklyn Bridge. My friend, Bob Side, wrote a column for the Heights Press, "Five minutes from Wall Street." Actually, on a good day, I could run it in seven.

In those days, the editors of literary magazines wanted the typed originals of the poetry that was submitted, but they were pretty good about returning them along with their rejection notes. Three of my favorite rejections were amazingly different.

One was a printed form with four boxes. Next to the first box was written: Your submission has been accepted. Next to the second box: Please resubmit with the following revisions. Next to the third box: Thank you for your submission. Please let us see your future work. And the fourth box: We wish you luck in submitting your work elsewhere.

The fourth box was checked. A check mark in the third box had been crossed out.

Another rejection was better than most acceptances. Here it is as I remember it: "'Poetry Today' has gone out of business, and the editors moved away. We are three college students now living in the attic where the magazine editors had lived. We wanted to return your poems, and, for what it's worth, we enjoyed them."

The third rejection was from a magazine in Alabama. The editor explained that his magazine had a local focus, and that my poetry clearly was about Brooklyn and New York. In fact, he had recently seen a submission from someone else in Brooklyn, whose work was very similar to my own. His last name was Nurkse, and he lived just a couple of miles from me.

I remembered this name only because I had read a book on economic development by a Norwegian economist named Ragnar Nurkse. But it certainly *was* interesting that both of us

245

had submitted to the same magazine in Alabama, and that the editor saw similarities in our work.

Maybe fifteen years later, I went to a restaurant in Park Slope, a toney Brooklyn neighborhood, to have dinner with other members of the National Writers Union. There were several of us sitting around a table, having some wine before dinner. Seated next to me was another bearded writer, who I began to chat up. But it was impossible to talk to him. His answers discouraged further questions. So I just ignored the schmuck and talked to some of the others.

After he finished his wine, he stood up, and without bothering to say his goodbyes, he left. Good riddance! We were all having a fine time, and he enhanced our merriment by leaving. When we finally got to dessert, I asked the woman who organized the dinner if she knew who that disgruntled guy was.

She said that he told her he was a poet, and she felt so sorry for him that she bought him a drink. And he probably didn't have enough money for dinner, so that's why he left. I told everyone what a complete asshole the guy was. Did anybody know him?

Someone else said, "I don't *know* him, but he's a member and he lives around here. I think he's on Prospect Park West." That was probably the most expensive block in the neighborhood.

And then, the woman who had paid for his drink said, "*Really*! Maybe he's not so poor after all. I know that his last name is Nurkse, but I can't remember if he told me his first name."

Oh my God! That's the guy! I told everyone the story about the rejections we had both received from the same Alabama literary magazine, and we all had a hearty laugh.

A few years later, the Borough President of Brooklyn made an important announcement. He had selected the Poet Laureate of Brooklyn. It was someone named D. Nurkse.

# MEALS À LA CARTE

Francine Retchnik never in her life ordered à la carte. In fact, she never ordered at all. "Hey, let someone else pay for my meal! After all, what are friends for?"

A classic *schnorrer*, Francine figured that she was she was just eating food that would otherwise go to waste. And face it: with friends like her, you never had to worry about what to do with leftovers.

You don't have to be Jewish to know that eating is central to our existence, which makes Francine Retchnik a very good Jew. In fact, she is such a good Jew that she devotes most of her waking hours to acquiring large quantities of food. And that brings us to "Meals à la carte."

Francine's life revolves around her shopping cart, which is why she never leaves home without it. Wherever she goes, her shopping cart goes. Can you guess why she needs it? If she has a good day as a *schnorrer*, she'd have too much to *schlep*.

Francine lives in a nice home in the Midwood neighborhood of Brooklyn. Unlike the teeming and intense "black hat" neighborhoods of South Williamsburg, Borough Park, and Crown Heights, where *Yiddish* is the lingua franca, the modern orthodox of Midwood mingle effortlessly with nonobservant Jews, Pakistanis, and whoever else is shopping on Avenue J or on Coney Island Avenue. In fact, you rarely hear Yiddish spoken – and even then, just when a couple of old friends stop to schmooze.

247

But if you're not from New York, you may not be familiar with the term, "black hat." Religious Jewish men wear *yamulkas*. The least religious among them wear colorful and elaborately embroidered *yamulkas*. The more devout wear plain black *yamulkyas*. But the rigorously religious wear black hats. They dress entirely in black, except for their white shirts. If someone asked, "So who's more religious, you or Akiva?" You might reply, "Akiva is even more black-hat than I am."

Francine has never held a job, but her husband, Howard, has always been a good provider. Together, they raised a son and a daughter, married them off, and now rattle around in their big house by themselves. Separate, but comfortable. Sometimes they don't run into each other for days. In fact, once Howard was away on business for a week and Francine never noticed that he was missing. So, all things considered, they both feel that they enjoy a good marriage. "He don't bother me, and I don't bother him. So what's not to like?"

It turns out that Francine and her husband actually own a second house on the same block, which they rent out to an orthodox family with twelve children. Why did they buy *two* houses? Who knows? Maybe they were on sale.

Every morning Francine would leave the house with her shopping cart. She knew that what she didn't do in shopping, she'd make up for in carting. Her first stop was usually *Top Banana*, a large fruit and vegetable store on Avenue J. She loved *hondling* with Leib, the owner, and walking away with some decaying fruit and vegetables for almost nothing. "Here, just take it!" he would yell. "I was going to throw it out anyway." She would make a show of handing him a few pennies, knowing that he would dismiss her offer.

At *Met Foods*, which was part of a chain, they didn't *hondle*, so she refused to give them her business. She often hit the jackpot at *Bagels and Bialys* when they were throwing out their two-day old stuff. "You have to know exactly when to shop there, because if you're too early, they won't give you nothing – and if you're too late, the garbage truck got there first."

Francine is the first to admit that she isn't above picking through the garbage put out by some of the best food stores on Avenue J. "You never know what you'll find. But you *do* have to be careful with stuff that might be spoiled. I have a rule never to take anything with mayonnaise no matter how good it looks, especially if it's left out in the sun."

By noon, she was home for a nice lunch. And she was happy that there was plenty left over in case Howard got hungry. Then it was off again with her cart. A women's group had invited an important rabbi for a lecture. And then they'll put out a nice *nosh*, which she could never refuse. . "I mean, if it was just him talking – that I could do without. But if they have food, it would be a sin to just let it sit there uneaten."

She arrived a little early, parked her shopping cart in the hallway, blocking everyone else from getting in, and asked Mrs. Feinstein, the hostess, if she could have a glass of seltzer, and maybe a few cookies.

"Francine, you know we're going to have a nice spread after the rabbi's lecture."

"I know, Sarah, but I'm starving. Don't worry: I finish it so fast, no one else will know. So they won't ask you for anything, those *schnorrers*."

"Francine, what am I going to *do* with you? The rabbi will be here any minute… Look, why don't you go into the kitchen and just help yourself. You know where everything is."

"Thanks, Sarah. You're an angel."

She enters the kitchen and a minute later the bell rings. Sarah buzzes, the door opens, and then a woman yells, "I can't get in! There's a shopping cart blocking the hallway."

"*Oy!* That must be Francine's. Let me get her to move it." She goes into the kitchen and sees Francine sitting at the table with a glass of seltzer, a plate of cookies, and a huge sandwich."

"Francine, I need you to move your shopping cart."

"I can't right now. I'm eating."

"People can't get in."

"They can walk around it. When I finish, I'll go and fold it up."

249

"*Oy*, Francine, for just once you can't put yourself out?" Sarah leaves the kitchen, goes out into the hallway, and rolls the shopping cart into the living room. She is followed by the woman who had been stuck in the hallway. The doorbell rings again and another woman comes in.

A few minutes later all the women find seats and the rabbi begins his talk. He has a low, mellifluous voice, but sometimes he's a little hard to hear. Still, his talk is very interesting, and he has their undivided attention.

And then Francine makes her entrance. "Who moved my shopping cart? I left it out in the hall for a reason." Then she rolls it back into the hall where it once again blocks the door.

The rabbi stops speaking and asks, "Is everything all right?"

"I'm so sorry for the interruption, Rabbi." says Mrs. Feinstein. "Please continue."

Francine returns. Ignoring the rabbi, who has resumed speaking, she says in a loud voice, "Can someone move from the couch? I need to sit there. My back is *killing* me! The pain kept me up all night!"

Two women get up from the couch and Francine plunks herself down. The rabbi, who has stopped again, looks around a little nervously.

"Please go on, rabbi," says Mrs. Feinstein.

After a brief pause, he resumes once again. A minute later, "Rabbi, could yuh talk louder? I can barely hear you."

"I'm so sorry, but this is as loud as I can speak."

"What, do you have a cold or something?"

"No, I'm fine. I just don't have a loud speaking voice."

"How do they hear you in *shul*?"

"FRANCINE!" says Mrs. Feinstein. "Enough, , already! Rabbi, please excuse her. I think maybe she drank a little too much seltzer."

"*What*? I told you I was starving and needed some seltzer and a couple of cookies, which I need when my blood sugar drops too low. By the way, when do we eat?"

Somehow, the rabbi was able to get through the rest of his talk, and when Mrs. Feinstein put out the food, Francine managed to get seconds of everything. And then it was time to load up her shopping cart with all the leftovers. Of course no one could get out until she was ready to leave.

When Francine got home, she was still stuffed from all that food. But that poor rabbi: what was wrong with his voice? He probably *did* have a cold. I hope I didn't catch something.

Anyway, she would skip supper because she had another talk to attend. So much education in one day! She knew that at the next house they would have even better food – and more of it! And this time she would bring her shopping cart all the way inside. If she left it out in the hall, someone could steal it. So when she got there, she wheeled it all the way in and left it in the middle of the living room. When Mrs. Rabinowitz asked her to move it, she replied, "Don't worry, it's fine right where it is."

Another rabbi would be speaking. Francine hoped he would be louder than the first one. And luckily he was. But there was another problem. It was too hot in there. "Could someone put on the air conditioner?"

"Francine, please! The rabbi is speaking."

"Boy am I hot!"

"Is anyone else hot?" All the others just shook their heads no. "Rabbi, please excuse the interruption."

The rabbi resumed his talk. A few minutes went by.

"*Oy*, it's like a furnace. I'm *switzing* so much, you could ring me out and throw me over a clothes line!"

"STOP already!"

"I'm so hot I could *plotz*!"

"Francine! If you're hot, please go outside. Rabbi, I must apologize. Could you please continue?"

Mercifully, there were no more interruptions. When it came time for the rabbi to answer questions, Francine had the first one. The rabbi was left speechless by her question.

"Rabbi, do you think I should switch my cable to Verizon or stick with Comcast?"

Finally, they were ready to eat. And indeed the food was even better and more plentiful than the spread that Mrs. Feinstein had put out.

After about half an hour, people started leaving. "Mrs. Rabinowitz, could you put out some more chicken? It was delicious, but all I got was a couple of small thighs. Maybe you got a nice breast? If you don't, that's OK. I'll take whatever you got."

Francine was the last one to leave. She had filled her shopping cart and Mrs. Rabinowitz looked really tired. As she stood, waiting for Francine to push her cart out the door, she had a premonition. Then she saw that look on Francine's face.

"So your husband? He must have been very tired that he went to bed so early?"

"Yes, he has to get up very early every morning."

"Could you wake him up so he can walk me home?"

"Francine! He's asleep. He works very hard, and he has to get up at five o'clock."

"So how am I going to get home? It's dangerous at this hour. Wake him up! And while you're at it, I need your help with something else."

"I don't believe my ears! Francine, you're not normal. You need help!"

"You're telling *me*? That's what I'm trying to tell *you*. So could you lend me your shopping cart? All this stuff I'm taking is too heavy for my cart. I don't want it to break."

Francine! I have just about *had* it with you! Your behavior is completely unacceptable. You are rude, and you are a *schnorrer* – you just keep taking and never giving back."

"Is that all that's bothering you? You should have said something. If lending me your shopping cart is such a big issue, you don't have to worry. After I unload it, your husband can bring it back home with him."

## GOLLAH DEAD; SHINK HELD

(Brooklyn, New York) – At 9:06 this morning, Pant S. Gollah, 41, a postal employee at Brooklyn's General Post Office, was stabbed to death by Dr. Sheldon I. Shink, 35.

The murder weapon was Shink's umbrella which he allegedly pushed through a stamp window when Gollah took too long handling a transaction. He stabbed Gollah right in the jodhpurs, which are part of the standard uniform in the Indian postal service.

Mr. Gollah had originally been hired in his native country. Records had been fouled up at the Bombay G.P.O. and a Mr. George Armstrong was sent to Bombay and Mr. Gollah, here.

Gollah is survived by his wife, Pandet, his forty-six children, who cannot be named here, as well as by his father, also known as Pant S. Gollah. The elder Mr. Gollah resides in Uttar-Pradesh State, where he owns and operates a turban repair shop. Most of his business is walk-in trade – from those whose turbans have unraveled and become tangled.

Dr. Shink is a computer programmer, and not, as first reported, an Indian national.

There have recently been several unpleasant incidents at the Brooklyn G.P.O., involving a group of postal employees supporting the separatist movement of the border regions along India's Northwest Frontier. That Dr. Shink was wearing an unraveled and knotted turban when apprehended lent some credence to rumors that he was part of this movement.

However, Shink stated that he had merely been in the post office to purchase some plate blocks for his collection.

There were several witnesses to the slaying. According to Mrs. Kevin O'Neill, the night supervisor of a cigar store, "I saw everything. The gentleman with the umbrella couldn't understand what the other gentleman was saying. Then he stabbed the other gentleman with his umbrella. I don't think he meant to kill him, you know? Maybe just poke his eye out or something."

Another witness, Franklin T. Robinson, a New York City bus line executive, also claims to have seen the entire incident. "The cat in the red turban lays it on the cat in the white turban, like, never mind that soft shoe number; just come across with the stamps. Well, this cat with the white turban, he just keep mumblin' sumfin' in Indian. Now it look from here like the cat in the red turban dint mean nuffin' by stickin' him with the umbrella, jus hurry um up a little. But dis lady scream and everybody come runnin'."

A third witness, Hyman Finger, a retired manufacturer, saw only the slaying itself. "Vel, dis fel gives the other fella a real klop mit hiss umbrella. Like that Negro boy mentioned, the lady starts hollering and the postal man falls down on the ground."

The American ambassador was called in by the Indian Foreign Ministry and a strong protest was lodged. The Indian government termed "critically inadequate" the measures taken by the American postal authorities to protect its employees against irate patrons. The protest went on to note that this constituted an international incident, not only because an Indian national had been slain, but because of the large number of foreigners working for the United States Postal Service.

A strongly worded press release was issued by the Jewish Defense League, stating that Dr. Shink was not a member of that organization, nor was Mr. Gollah an Arab or an Arab sympathizer. A group calling itself the Sheepshead Bay chapter of the Fourth Route Chinese Liberation Army sent a telegram to the Jewish Daily Forward claiming credit for the assassination, while 119 other groups reported that they would issue statements within 24 hours.

Sheldon I. Shink, the son of Russian Jewish immigrants, is an Episcopalian. He attended Brooklyn public schools and was in the same James Madison High School graduating class as Eddie Grace, who shot eight people in a New Jersey shopping center parking lot several years ago. Like Eddie, neighbors and relatives remembered him as a quiet, gentle boy.

After graduating from the New York University School of Commerce, Shink went to North Dakota State Teachers College, where he got his Ed.D, taking an introductory computer course as an elective. Seven years ago he moved with his wife Sybil, the former Sheila Schlokowitz, from their Borough Park apartment to their present home in Westport.

Dr. Shink is employed by the Daughters of the American Revolution as a programmer. He is engaged in an information retrieval project, the purpose of which is to reconstruct family trees of the entire membership. The Daughters are rumored to have another project for Dr. Shink, which has something to do with making clocks run counterclockwise.

No one has come forward with any information as to why Shink was wearing a turban, nor was there any explanation as to how it had become unraveled and knotted. Police originally speculated on the possible connection between Shink and the elder Mr. Gollah, but they subsequently discovered that turban trouble is fairly common, not only in India, but in large areas of the upper westside of Manhattan.

A spokesman for the DAR gave the press a statement which turned out to be, verbatim, a speech George Washington once gave on the dangers of "entangling alliances." Mrs. Shink was unavailable for comment, having gone back to her mother's apartment near Tremont Avenue in the Bronx. As for Dr. Shink, he has refused to make any further statements, except to request that the *New York Post*, which was delivered to his Westport home, be forwarded to the 61$^{st}$ Precinct, where he is being held for questioning.

# Part VI

## ODD ENDINGS

It is said that all good things must come to an end, whether it is a relationship or even a life. Thankfully, all *bad* things also must come to an end. But very little is entirely good or bad, so the endings can be complicated.

# HOW BERNIE WON

Do you want to hear how Bernie *really* won the election? Some insiders say the story goes back to the New York primary, and that's certainly plausible. Because, looking back, Bernie's big win in that state was the beginning of the end for Hillary. But I'm going to give you the *real* inside story. And that goes back to the 1950s, when Bernie was a student at James Madison High School in Brooklyn.

Now don't tell me you never heard of our school. Let me drop a few names on you *besides* Bernie Sanders. Here's just a few you might have heard of – Supreme Court Justice Ruth Bader Ginsburg – who, believe it or not, was a cheerleader at Madison. And you know who Senator Chuck Schumer is – *besides* being the cousin of Amy Schumer. No doubt you've heard of Carole King and Judge Judy? And Chris Rock went to Madison for a couple of years. Oh yeah, we even have four Nobel Prize winners. Not bad for a neighborhood school.

A whole group of really smart kids went to our school. No one can say who was smartest, but when Bernie went to Madison, everyone agreed it was Shelly (short for Rochelle). Sometimes she was called "Shelly the fixer," but the nickname never really stuck.

Before we talk about how Shelly got involved in Bernie's presidential campaign, I want to tell you about a few things Shelly did was when she was a kid – just so you'll have some idea of who we're dealing with.

One day Shelly, who was about ten, her younger sister, Bonnie, Bonnie's friend, Susie, and the sisters' dog, Teddy, went for a walk. Teddy, a brown and white cocker spaniel, grew increasingly tired. The girls, realizing that they were miles from home, agreed that they would have to get home by bus.

But there was a big problem. No dogs allowed. What could they do? Shelly told Bonnie and Susie to get on the bus and walk to the back to find seats. But whatever they did she warned them, "Don't look back!"

So Bonnie and Susie did as they were told. After all, Shelly was a couple of years older, and she was very wise. As they approached some empty seats, they heard people murmuring, and making tsk tsk sounds. One woman sadly noted that it was "Such a shame!" To which a man added, "And so young!"

Bonnie and Susie noticed that the bus wasn't moving. They just *had* to see what was going on. Shelly was slowly making her way to the back of the bus, holding Teddy's leash with one hand, and her other arm held out straight in front of her. Her eyes were open but she was staring straight ahead. Teddy was sniffing along, his nose almost dragging on the floor. After Bonnie and Susie helped Shelly into a seat, the driver started the bus.

OK, maybe you're not convinced from this one incident that Shelly was a genius. So if I told you that she won almost $50,000 on a children's quiz show, you'd probably think that maybe she was just lucky – or that the show was fixed.

Shelly and I happened to be in the same math honors class, and she would call out the answers before the teacher could even begin asking the questions. He finally worked out a deal with her. She would cease and desist if he got all the teachers in the math department to refer their failing students to her for tutoring.

What did a sixteen-year-old do with all that money? She played the stock market. Before she graduated, Shelly was worth several million dollars. Not bad for a kid from the projects.

Madison was very overcrowded. So we had to wait in long lines to get into school, get into the cafeteria, pick up our textbooks, and turn them in. If Bernie had a list of "issues" back then, the long lines we were forced to wait on might have topped that list. I can still picture Bernie in his graduation gown, just seething as the hour-long procession filed into the Loews Kings, a huge movie theater that was rented for the occasion. I laughed when I heard Shelly asking him if had had brought along anything to read.

No one knew what happened to Shelly after high school. In fact, even her closest friends were clueless. And then, two weeks before the New York primary, Bernie got a note from her.

He called her immediately, and within a couple of days, the campaign put her plan into action. Now you can probably figure out what her plan was, because of how radically altered his campaign was. But just in case you were on another planet for the last few months, I am going to spell out everything for you.

Shelly met with Bernie, his wife, Jane, and four of his other most trusted advisors. Shelly began by pointing out that Bernie drew huge crowds wherever he went. Was this because of his movie star looks? His friendly disposition?

They kind of chuckled. "OK," she went on. Everyone was there to hear Bernie's message. "The rich are getting richer.... The poor are getting poorer... The middle class is disappearing. Blah, blah, blah."

"So you think we should change the message?" "No!" she screamed.

Everyone looked at everyone else and kind of shrugged. Shelly waited. And then she *really* surprised them. "Bernie, they loooove your message!"

They waited.

"They love your message so much, they've memorized it. *You've* memorized it! Watching you give a speech is like watching the Rocky Horror Picture Show. The audience recites the lines along with the actors. 'The rigged economy!' 'Enough

261

is enough!' 'The top one tenth of one percent owns almost as much wealth as the bottom 99 percent.'"

"So what you're saying is that they can't get enough of Bernie delivering the same speech."

"You *got* it!"

"Yeah, it's terrible! Sometimes people have to wait five or six hours just to get through security."

"OK, now Bernie, I want you to think back to when we were at Madison. Remember all those lines they made us wait in?"

Bernie just smiled, nodding his head.

"You didn't like waiting in those lines."

*"Like? Like!* I *hated* waiting in those damn lines!"

"So what about the lines that you make all your supporters stand in for hours?"

"It's not our fault!" said one of the managers. "It's the fuckin' security check points that the Secret Service set up."

"Right! It's not your job."

Shirley noticed Bernie turning beet red, but she just plunged ahead.

"These are *your* supporters forced to stand out there for hours like complete schmucks waiting to hear the golden words of their great hero."

Bernie opened his mouth, but before he could get out a word, Shelly shouted, "Here comes the old bullshit!"

All of them were stunned. How many times had they heard this outburst, word-for-word? Soon they were all laughing – even Bernie.

"Yeah, Shelly," said Jane, "You can take the boy out of Brooklyn…."

Then Shelly went on. "So Bernie, do you see where I'm going with this?"

"You're one hundred percent correct, Shelly! *I'm* responsible for exactly the same thing that I used to bitch about."

"Shelly," one of the others said, "we all feel like complete shit for making these long lines of supporters go through all this security crap. But what can we do?"

"OK," said Shelly, "we all agree that the quality of life of Bernie's supporters would be greatly enhanced if they didn't have to wait on those fuckin' lines."

There were a few more complaints about the long lines. Shelly waited until everyone had a chance to comment. Then they all looked at her expectantly. She knew that this was the moment when she would actually change the course of history. She made eye contact person-by-person. Then she cleared her throat.

Here's our problem: There's only one Bernie Sanders. And there are millions of people who would love to hear him speak. But most of them never will. If Bernie went out there twenty-four hours a day, seven days a week, he *still* would reach just a tiny fraction of the people who want to hear him give that speech."

She waited. No one had a clue where she was going with this. She just stared at them. And when they began to think she would just leave them hanging there, she said the two magic words.

"Larry David."

*Brilliant!*

They looked at her, anticipating what she would say next. But instead, she said, "But *not* Larry David."

What was she talking about? Was that some kind of Zen bullshit? Was she nuts or what? After all, there's not a whole lot of real estate between genius and insanity. Still, maybe there was something that *she* saw that they didn't.

"OK, let's just say that we *did* get Larry David to give one speech. Bernie, you could lend him those long yellow legal sheets you've always dragging around with you."

Bernie laughed. "Yeah, he could probably do a better job than *I* do."

"Yeah, Bernie, he kind of *does* have you down."

They waited for Shelly to go on. Again, she cleared her throat. She knew that they were primed to make the leap of logic.

"So suppose we *don't* get Larry David. Suppose we hire ten actors – men, women, blacks, whites, Hispanics, Asians, American Indians. Maybe we give them Bernie's hair and glasses. But all these folks are actors. They give the speech. Maybe they even give it in Brooklynese."

They were hooked. They looked at each other and nodded. Now all she needed to do was reel them in, close, and have them sign on the dotted line.

"OK, we hire ten – or, who knows, maybe twenty – of these actors. They learn the speech. We schedule hundreds of rallies a day all over the state."

"*Yes!*"

"No more waiting on long lines to go through security!"

"*Amen!*"

"No more Secret Service!"

"*Preach it sister!*"

"Bernie, your public wants you 24/7. They can have you 24/7!"

Bernie and Jane, followed by everyone else, stood up and hugged Shelly. They all knew at that very instant that they had changed the course of history.

And indeed they did. Bernie impersonators, many of them quite comic, fanned out all over New York State. For the next two weeks no town or village was too small for a rally, complete with "the speech." His supporters continued to be full participants, mouthing the words along with the Bernie impersonators.

The last poll, just two days before the primary, had Hillary still ahead by three percentage points. But that was down from twelve just ten days ago. Clearly she no longer had the home field advantage.

On Primary day there were reports of over 100,000 voters in Brooklyn whose names had been mysteriously removed from the voting rolls. Although there were just two candidates, the New York City Board of Elections managed to create a paper ballot that even the election workers were unable to explain to voters.

It looked as though the Board of Elections might be trying to steal the primary. Weren't they part of the Democratic machine, which everyone knew was in Hillary's pocket?

"Don't worry," said Shelly. "These guys are far too stupid to steal the election. She was right. Bernie won by five percentage points. And poor Hillary began to channel Yankee baseball great, Yogi Berra. It was indeed déjà vu all over again. She didn't win another primary, and quietly dropped out of the race before the convention.

In January, when Bernie took the oath of office, there wasn't that big a crowd. Why schlep all the way to Washington when you could go to the oath-taking in your own city or town? Millions of Americans will remember the stirring words that would become the rallying cry of our nation: "*Enough is enough!*"

# TUNNEL VISION

## 1

Glad to meet you! I'm Ernie the attorney. Here, take a card.

What kind of cases do I handle? Mostly personal injury. I'm constantly suing hospitals, doctors, insurance companies, and sometimes city agencies. None of my clients are rich, so I take my cases on contingency. What does that mean, exactly? It means that you don't have to lay out any money. And if I win the case, I get one-third of the pay-off.

So let me set you straight: I ain't no Robin Hood. Yeah, I do take from the rich and give to the poor, but I'm really in this just for myself. And let me level with you: I make out OK. In fact, more than OK.

I want to tell you about one of my cases. In fact, this was one of the strangest cases I ever came across – and *believe* me, I've seen pretty much everything.

There were these two brothers – Donnie and Frankie Johnson – one crazier than the other. They were in their early forties, and were almost inseparable. In Kuwait during Operation Desert Storm, they spent weeks putting out fires in the oil fields while inhaling a lot of smoke. The VA wouldn't help them and Social Security turned them down for disability. And now they were homeless.

You'll never guess where these guys lived. Are yuh ready for this? They lived in a subway tunnel. Twenty-four hours a day trains would go right by them. It turns out that both of them were nearly deaf, probably from all that noise.

So one day, they turned up at my office. My secretary, Gladys – she was holding her nose when she ushered them in. I happen to have a terrible sense of smell which, frankly, can be an asset in my kind of business – so I didn't even notice anything.

Donnie handed me an eviction notice obtained by the Metropolitan Transit Authority, which owns and operates the New York City subway system. It took me only a minute to spot the good news and the bad news.

The good news was that the idiot lawyer for the Transit Authority had filed the wrong case in the wrong court. The bad news was that since there would be no monetary settlement, I couldn't make any money.

But these poor guys were homeless veterans. I just felt so bad for them that I decided to handle their case pro bono. They were so happy, they came over and hugged me.

Now I ain't no constitutional lawyer, but I've been around the block a couple of times. Besides, it was just common sense that you can't be evicted from a home if where you live is *not* a home. And I also knew that the MTA didn't want this case to go to trial for two main reasons.

First, they didn't want anyone to know that there were actually people living in the subway tunnels. And second, they probably realized by now that they had no case.

And sure enough, the MTA quickly agreed to a settlement that satisfied both sides. The brothers could stay put, and both were given free metro cards for life. And what was in it for me? The biggest payoff I would get in my entire career.

## 2

About six months later I got a call from Roosevelt Hospital. Donnie and Frankie had both been hit by a subway train. They had sustained very serious injuries but were expected to recover. Could I come to see them?

I felt really guilty. I had never even said anything to them about not going back to live in the subway tunnel. But what were their alternatives? And would they have even listened to me?

On my way to the hospital, my brain was already working overtime on the case that I would be presenting to the jury. Dollar signs danced before my eyes. Still, I began to feel a little ashamed. I mean, look: these guys almost died, and all I could think about was money.

When I arrived at the hospital, I was directed to a small private room on the eighth floor. Thankfully, they were not in intensive care. I peeked into their room and saw Frankie lying on his back, fast asleep. His elevated leg was in an ankle to thigh cast. Donnie was sitting up, but he looked kind of out of it. There was a bandage wrapped around his head just above his eyes, and his arm was in a sling.

I slipped into the room and looked at their charts and began taking notes on their injuries. None appeared to be life threatening, but the Johnson brothers would certainly need to spend a few months in rehab. But *then* what?

When I came back the next day, the brothers were both awake and happy to see me. "Can we sue?" asked Frankie.

"*Sue?* Of course we can sue!"

"How much will we get?" asked Donnie.

"A lot! ... A *whole* lot!"

# 3

As soon as the jury ended their deliberations and entered the courtroom, I knew that we had won and won big. A few of them were even smiling. But when the judge read the amount of the award, even *I* was shocked. It was $12 million. My share was one-third of that... $4 million.

The brothers were overjoyed. They high-fived each other, high-fived me, and even managed to high-five the bailiff. If I hadn't restrained them, they would have high-fived the jury, and maybe even the judge.

I received still another shock the next day when I learned that the MTA would not appeal the amount of the award. I guess they really wanted this case to disappear. But I had a sneaking suspicion that just maybe it wasn't over yet.

What would the brothers do with all this money? I've had plenty of clients who ran through settlements of hundreds of thousands of dollars in just months.

But before we worried about their long-term financial security, they needed to decide what they would be doing in the immediate future. I proposed setting up checking accounts for each of them and renting a small apartment. That was fine with them.

I sent them to talk an estate lawyer who would figure out what to do with their money, and to draw up their wills. Dara and I had remained casual friends since law school, but unlike me, she was completely ethical. Despite my pretty obvious curiosity, she never disclosed any of the details of their wills.

From time to time I dropped by their apartment, but they either weren't home, or maybe didn't hear the bell. Perhaps they had both gone completely deaf. After a while, I began to lose interest. If they needed to see me, they knew where to find me.

Almost a year later, Gladys dropped a copy of the *Daily News* on my desk, and then walked out of my office without a word. I glanced at the headline on page 3: Tunnel Dwellers Killed by Train.

Gladys returned with a glass of water and a box of tissues.

"Ernie, do you want to talk about it?"

"You know? I really *did* have a premonition that this would happen."

"But you set them up in that apartment."

"Yeah, Gladys. But I wonder if they ever lived in it."

"So they were more at home living in a subway tunnel?"

"Yeah, I guess they were."

The next day I got a call from a lawyer with the MTA. He wanted to know if he and a couple of other lawyers could meet with me. A day later they came over to my office, and we sat around my small conference table.

They asked if I would consider a settlement offer. I knew exactly why they were so reluctant to go to trial. It was so obvious, no one needed to say anything. But I'll say it anyway: The longer this dragged on, the worse it would look for the MTA.

"All right," I said. "Here's what we're going to do. You're going to go back to your office and have a nice long talk with the bigwigs who make all the decisions, OK?"

They looked at each other and then nodded.

"Good! Then I think we understand each other. Now here's what I want you to say to them. I will be very happy to hear their settlement offer. I completely understand why the MTA would like all this behind them.

"But this will be a take-it-or-leave-it offer. The MTA makes the offer, and I take it or leave it. If I take it, then this business is all over."

"And if you don't?"

"Then I'll see you in court."

## 4

The next day the MTA proposed a $20 million settlement. I jumped on it! It was even more than I had hoped for. I called Dara with the good news. We decided to go out for drinks after work.

After our second round of drinks, Dara gave me one of her patented no-nonsense looks and said, "I'm about to break my most important rule."

*Now* she was talking my language! But what was she going to tell me? Maybe that Donnie and Frankie had left *me* all their money?

"Ernie, you know how important confidentiality is in estate law."

"Trust me, I am painfully aware of that."

271

"Good. I'm glad we understand each other. I know that you've been dying to hear who the Johnson brothers have left their money to."

"You're a mind-reader!"

"Ernie, you give me much too much credit. So here it is in a nutshell: They have left their entire estate to the Coalition for the Homeless."

I didn't say anything. Dara tried reading my expression and then tried to offer a few words of consolation. But I cut her off.

"No! You don't understand! Sure, I *was* hoping they left me some of their money – or even all of it. On the other hand, I already have much more money than I'll ever spend.

"But what a great thing they did! I truly underestimated those guys."

"Well, Ernie, I certainly can't take credit any of this. I just followed their wishes. Do you know how the Coalition will use the money?"

"Actually, I do. They're buying about twenty abandoned buildings in the South Bronx, having them refurbished, and will be providing permanent housing for about 2,000 homeless veterans."

"That is amazing! And that was all Donnie's and Frankie's idea?"

"That's right! And each of the buildings will be named for a veteran who was homeless when he died."

"Dara, that is so symbolic!"

"Yes, they really thought of everything... Oh, and one last thing. There's going to be an office in one of the buildings – Ernie the Attorney Free Legal Services."

# A DOG'S LIFE

May I ask you question? Would you keep a large dog cooped up in a small apartment all day?

What kind of a person would treat an animal so badly? But who am *I* to judge? Especially after what I did.

It all began very inauspiciously. I had made a dinner date with a woman I had met at a party. She lived on the 37th floor of a high-rise building on the Upper Eastside. Why do I remember what floor she lived on? Funny you should ask.

Often, at least on a first date, a woman will ask you to meet her in the lobby. But when I gave the doorman her apartment number and my name, he just pointed me to the bank of elevators.

I rang the bell and waited. A few seconds later she opened the door just a few inches and asked if I liked dogs. "Sure, I'm a regular dog person."

"Well, I need to warn you. I have a large dog. In fact, Jeff is a very large dog."

"No problem. The bigger, the better."

As I stepped into the apartment, Jeff, a tan Great Dane, took one look at me, and then placed his paws on my shoulders and looked me right in the eye. I could not help but notice a great glob of saliva hanging from his chin. Lovely.

"Jeff! I must apologize. Jeff can be overly friendly. I'm really glad you're a dog person. There have been some guys who were afraid to come into my apartment. But don't worry, I can see that Jeff really likes you."

"I'll be ready in a couple of minutes. So in the meanwhile, why don't you just toss this ball to Jeff. He loves to retrieve."

And she handed me this soggy sponge ball. I was left there holding it as she went into the bathroom to finish her preparations. Jeff looked at me expectantly, so I threw the ball a few feet away. Jeff gave me a look like, "That's *it?* You can't throw any further than *that?*" Had he been a sexist, he might have accused me of throwing "like a girl."

But he decided to give me another chance, so he slowly walked over to the ball, got it into his mouth, brought it over to me, and deposited it into the palm of my outstretched hand.

Strings of saliva hung from the ball. I tried to ignore them as I looked around the apartment. It was basically just one room, about 15 by 20 feet, and a short hallway leading to the bathroom. I began to feel sorry for Jeff, so this time I threw the ball across the room, and Jeff rushed after it and quickly returned it to me.

Soon we got into a rhythm − throw and retrieve, throw and retrieve. For poor Jeff, it was the only game in town. But for me, it was getting increasingly boring.

And then I had an idea. Or actually, a fond memory. When I was around sixteen years old, I went to a small party in some girl's apartment. Her parents were away and she invited a couple of her girlfriends over and I invited a couple of guys I knew. We ended up having a huge pillow fight in the living room − the boys against the girls.

We were laughing so hard that we got a little careless. Someone knocked over a lamp, but the hostess was in hysterics, so we figured she didn't mind. The pillow fight continued. Then another lamp was smashed, and still the fight went on. With each breakage, we laughed even harder. When the fight was finally over, there were feathers, glass, porcelain, and other elements of breakage all over the living room.

And yet the hostess did not seem upset. Finally, the five guests all thanked her and we left. I don't remember what happened to her when her parents returned, or if I ever found out.

Back to me and Jeff. I decided to see if I could get him to knock over a lamp. So I threw the ball off the wall, and sure enough, it bounced right behind a large floor lamp. But for a huge dog, Jeff was quite agile. He leaned in and secured the ball without touching the lamp.

I tried again and again, but Jeff never came close to knocking over the lamp. So then I threw the ball over the couch. This time Jeff leaped onto a couch seat and then jumped over the back of the couch. He reminded me of basketball players who rarely use the backboard when they shoot. Swish. Just net.

I threw the ball off a wall, off the ceiling, under a table, and almost anywhere else in the room, but Jeff managed to retrieve it without doing a bit of damage.

I really needed to wash my hands. And there were saliva stains all over my shirt and pants. Lovely. Finally, she came out of the bathroom.

"You know, I could hear you and Jeff playing. Well, I am so glad he got that workout. OK, ready to go?"

Boy was I ready. As we stood by the apartment door, I gave the ball one last throw and saw Jeff running after it. As she opened the door I glanced back and saw the ball bounce out the window. No! And then I saw Jeff leap.

By now I was out in the hall and she was locking the door. Then she looked at me. "What's the matter?"

I had to think of something to say. But what? "Excuse me, but could we go back into your apartment so we can check to make sure your dog is still there?" No, too alarming.

And then I hit on it: "I was just wondering about something?"

"Yes?"

"Did I see your whole apartment?"

"Oh, did you have a look around?"

"Well, yeah, sort of. But Jeff kept me pretty busy."

"Yes, I know what just you mean. If he likes you, then he's your friend for life."

"That's nice. He's a great dog. So tell me, do you have a terrace?"

"Why do you ask?"

"Well, you're up on the 37$^{th}$ floor. You must have some view."

"Yeah, the view's nice, but there's no terrace. This is all I could afford. In this building an apartment with a terrace would have cost me an arm and a leg."

And I thought: Yeah, but having no terrace just cost you a dog.

By now we were in the elevator. It stopped several times as people got on. People usually don't like to talk on crowded elevators, so we rode down to the lobby in complete silence. As soon as the doors opened, I asked her if she lived in the front of the building or in the back.

"The front. Why do you ask?"

"Just curious. So I guess you have a view of the midtown skyline."

"Yeah, but don't bring that up. It makes me envious of my neighbors who have those great terraces."

As soon as we got outside, it looked like Times Square on New Year's Eve. There were, literally, thousands of people. And there were police cars, an ambulance, and from the sound of sirens, still more on the way.

"I wonder what happened?" she said.

I just shrugged. Then I answered, "How should *I* know?"

Poor Jeff. He *was* such a nice dog. The two of us had really made a connection. And yeah, we had been friends for life … his anyway.

We needed to get out of there. If we stayed any longer, she'd find out. So I told her that whatever had happened, we shouldn't let it spoil our evening.

So we walked to the restaurant where we had a reservation. But when the food came, I couldn't eat. I pictured Jeff falling, floor by floor, all the way down, all thirty-seven stories. I wondered if he felt any fear. Did he know he was about to die? Did he feel pain or did he die instantaneously?

I knew I must be terrible company, but she didn't seem to notice. She was going on and on about how much she hated her job, how she was so underpaid and underappreciated, and how her parents kept pressuring her to move back to Long Island. I smiled a lot and nodded yes or shook my head no at the right times.

Then she reached across the table and placed her hand on mine. "You're such a sensitive and caring man." I shook my head no in complete disbelief, but then she said, "Look, I've met a lot of guys, so I'm a pretty good judge of character. So don't sell yourself short. You are honest, and you are the kind of man who always takes responsibility. I'll bet you never take the easy way out."

I just smiled. I mean, what could I say? "I think I just killed your dog?" She squeezed my hand.

When the waiter came by to clear the table, I asked him to wrap up my food. And only then did she notice that I hadn't eaten anything.

When we returned to her building, there wasn't a soul in the street. Evidently the terrible mess had been cleaned up as well.

Does the Sanitation Department have a special group of employees to do that kind of work, or was it left to the apartment building's janitors. And where do they take the body if the deceased happens to be a very large dog? Do the police do an investigation to determine if it was a suicide or a murder?

"Would you like to come upstairs?"

"Thank you! I would really love to, but I seem to have an upset stomach."

"I noticed something was wrong. You didn't touch your food."

Then I kissed her on the cheek, flagged down a cab, and gave the driver my address. The whole ride home I kept thinking of poor Jeff falling through space. And for what? A chewed up old sponge ball covered with his drool? A ball that *I* had thrown out the window?

When the cab dropped me in off in front of my building, I rushed up to my apartment and checked my answering machine. *Hallelujah*! Not one message! I quickly unplugged the machine and turned the ringer off on my phone.

After a few weeks I figured the coast was clear, so I came out of hiding. Soon after, I met a guy at a party who knew the woman. In fact, he had gone out with her last Saturday night.

How could I ask him discreetly if Jeff was still live? Then I knew just what to ask. "She lived in a high-rise on the 37th floor, right?"

"Yeah, that's her."

"What did you think of her apartment?"

"Huh?"

"You know, did she have a nice apartment?"

"To tell you the truth, I never found out"

"Didn't she invite you up?"

"Yeah, but I never went inside."

"Why not?"

"Well, as soon as I rang her bell, I heard this dog growling."

# MISTAKEN IDENTITY

## 1

I have a rather unusual name. If you checked the residential phone listings in all five boroughs of New York, you would find just sixteen Kanadlehoppers.

You might assume that someone with a name like that must be some kind of nerd. But nothing could be further from the truth. OK, maybe I haven't had an actual date in eleven years, but that's just because I happen to be extremely selective. Just the other day I got a call from a young woman, and I could tell from the sound of her voice that she was very attractive.

"Hello?"

"Marty?"

"This is Marty."

"Are you sure you're Marty? Marty Kanadlehopper?"

"Trust me, no one pretends to have that name."

I could hear her laughing. "I am soooo sorry. I didn't mean to laugh, but you're very funny! "Anyway, I must have the wrong number."

I didn't want her to hang up. "May I ask what you're calling about?"

"I'm afraid it's very personal. I'm sorry to have bothered you." Then she hung up.

I stared at the phone, listening to the dial tone. You know, I really should get caller ID. Then I wondered who this other Marty Kanadlehopper could be. I had an old Brooklyn phonebook, practically a collector's item, so I looked him up. It turned out there was a Martin Kanadlehopper who lived way on the other side of Brooklyn.

A few weeks later I got a call from another woman.

"Hello?"

"Martin?"

"This is Martin."

"Martin Kanadlehopper?" Boy, this was getting old.

"The same. May I ask who's calling?"

"This is *Mrs.* Martin Kanadlehopper."

"Is this some kind of joke?"

"I think I had better explain. No, I am certainly not married to *you!*"

"Well, I already *knew* that."

"You see, I am married to a different Martin Kanadlehopper."

"You mean, the Martin Kanadlehopper on East 93$^{rd}$ Street in Canarsie?"

"That is correct."

"So how can I help you?"

"Well, for some time we have been getting calls from women we don't know, plus frequent hang-ups. And since you're the only other Kanadlehopper listed in Brooklyn with a first initial, M, we would like you to consider changing your listing to *Martin* Kanadlehopper. That way, you would not be missing those calls, and my husband and I could have some peace."

"I don't think so. This was my parents' number from before I was born. My father's name is Max.

"Look, Martin, your social life is none of my business; I am not a judgmental person. But evidently some of the women in your harem are calling our number by mistake. And just for your information, Martin and I have been happily married for eighteen years."

"Mrs. Kanadlehopper, if I told you about my social life, you wouldn't believe me."

"Look mister social butterfly, I'm going to level with you. I want all these phone calls to stop! I don't care how you do it.

Just tell all your lady friends to stay away from my husband!" And then she slammed down the phone.

## 2

About six months later I got another call.

"Marty?"

"Yes."

"Remember me?"

It was the young woman who had been looking for the other Marty Kanadlehopper. I'd recognize that voice anywhere. That beautiful young woman.

"Of course I remember you."

"I am so flattered."

"Why, thank you."

"You're welcome! Marty, could you do me a great big favor?"

Anything, I thought to myself. Anything!

"Could you give me the other Marty's phone number? I must have misplaced it."

"As a matter of fact I can. Just give me a minute. I have an old Brooklyn phone book."

"You're an angel!"

"Thank you. By the way, may I ask you what your name is?"

"Nona."

"Nona. What a beautiful name."

"Thank you, Marty."

"Here's the number. Area code 718-772-0426."

"Thank you, you've been so kind."

"Wait! Nona, I need to tell you something."

"Yes?"

"I got a call from his wife."

"*Marty's* wife?"

"Yes, it was a few months ago. She said that all these women were calling her husband and she demanded that the calls be stopped."

"What did *you* have to do with any calls *he* was getting?"

"How should I know? Besides, I'm not even related to him."

"Well, thank you for telling me. You're a sweetheart." Then she hung up.

Boy, my social life was really picking up. I might even be able to get a date out of this.

## 3

A few months later she called again. As soon as I heard her voice, I was in heaven.

"Marty?"

"Nona!"

"I am so amazed that you remembered me."

"I will always recognize your beautiful voice."

"Well thank you. Marty, I was wondering if you could do me a big favor."

Anything! Anything! Just *say* the word!

"Remember how sweet you were the last time we talked? Well, it turns out that Marty moved, and I don't have his new number. Is there any way you can help me figure out where he is?"

I would do anything for Nona. Even if it meant helping her find another guy.

"Look Nona, it might take me awhile, so could I call you back?"

"No, Marty. How about if I call you in an hour?"

"OK, I'll do my best."

I tried all kinds of computer searches, but no other M Kanadlehoppers turned up. I printed out a list of Kanadlehoppers all over the country, figuring that maybe he was related to some of them. When the phone rang, I was prepared.

"Marty, it's me. Could you find his new number?"

"No, I'm sorry. But I did manage to print a list of Kanadlehoppers all over the country. Maybe he's related to one of them."

"Thank you, Marty. Look, I'm going to level with you, OK?"

"Sure."

"I know Marty's married, but I've been very discreetly seeing him on the side. It's not so hard because his wife works days and he works nights for the Sanitation Department. So there are certain times when I can call him when she's not at home."

"Yeah?"

"The problem is that Marty is a complete screw-up. It's bad enough that he has other girls on the side, but *they're* the ones who are calling the house when the wife's there."

"I see."

"Anyway, I didn't hear from Marty for a while, so one morning I called him. The phone was disconnected. So I went out to where they lived. And would you believe that they moved – and left no forwarding address?"

"I'm sorry."

"Thanks, Marty. You've been so understanding."

"Nona, could I tell you something?"

"Sure."

"I would do anything for you."

"Ops! Sorry, Marty, I just got another call."

I sat there staring at the receiver. I knew then that I would never get to meet this beautiful woman.

## 4

A year later I was still fantasizing about Nona. And wishing that I could have been the other Marty Kanadlehopper – except, of course, for that awful wife. As always, I got up at six a.m. and was the first one into work. As I walked down the dimly lit hallway, I saw a woman walking toward me. It was Vivian, a very sweet older woman I sometimes chatted with. She had the strangest expression on her face and she was walking very slowly.

"Viv, are you OK?"

"Are *you* OK?"

"Sure, I'm fine. But Viv, you look like you've just seen a ghost."

She began to shake. I led her to a chair and helped her sit down. She just kept staring at me and shaking her head.

"Should I get you some water?"

"You're *alive*, Marty! You're *alive*!"

I went into a little comic routine, patting myself all over and saying, "Yes, I'm alive! Glory be, I'm *alive*!"

"Marty, are you really alive?"

"Yes, Viv, I'm very much alive!"

"But you're supposed to be dead! On the way to work, I heard it on the radio. They said you were killed in some kind of traffic accident."

"Let me see if I'm hearing you correctly. They said 'Marty Kanadlehopper is dead?'"

"That's what I heard."

Just then, Jerry came down the hallway. "Marty, you've alive!"

"You heard it on the way to work?"

"Yeah, I know that on the news they lie all the time, but this is ridiculous!"

"Hey listen, I've got a radio in my office. Let's see if we can get some more details."

So we went into my office and I turned on WINS 1010, the all-news station. We didn't have long to wait.

"We now have an update on this story. Here is a statement from the Sanitation Commissioner about this tragic death. 'Martin Kanadlehopper worked for the Sanitation Department for twenty-one years. Last night he left his truck to assist a motorist whose car had stalled at an intersection. Witnesses saw the car lurch forward, striking him. He died before the paramedics arrived. Martin Kanadlehopper and his wife would have celebrated their twentieth wedding anniversary this Sunday. Instead, on that day, his family will bury a hero.'"

The newscaster went on to say that the driver, identified as Wynona Scott, had appeared to be in shock, and was taken under police escort to Coney Island Hospital for observation.

# NO CHEMISTRY

Earning a PhD could be described as a running along a very long and arduous obstacle course. But for women who majored in chemistry at one New York school, that race included an additional obstacle – Professor Marcus Helm.

The Professor seemed to take a special interest in female students. One might even get the impression that he was a man far ahead of his time. When asked about it, he would simply observe that he just happened to feel an affinity toward women.

Can you guess where this is going? It turns out that there was an unwritten rule in the Chemistry Department that no woman could receive a PhD unless she went to bed with Professor Helm.

How could this be allowed to happen? Why didn't anyone *do* something about it? The most obvious answer is that back in the 1970s and 1980s, hardly anyone had ever heard of the term, "sexual harassment" – let alone tried to do anything about it. At best, if a professor was too ardently demanding "a lay for an A," perhaps his Department Chairman had a talk with him, and maybe even suggested that he try to be a little more tactful.

There *were* complaints, of course. Two students even facetiously suggested to the Chemistry Department Chairman that going to bed with Professor Helm be listed as a prerequisite for a PhD. But his department colleagues and the university administrators dismissed these accusations as merely "he said, she said" disputes. When pressed by one irate student to do something about the lecherous professor, the Academic Vice President blandly observed that "Nobody's perfect."

Whatever else might be said about him, Professor Helm could not be described as anything but extremely well mannered. A highly respected chemist, he brought the university millions of dollars in grant money, and his former students held teaching and research positions at many of the nation's most prestigious universities. His manners were impeccable, and he was a brilliant and highly entertaining lecturer.

And yet, the Professor's standard operating procedure was pretty much an open book. It was even a source of some amusement among his colleagues that his presence invariably graced the dissertation committees of all the female PhD candidates. He would often suggest additional research, or even persuade a colleague to do this *for* him. And any criticism was always labelled as constructive.

It fact, Professor Helm even seemed to consider himself as something of a feminist. Acknowledging that in academia – and especially in the sciences – women were almost always held to a higher standard, he wanted the department to ensure that the scholarly reputation of *all* of its PhDs – male *and* female – be of the highest order.

But the bottom line remained: Over the years, of the dozens of women who had been PhD candidates, not one had completed her degree without having had sex with the Professor. He rented a two-room suite on a monthly basis at a sleazy motel on Tenth Avenue in the West Forties, where he would "meet" with his students. One room was set up as an academic office, and for many years he took it as a tax write-off.

How would he have justified this business expense, had he been questioned by an IRS examiner? Why did he need additional office space when the university provided him with a perfectly adequate office?

He might have pointed out that in his university office there were frequent interruptions, and that he sometimes needed to spend hours at a time with some of his students. Indeed, he might even have modestly observed that had some of these students not spent this time with him, they would not have been able to complete their degrees.

If you happen to be one of those nerds who compile lists of the most outrageous horror movies of all time, then you'll remember "Motel Hell," which made quite a splash when it was released in 1980.

It didn't take long for the Chemistry female grad students to come up with a nickname for their esteemed professor. In fact, to this day, they still refer to him as "Motel Helm."

By 1992, the university found itself under growing pressure to finally put a stop to Professor Helm's extracurricular activities. But no one, from the president on down to the Chemistry Department Chairman, seemed ready to take action. And then, quite unexpectedly, a decision was made *for* them.

While the blockbuster TV series, "Breaking Bad" was still years from production, the New York City Police Department was hot on the trail of an offshoot of the notorious Irish-American gang, the "Westies," that had served as a model for the Jets in "Westside Story." They were strongly suspected of distributing meth through a network of flea bag hotels in the West Forties and Fifties.

So an eminent chemistry professor renting a motel suite in that area was sure to arouse some suspicion. The NYPD quickly obtained a search warrant and planted several video surveillance cameras in his rooms.

When viewing the tapes, the police first assumed that the women in the videos were prostitutes, and that they were simply paying for their drugs with sex. But no drugs were exchanged. Since the police did not want all their hard work to go to waste, they decided to arrest one of the "prostitutes" as she left the suite, and then arrest the "john" for good measure.

When it was discovered what had really been going on, one of the tapes found its way to a public access TV station, where it was played twenty-hour hours a day, quickly becoming the most popular show on cable.

The Professor was immediately fired, and the women who had refused to go to bed with him were granted their PhDs. The university also announced a policy of zero tolerance of sexual harassment.

Then, of course, came the lawsuits. The university quickly agreed to a multi-million-dollar settlement to avoid a class action case including every student who had been preyed upon by Motel Helm. In addition, he agreed to pay a substantial sum of money and to issue a highly public apology to the women he had preyed upon.

But it did not end there. The women then sold the production rights to a major Hollywood studio for a sequel to the 1980 horror film. Now Motel Helm would earn even greater notoriety as a sexual predator than he had as a distinguished chemistry professor.

# THE GIRL WHO WOULD STOP TIME

## 1

One two three four,
We don't want your fuckin' war!
One two three four,
We don't want your fuckin' war!

Again and again they chanted the couplet as they slowly made their way downtown along Fifth Avenue, and then crosstown on 42$^{nd}$ Street to the United Nations. There they would hear Martin Luther King and several other luminaries express these same sentiments, albeit in somewhat different language.

Donna and her cohort of anarchists had settled in at the ass end of the parade behind the Unaffiliated banner, which best described their feelings about the quasi-military organization of the parade. It was kind of weird to hear all the onlookers cheering wildly for their group. Walking next to Gary, Donna remarked, "I mean, I can understand their cheering Medical workers for peace, or Students for peace... but Unaffiliated? What does that *mean*?"

"Unaffiliated means unaffiliated. Affiliated anarchists would be oxymoronic."

"Gary, can you believe the parade organizers call those schmucks with armbands 'parade marshals?'"

"What *should* they be called?"

"Why not just put swastikas on their arm bands and call them the Hitler Youth?"

"Perfect."

What do we *want?*
Peace!
And when do we *want* it?
*Now!*
What do we *want?*
*Peace!*
And when do we *want* it?
*Now!*

This was, by far, the largest anti-war march in history. Donna, Garry, and their anarchist buddies could not help but be impressed by this vast sea of humanity surging against the American war machine. Indeed, it seemed as though the whole world *was* watching.

A group of puppeteers marching among the unaffiliated carried huge paper machete masks of President Lyndon Baines Johnson, Defense Secretary Robert McNamara, and Secretary of State Dean Rusk. Each wore a placard that read, "War Criminal."

Hey, hey, LBJ!
How many kids did you kill today?
Hey, hey, LBJ!
How many kids did you kill today?

As the parade marshals shouted cadence, everyone among the unaffiliated picked up on the words, but refused to march in step. What was this supposed to be – a fuckin' *military* parade?

## 2

A year later, Donna had joined the Yippies, a group started by Abbie Hoffman, Jerry Rubin, and a few other Lower

Eastside radicals. Also known, in a not entirely derogatory way, as the "Groucho Marxists" because of their humorous anti-establishment protests, the Yippies had decided upon an uncharacteristically practical action plan.

They were going to shut down the nation's war machine by stopping time. If they could stop all the nation's clocks from working, then our Military-Industrial Complex would be unable to function and we would have to end our war against the Vietnamese people. And this action would begin by holding a giant Yip-In at one of New York's most famous landmarks.

On the evening of March 22, 1968, some five or six thousand hippies, Yippies, Yippie sympathizers, anarchists, and curiosity seekers descended upon Grand Central Terminal. There was a circular information booth about sixty feet in diameter in the middle of the central concourse of the terminal with a clock above it. Donna and another young woman were boosted to the roof of the booth. Meanwhile, hundreds of policemen surrounded the group, awaiting orders to begin making arrests. Once on the roof, Donna realized that she had lost a sneaker, but she knew what she had to do. She and the other woman pulled the hands off the clock.

Cheers from the crowd echoed throughout the terminal as they held up the clock hands for all to see. Then some of the Yippies started throwing lit firecrackers and the police quickly moved in to make arrests. But then something went horribly wrong. The police started indiscriminately beating the Yippies and innocent onlookers with their nightsticks. Scores of people were injured, dozens were hospitalized, and there were more than one hundred arrests. Days later, the incident was described as a "police riot."

Despite being arrested and spending the night in jail, Donna was ecstatic. It wasn't so much because of her fifteen minutes of fame, but that she and the other young woman had actually done what they had set out to do. If their goal had been to stop time, then at least they had taken the first step.

But the rest of the nation's clocks were never stopped. The war would drag on for six more years, and hundreds of thousands of people would die. So in retrospect, what had all their marches, demonstrations, and be-ins really accomplished? Still, while the protesters may not have ended the war, they sure gave it a try. When their children and grandchildren asked what did *you* do to end the war, at least they would have a legitimate answer.

**3**

Today is May 16, 1978. It is a day that marks an end, if not a new beginning. When Donna got up that morning, she smiled as she recalled the mantra that she and all her friends would mindlessly proclaim, "Never trust anyone over thirty." Well guess what today is. Yup – that's right!

She glanced in the mirror. Thank God! No gray hairs. And no perceptible wrinkles. But numbers don't lie, and thirty will always equal thirty. There's just no stopping time.

That evening, a bunch of friends took her to the Russian Tea Room, just down the block from Carnegie Hall. An ornate five-story restaurant designed to recall pre-revolutionary Russia, it seemed an ironic choice for an anarchistic birthday celebration. But after a few vodkas, even Donna no longer noticed.

An elaborately uniformed waiter approached their table. Looking like a member of the czar's palace guard, he carried a large birthday cake which he ceremoniously placed in front of Donna. Almost everyone in the dining room joined in singing happy birthday. After blowing out the candles, she closed her eyes and made her secret wish. She thought back to the clock in Grand Central and remembered how she had felt that evening. Her wish was very simple: If only I could go back just one more time.

Her friends all raised their glasses and shouted, "May your wish be granted!" Then it was bottoms up! If any were tempted to fling their glasses against the wall, they managed to restrain themselves.

Just then, a man about Donna's age approached the table. He looked vaguely familiar, and he was grinning widely.

"Do I know you?" she asked.

"I doubt it. I mean, we never really met."

"So how do you know me?"

"Aren't you the girl who pulled the hands off the clock?"

She smiled and threw her arms around him. They hugged like old friends. Then he said, "I have something that belongs to you." And he handed her a sneaker.

## MAGAZINE MADNESS

It seemed a mistake when I received a copy of *Modern Bride*, since I'm not planning to get married, and also because I'm a guy. But there was my name on the mailing label. The next day, when *Good Housekeeping* and *Woman's Day* arrived, I knew that something funny was going on. It had to be Andy, my closest friend. Although now in our thirties, we still "live at home," and have been playing practical jokes on each other since the second grade.

A day later, the postman rang the bell – not twice – but *six* times. He handed me copies of *Vogue*, *Woman's World*, *Redbook*, *Glamour*, *Elle*, and *Seventeen*. We just stood there, silently eyeing each other. Then, in a very plaintive tone, he asked, "Who *does* this?

Later that day, when Andy and I got together, I asked him what was going on with the magazines. At first, he played innocent. But when he couldn't contain himself any longer, he gleefully admitted that he had been sending magazines to a few select friends and family members.

"You are a deeply disturbed individual, Andy. But you already know that. So permit me ask: Why are you doing this?"

"Because I can!"

"That's a cop-out if I ever heard one."

"Because it's fun?"

"*Now* you're talking!"

But then I realized his subscription plan did have one serious drawback. "Andy, isn't this costing the magazine publishers a bundle for printing and postage?"

"Sure. But they can more than make up for that by charging higher advertising rates."

"I don't think I follow."

"The more magazines they sell, the more they can raise their advertising rates."

"But they're not selling these magazines. No one is paying for them."

"True, but as long as the magazine publishers don't tell their advertisers, these subscriptions will count as paid.

"Are you sure about this?"

"I am, Tom. You know those discounts that are offered to college students?"

"Would you believe I got an offer in the mail the other day? The headline was something like, "Deep discounts: up to 85 percent off many magazines."

"Shit! That's almost as good as the deal I give *my* quote unquote subscribers."

"So it doesn't matter whether people pay full price, half price, or none of the price: They're still counted as paid subscribers?"

"Correct. And as long as they're paid subscriptions, the advertisers don't care."

Still, there was something about Andy's scheme that wasn't adding up. "You're telling me that when I got *Modern Bride*, someone actually paid for it?"

"Well technically, *you* did."

"How?"

"The card that I filled out for you had a box which I checked off. It said, 'Bill me later.'"

"I don't believe this!"

"So, in a couple of months, you'll get a bill, and then, a second notice, and maybe even a third notice. But don't worry: If you don't pay, they probably won't cut you off for another few months. And in the meanwhile, you'll be carried on their books as a paid subscriber."

"You're actually serious?"

"Look at it this way: Everybody wins. Subscriptions go up, sales of the advertised products go up, magazine advertising rates go up, and you get to read *Modern Bride* for free."

"And you want *me* to participate in this fraudulent undertaking?"

"Exactly!"

"When do we start?"

We spent the rest of the day at the neighborhood library pulling post card ordering forms from hundreds of magazines. And then we went back to my house and began sorting them. My parents never asked what we were doing, and we never told.

One of our favorite ploys was sending a gift subscription of *New York Magazine* to a friend, and the bill to someone he or she knows. So Mel sends it to Sue and gets the bill. Then we reverse the process and have Sue donate a subscription to Mel. Repeating this process dozens of times, we solidified many friendships, while expanding cultural horizons.

Next, we started messing with people's heads by signing them up for magazines they probably hated. We sent gay magazines to straight guys, retirement magazines to teenagers, and sex magazines to fundamentalist Christians, Orthodox Jews, and deeply devout Muslims. Did we *miss* anybody?

Then, we wanted to see how subscription departments would handle unusual names. Their employees sometimes assumed the names had been misspelled. And so, Hitlerella Olson was changed to Hilterella Olson. Come on now, did you ever meet someone name Hilterella? Colonel Bloodstock-Shit became Colonel Bloodstock-Smith. But M. Cowflop Putzhead actually went through unchanged. As did Jesus Mohamed Schwartz, Colon Oscopy UpJohn, Mao Tse O'Connor, and T. Thomas Thimblecock.

One day I got an urgent phone call from Andy. You've got to get over here right away! There's been a new development."

When I got there, instead of inviting me in, he said we needed to go for a walk.

"Andy, are we in trouble?"

"No, I don't want my parents to hear this conversation."

"What happened?"

"I got a call today from a lawyer. She represents one of the big magazines we've been ripping off."

"Are they suing us?"

"No, just the opposite! She said that they had finally figured out what we were up to, and that their advertising revenues were up twenty percent in the last quarter. So the publisher wants to arrange discrete quarterly payments that would be kept strictly confidential."

"I can't believe this! How much will we get?"

"Tom, would you believe they're giving us ten thousand dollars every three months?"

"That's amazing!"

"There's more! She has agreed to represent three other magazines which would also like to send us payments."

"And there's no catch?"

"Just that if we keep doing what we're doing, they'll keep paying us."

"You know, with this deal, we can still live with our parents while we're paid to have fun."

"That's right, Tom. We never have to grow up."

## THE TOKEN CLERK'S TALE

Long, long, long ago, before Brooklyn got hot, there was a guy named Rocco who found himself in quite a bind. First he got his girlfriend pregnant. Then he did the right thing and married her. At the time they were both freshmen at Brooklyn College. With a little help from their parents, they found a nice three-room apartment in Bensonhurst, and Rocco managed to get a decently paying job as a subway token clerk.

But not long after Anthony was born, Dolores was pregnant again. "Don't you guys ever use protection?" asked her best friend, Rosalie. Evidently not. Four years later they had four kids, but somehow, they both managed to stay in Brooklyn College, move to a much larger apartment in Dolores' uncle's house on Bay Parkway, and, in Rocco's words, "put food on the table."

A bunch of us hung out in the cafeteria around noon every day. We had our own table, but anybody was welcome to sit with us. While other students spent their breaks studying in the library, we would sit around and bullshit. Although not exactly *cafeteria majors*, we'd tell people we were studying astronomy since we were taking up time and space.

It was amazing that Rocco and Dolores had the time, but it was probably their only chance to socialize. And they did have a great support system of babysitters, spearheaded by two doting Italian mothers, plus dozens of brothers and sisters, uncles, aunts, and cousins.

But all was not well in paradise. One day, Rocco took me aside. I knew something was up when he used the indirect approach.

"You know where I work, right?"

"You work at the Park Place stop of the Franklin Avenue Shuttle."

"How do you remember that?"

"Because you mention it every day."

"So you know how much I hate my job."

"Rocco, another year, year and a half and you can quit. You and Dolores will have your teaching licenses. You'll be home free."

"I think they're gonna fire me."

"Aren't you past your probation period?"

"Yeah, but something happened."

"Seriously?"

"Look Harry, you know how I sometimes fool around a little on the side?"

"A *little?*"

"OK, whatever."

"Don't tell me!"

"No, Harry, it's not what you think."

"So what then?"

"You know."

"Well, maybe it's a little like what happened between you and Dolores?"

"No! Of course not! Listen, Harry, you're one of my oldest friends. I know I can count on you to keep this just between us."

"So what happened?"

"Well, every so often I get lucky. I mean, think about it! I see some good-looking chick who's buyin' tokens, and all she can see is my hands. So I gotta charm her with my winning personality."

"Don't you have a plexiglass window?"

"No, the Shuttle will probably be the last line in the entire subway system to get them. It feels like you're inside a sardine can, except instead of fish, you're packed in there with thousands of subway tokens."

"Well at least you can study — I mean when you're not coming on to women."

"Very funny. Well, even though it's a pretty rough neighborhood, it's usually very quiet. And it's especially quiet on Sundays."

"So what happened?"

"Well I was just finishing my calculus homework when this bimbo walks over to the booth and starts chatting me up. And she was a real looker."

"Yeah?"

"I could see she was pretty hot tuh trot, so I took her into the ladies' room. And I left a pile of tokens where customers could take 'em. If they were honest enough, they'd even pay for 'em. I mean, it doesn't matter that much. Half the guys don't even bother to pay. They just jump over the turnstile."

"OK, so you're in the ladies' room with this woman."

"I'm reaching into my wallet for some protection and she tells me I don't need any. And get this: she says she's three months pregnant."

I just stood there with my mouth open. Rocco smiled and went on.

"Shit, Harry! I never had anything like this one. So we're really goin' at it, and then I heard this terrific racket outside. I figured they must be takin' apart the station."

"What was it?"

"Harry, would you believe it was a Girl Scout troop?"

"*They* were making all that noise?"

"No, not the little girls. It was the scout mistress — or whatever they're called."

"What was she doing?"

"She was this little old lady. And she was whacking the booth with her umbrella."

"Why?"

"She wanted service. She was in a rage. And when she saw me coming out of the ladies' room, she started screaming at me."

"Why?"

"Well first, she wanted to know why I was pulling up my pants. And then she wanted to know why I was in the ladies' room instead of the men's room."

"What did you say?"

"I told her the toilet in the men's room was out of order."

"Fast thinking, Rocco."

"But not fast enough!"

"Well, why not?"

"Because then the chick comes out of the ladies' room, and she's pulling on *her* clothes."

"Shit!"

"You're tellin' *me*!"

"So then what?"

"Well, I told the old lady that because I had inconvenienced her and her girls, they could ride for free."

"Was she OK with that?"

"Well, I went inside the booth and rang the buzzer opening the exit door. And all the girls marched through. But as the scout mistress went through, she waved her umbrella at me and said, 'Young man, you'll be hearing from *me!*'

"And did you?"

"I think so."

"What do you mean, you think so?"

"My supervisor and *his* boss are meeting with me this afternoon. He said they had gotten a letter from a passenger, and they wanted to get my side of the story before they took any official action."

"Rocco, I don't want to say that I told you so, but you've got to learn to keep your cock in your pants."

"Tell me about it! It's the story of my life."

The next day when I got to our table, Rocco and Dolores are already there, along with a bunch of our friends. He had his arm around her and they were both smiling. And then Dolores asked us to raise our drinks in a toast to Rocco.

After we toasted him, Dolores explained. It turns out that the scout mistress had been so taken by Rocco's kindness and ingenuity, that she wrote a glowing letter of commendation to the New York City Transit Authority.

"That's great!" we all agreed.

"But wait!" shouted Dolores. "There's more! On that same day, a second passenger wrote another letter of commendation. She was having a bad bout of morning sickness and Rocco was kind enough to unlock the ladies' room for her.

Rocco was named the New York City Transit Authority employee of the month. Millions of subway riders saw his smiling face taped to the windows of token booths. And at the awards ceremony, the commissioner observed that in just one afternoon Rocco had more social interaction with subway riders than most transit employees had in a lifetime.

## ABOUT THE AUTHOR

Steve Slavin has a PhD in economics from New York University, and taught economics for 31 years at New York Institute of Technology, Brooklyn College, and New Jersey's Union County College. He has written 16 math and economics books. These include a widely used college textbook now in its eleventh edition, and the bestselling All the Math You'll Ever Need. His short stories have appeared in dozens of literary magazines.

CPSIA information can be obtained
at www.ICGtesting.com
Printed in the USA
BVHW041855030321
601628BV00018B/456

9 781625 530974